The Nickel Loop

Nancy Houser-Bluhm

The Nickel Loop is a work of fiction written without assistance from artificial intelligence. Although historical persons were cited, the circumstances and connections are fictional. The town of Glenwood Springs, Colorado was the inspiration for this fictional story. Other than street names, mentions are works of the author's imagination. The flavor of the 1938 era is based on historical information gathered from newspapers, photographs, and documents.

First edition 2024

Contents

Also by Nancy Houser-Bluhm

Whispers for Terra

This book is dedicated to all those who appear in our lives at the most perfect of moments.

Author Note

The Nickel Loop is a work of fiction. The author took literary license while trying to remain historically consistent with the era of the late 1930s America. Details such as telephones in hotel rooms may not have been true to the named towns but were true other places in America during that time. To satisfy curious readers, but avoid spoilers, a list is provided in the back of this book.

Chapter 1

The Arrival

Emmeline was being watched. It began a few minutes earlier when the train left the Winter Park station. She always chose a window seat and put her bag in the adjacent seat to signal she wanted to be left alone. She peered out the window while sneaking a glance at the reflection of a middle-aged woman across the aisle. Emmeline knew she shouldn't turn her head to look, but she did.

The woman adjusted her red-framed glasses and smiled a toothy smile. She was ready to jumpstart a conversation. "Hi, I'm traveling from Kansas out to Utah. How about you?"

Emmeline smiled politely even though a cringe slipped through her body. She enjoyed her thinking time on the train. "Oh hi, I'm heading to Glenwood Springs from Denver."

"I'm surprised you take the train, since this ride takes longer than the three-hour drive from Denver to Glenwood Springs."

"You never know what the roads in Glenwood Canyon will be like. I don't need a car when I get there. Besides, I like this quiet time to think things through."

Unfortunately, the woman didn't take the hint. "Me, I love to meet people and hear their stories."

Emmeline thought it was probably more about her telling her own. She hoped to squelch the interaction. "The train's gentle sway calms my mind and I'm not much of a storyteller."

The woman wasn't deterred. "When I got back on after the break at Winter Park, I couldn't help but notice you running your fingers over that book."

Emmeline's attention shifted to the coin book in her lap, which she had been stroking to sooth her irritation. Her sister Hannah had been contacting buyers for her father's coins before they even discussed whether to sell.

"This was my dad's coin book," she blurted to her surprise. "Our shared interest in collecting was one way we connected."

"You said connected in past tense."

Emmeline's breath hitched. It'd been two years, but the reminder pierced the shield she'd constructed to avoid ever living that pain again.

"This was his favorite resource book. I can still see him sitting with his reading glasses half down his nose, running his finger across the page, hopeful the coin he held would lead to retirement. Coins were his version of a lottery ticket." She was quiet a moment, holding the memory. Then she said, "He died two years ago."

The woman tapped at her heart. "Oh, I'm very sorry. You are too young to have lost a parent. Did that deepen your interest in old coins?"

An opportunity to tell a dad-story soothed her heart. It was becoming harder to see his face and talking ushered in vivid memories. "It was a much-anticipated ritual for my dad and me.

He'd often pay in cash so he could get change back. When we could, we'd sit down, dump the saved coins on the dining table and sift through them as if panning for gold. He had me use my 'young eyes' to search for any tiny symbol or mark which added to the coin's value."

Emmeline had been wrong. The stranger's intent wasn't to dominate the conversation. She was simply curious. The woman tilted her head to one side. "Losing a parent at any age causes a rift in our plans. I can hear wistful nostalgia as you talk about him." The woman eyed the next car. "I'm suddenly famished. I'm going for a snack. Maybe we'll chat again."

Emmeline never would have expected the words that came out of her mouth. "I look forward to it."

As the woman stood, she added, "I love your dress. It reminds me of something I see my grandmother wearing in old photos. Everything comes back in style."

Emmeline glanced at her belted emerald, bias cut dress and saw an image of her favorite store, Rewind. She rose and leaned in with a soft smile. "Thank you. I truly enjoyed our conversation." Emmeline went the other direction, heading to the restroom. She took note of an unexpected lightness.

Emmeline touched the top of the blue leather high-backed seats, as she walked back from the restroom. Her toe nudged something. She bent and scooped a worn nickel. Never passing up a found coin, heads, or tails, she slipped it in her dress patch pocket. As time ticked by, the woman did not return.

● ● ●

The "All Aboard," shout jolted Emmeline awake. Her head swiveled, finding the train empty. She must have dozed. In a flurry, she tossed the books into her suitcase, threw on her coat, and dashed to the exit. The cold air struck her as she stepped down from the warm train. She was glad for her tights and that her retro overcoat with wide lapels had been updated with a polar fleece lining.

The town of Glenwood Springs had a clever practice of choosing a specific era or theme for the holiday season. Some people dressed the part, and the town donned aspects of the chosen era. This year it was the 1930s. She had chosen to visit Hannah thinking it'd be fun to see what the period might have been like. She didn't know how precisely she fit the era, but she knew her outfit, except for her tights, allowed her to slide into the costuming.

She slammed to a stop when she rounded the train station. Glenwood Springs had brilliantly recreated itself. A light-yellow car with an elongated front end and long rounded fenders rolled up to the curb. A broadly smiling man dressed in a pair of cuffed pants with an argyle sweater popped out of the driver's seat. Dashing to the other side, he opened the passenger door, tipping his hat to an approaching woman in a pair of high waisted, wide-leg woolen pants. Emmeline stared as they drove away, acknowledging she didn't hold a candle to their vintage shopping. She marveled at the changes before her. Even the Hotel Denver pulled out its old Star Hotel sign.

Her attention fell to the unpaved street while she watched them drive down the road. It was dirt, smoothed, but still, dirt. She noticed Grand Avenue was paved but Blake Avenue was not.

She wondered if the early cold spell had stalled seasonal road improvements. It did add to the vintage flair.

From the corner of her eye, she spotted a man walking briskly in her direction. She inhibited the head-jerking impulse his rough appearance stirred; she slid her head toward the man wearing a pair of jeans and a thick flannel shirt with a satchel attached at his waist. A coat of some kind was over one shoulder. It was the wild blonde hair parted in the middle and the vintage rifle over his other shoulder that drew her attention. He hastily passed within two feet of her. Oblivious to her presence, she took a step back. She wasn't a fan of open-carry laws and she saw hysteria in his deep teal eyes. As she shook her head at the strange sight, she watched him head west in long, forceful steps. Something was off about him. Even if he had gotten the wrong memo about this year's enactment, something else was peculiar.

Emmeline grabbed her cell to let her sister, Hannah, know she was on her way. There was no reception. Not a single bar. Only the words No Service in the screen's corner. She shrugged it off as cell tower problems and headed east toward Hannah's house on Palmer Street. In the six months since her last visit, many houses had changed. The dark brown house with colorful art deco shingles in the peaks, was painted a creamy yellow. The pavement was only the first oddity. Surely, no one painted houses for the town's event.

From the sidewalk in front of Hannah's house, Emmeline noticed the short picket fence lining the front yard was fresh white, not dull and peeling. It was nice Hannah had finally done some updating. Her knocking reverberated a deep bang from her hand hitting the wooden door. Emmeline ignored her stomach tightening, and muttered, "Hannah fixed the door too?" The warped bottom usually caused a bounce with each knock.

She peered through the window into the foyer, then stepped back and inspected the small porch. She hadn't noticed the metal rockers that replaced the two Adirondack chairs. "Hannah must be going vintage too. These are old-school," muttering to herself. Emmeline adored towns that preserved their historical appearance. This home had been in her family for 120 years.

There was still no answer even though her sister was expecting her. She opened the screen and twisted the knob hoping Hannah had neglected to lock the door. She had not. She sat in a chair trying her cell once more. It continued with the 'no service' message. Was a tower down? The metal chair was shockingly cold, and she couldn't sit around. Maybe Hannah was running an errand.

She started toward Hannah's shop, the Amethyst. If she wasn't there, someone may know. It was a metaphysical shop filled with crystals, runes, affirmation cards and everything new age. At twenty eight, Hannah was five years older, yet at 23, Emmeline was the serious one. She oscillated between envying Hannah's carefree nature and finding her too frivolous. In personality, Hannah was more like their mom, Agnes. Emmeline viewed them as too nice. They were always doing things to help others. She thought it made them easy to take advantage of. Their dad's accountant demeanor was more analytical and practical. Emmeline resonated with that and attributed her similar directed and pragmatic personality to getting her through high school AP courses. She graduated college early, finishing up just weeks ago. Hannah was high school homecoming queen. Emmeline never desired the circle of friends Hannah had. Friends in college were more study, than drinking buddies. During college, she drifted from her high school friends. Emmeline had one serious boyfriend, Mick. He'd been on the studious side, too. Borderline addictive personality she realized later. They broke up when he became entrenched in drug use.

Emmeline was devastated when her dad died in the car accident. She had been robbed of her rock. A sophomore in college at the time, she cut herself off from her small circle of friends and burrowed into her studies. She resented her mom's efforts to talk about grief and the afterlife. It was the cavern of loss in this world that overwhelmed her.

After the initial flurry of post funeral family togetherness, Emmeline visited from college for expected special dinners and responded to texts. She couldn't bring herself to help clear out her father's closet. She left that for her mom and sister. She welcomed taking charge of the coin collection. Hannah seemed to recover from the death faster. She frequently drove to hang out with Agnes on weekends. The two became closer.

Deep in review of her family dynamics, Emmeline found herself standing where The Amethyst should have been but wasn't. The street appearance made her gasp. She had no idea how to absorb what she saw. The building structures were the same, but the names, and the store fronts, were different. First the streets, then the houses, now the stores.

Nothing made sense. Making sense of things was her style. Heart racing, she ducked into an alleyway for time to think. After Emmeline dropped her case to the gravel, she leaned against the brick wall. Bile rose in her throat as she squeezed her eyes closed to block out the changes. Her head pressed firmly against the brick, she took long inhales to slow shallow, frantic breathing. The town couldn't accomplish this just for the holiday theme. There must be a logical explanation. She conjured nothing.

Questions ziplined through her brain. What the hell was going on? Where was Hannah? Where was her store? "Where am I?", she stammered as she raised her head to stare at the sky, wanting to look anywhere but the street. It backfired. Above her were clunky thick wires spaced with knobs resembling old fuses. Most certainly not twenty-first century wiring. The bile roiled up her throat. Lurching her chest forward, she vomited.

A woman stepped into the alley. "Honey, are you ok?"

She heard herself murmur, "Fine, I just have such horrible morning sickness."

The woman gave the reassuring global statement, "Only a couple of months and you will be feeling wonderful." She stepped back as the stench filled her nostrils and offered a few hurried words before leaving the alley. Leaning another moment against the wall, Emmeline took an inhale to gather her courage. She pulled a tissue from a purse pocket and wiped her mouth. She tossed it to the ground and nudged it up against the wall dismissing the typical littering concern. Emmeline picked up her suitcase and headed further down the alleyway to avoid people and the main street.

●●●

Nicholas walked out of town with long strides, twisting his head left then right, trying to understand what he was seeing. He had seen brick roads, but not this smoother surface. It wasn't just the number of motor cars; it was their sleekness. He was relieved to get to the edge of town. There was a foreign sound overhead when he came to a stop, but he saw trees, blue sky, and a few clouds. The sound faded. His cabin came into view through the woods, but he halted at a chain crossing a wide path. Behind the chain, loomed a much newer version of his outhouse, and his chimney was freshly spackled. He had left only the day before to hunt on a friend's property. Yesterday, the tree beside the window reached the frame but it now stood roof high.

Bounding over the chain, with a few strides, Nicholas surveyed the door, his door. Its latch was now a knob, and it was locked. He never locked his door. He roughly rattled the knob, hoping it would shake normal back into his day. His knees buckled and he extended a hand to the house to steady himself. His back to the door, Nicholas slid down to a squat on the stoop. Even though it was cold, he wiped sweat from his temples.

As he looked back at the chain crossing his property, his mind replayed all he'd seen on his way out of town. There were so many houses. The women wore such short dresses. The automobiles were streamlined and engines rumbled with power. He hadn't passed one horse or buggy. His breathing became jagged.

Standing, he paced for a moment and decided to visit the one place that still held some resemblance of familiarity— the bar across from the railroad station.

Chapter 2

The Meet-up

The alley stretched to infinity. Emmeline was far from calm, but her nausea had settled. Somehow, someway, the impossible had happened. This was no town wide reenactment. This was no longer 2022. With dusk approaching, the temperature was dropping. Her toes were getting numb in her flats. She needed a plan. As she plodded through the alley, Emmeline clung to a vestige of hope and tried Hannah once more. Nothing.

Getting a room at what she knew as Hotel Denver was the logical choice. Emmeline typically entered through the brewery entrance, but in this time warp or quantum leap, the door opened to the hotel lobby. The desk stood to the right and the lobby was much smaller. Under different circumstances, she would have admired the detailed green mosaic flooring.

Sitting in the lobby was the possibly crazy man from the train station. In one hand he held a newspaper, and the other was rubbing back and forth over his mouth. His eyes were fixed a few feet out from him. She could see the coat over the back of the chair. The gun was nowhere to be seen.

She stood in the center of the lobby; her eyes roamed every inch over and over, confirming the unbelievable. The man's distraught expression mirrored her own desperate thinking. She approached slowly. "Are you okay?"

"Depends on who you are, where you're from."

"What do you mean...where I'm from?" He was now staring blankly at a newspaper headline. "Did something happen I should know about?"

Pulling the paper from his lap, he flicked it toward her. The design was black and white—no color. The headline read Statesman Embroiled in Scandal.

She shrugged. "That's hardly shocking news. Doesn't tell me anything."

"No, it's the date that defies logic." She still hoped to see 2022 but her breath hitched at the year 1938.

"I know something's wrong, but this can't be. It's not 1938. They make special papers for festivals or maybe someone left a vintage paper they bought at an antique store." Emmeline desperately studied the ceiling for cameras, still resisting what she dreaded was true. "Someone's trying to freak us out. We're probably live on Instagram."

"Freak someone out?? Insta what?"

Emmeline clarified. "Pranking us to believe it's real."

"So, you think it's not true? I can tell you this building did not look like this last time I was here."

Happy no one was in earshot, she sat in the chair opposite the man. If he was insane, she might be too. "How long ago was that? This building has been here since the late 1800s."

He shook his head. "Not looking like this. You will think I am insane."

"I'm beginning to realize if you are crazy, I must be too. Try me."

Quietly he spoke. "1898. Trains were coming across the states. No train station here, only a platform down the street. And that train I saw pull in today, it's *not* from 1898."

Emmeline stared at him, her mouth agape. Her thoughts swirling, still deciding if he was for real—if any of this was real. She popped up from the chair searching for something, anything, to confirm he was, in fact crazy, and this was all an elaborate reenactment of olden Glenwood Holidays. She stepped outside again. Unless there was also a classic car convention, something was very wrong. Stopping a passerby to ask the year didn't seem wise. She swung around and went back in.

She approached the desk and asked the clerk, "How much is a room for the night?"

The man's head lifted from his books, "$2.50."

Emmeline couldn't help herself. "Silly question but who's our president?"

The clerk eyed her quizzically. "Roosevelt-FDR, of course."

Her knees weakened as she uttered, "Didn't see that coming, but thanks." The clerk shrugged, returning his focus to the ledger. Emmeline craned her neck and saw rows of handwritten names.

Her eyes shot back toward the man, and their minds merged in disbelief. Returning, she dropped into the chair as the man asked in a gruff whisper. "What has happened to us?"

"I don't know, but I know I need a drink." He stared briefly then drew a flask from his side coat pocket and held it out to her. That wasn't what she meant, but she took a swig out of desperation, avoiding the mouthpiece as much as possible. At least it was whiskey, her go-to booze. He followed with a guzzle.

"Now what?" he asked.

"Not the foggiest idea. If we are not insane, then the situation sure the hell is."

His eyebrows raised. She didn't care if her language startled him. She could have said a lot worse. He asked, "Should we walk or stay here?"

Emmeline did not want to be alone. It made no sense to stay with the man, but he was appearing less crazy and more like she felt—shocked. "Neither, let's go into the bar. I don't want to carry my suitcase around with me."

She chose a corner table and said, "You don't have a bag?"

His tone bewildered, he shrugged. "I wasn't traveling. I was walking."

"Where were you walking?"

"Along the river, coming down from a homestead the owner allows me to hunt on. It's along a creek. Sometimes I fish." Emmeline had seen the Grizzly Creek sign along the highway during trips. That might be what he was referring to.

They both peered into their drinks in silence. Emmeline fought the urge to run back to her sister's house. A sinking reality settled deeper. She reached for her cell phone as she always did, many times an hour. With it in her lap she hit Safari seeking any sliver of evidence when she heard, "Apologies, miss, for my poor manners. I am Nicholas. May I ask your name?"

She shoved the phone back into her pocket. "Emmeline." She leaned in as she blurted, "Maybe I'm just dreaming. You aren't real, you're just in my dream."

13

"That'd be wonderful, but I believe myself, this place to be real."

She collapsed back against the chair. "My mind is scrambling to explain this. I don't dream in colors, and I see them all around."

Suddenly she sat up straighter. How were they going to pay for these drinks? Casually scanning the room, she was relieved the few patrons weren't staring. Her vintage clothes were paying off. Nicholas's clothes of jeans and flannel was ageless. She was believing the impossible more with each passing moment. It was 1938 and credit cards were out. Most of her cash would trigger astonishment and suspicion. She didn't even know if the bill size was the same. She knew there were coins in this era, but dimes were different, all silver.

With a swipe of her hand above the drinks, she asked, "How are we going to pay for these?"

Nicholas, dug inside his satchel and pulled out some paper bills and coins. They sorted out his newest coins and bills. She didn't mention her own.

Emmeline brought her phone out for another peek.

Nicholas's head jerked forward, his eye squinting. "What in tarnation is that?

Emmeline's brain captured a scene from Star Trek when Captain Kirk went back in time.

"It's a phone."

"I know about telephones. That is no telephone I have ever seen."

"Yeah, if it *is* 1938 and you are from 1898, there are more than a few things you haven't seen from my time or even this era."

"I didn't ask, but what is your time, your era?"

Emmeline was able to access her minimal knowledge of history, plus she'd seen movies of this era. She could picture older versions of her everyday items. Nicholas, on the other hand, couldn't even dream most of the advances which had transpired since the late 1800s.

"Are you ready for what I have to say?"

"I can assure you I am not ready for any of this but need to hear it anyway."

She leaned in and whispered, "2022."

"Damn." Nicholas slouched back into the chair and rubbed his hands in silence. Eventually, he flipped a few coins in his hand, "I hope these will suffice."

A burst of unfamiliar panic engulfed Emmeline. She shoved the chair back and stood. Her legs went rubbery, and she fell back to the chair. Her chest tightened. "That drink didn't help one bit." Her body shoved her mind aside. Her volume escalated, her hands trembled. Emmeline's voice was shrill. "What the hell am I going to do? I can't stay here." Patrons at the closest table stared. She didn't care.

Nicholas glanced at the patrons and whispered toward her. "Miss Emmeline. Please. Calm yourself. People are staring. We don't need to call attention."

She hissed her own whisper as her eyes narrowed. "Don't you tell me to calm down." Emmeline glared at the patrons, and they turned back to their drinks. She stood again. This time, her anger from being told to calm down gave strength to her legs. "It's getting late. I've got to find somewhere to stay." She leaned to fetch her suitcase.

Nicholas rose. "Miss Emmeline, please wait. I have an idea. Let me pay first. Please sit."

Emmeline sat sideways at the edge of her chair poised for a quick getaway. Her hand slipped to her pocket, tightening around her phone offering up security. "Go."

Nicholas tossed back the last of his drink and went to the bar. Emmeline watched with her chin held high working to regain her usual composure. The bartender looked past Nicholas to Emmeline and said something. Both men chuckled. He returned slipping silently back onto his chair.

"What did you say about me? What was funny?"

"Never mind. I was trying to distract the man from questioning the coins. The chat was just a decoy."

Emmeline squinted a look of skepticism. Nicholas continued. "Here's my idea."

She shook her head. "This may be a bizarre situation, but I don't know you. I want to know what kind of shit was said about me before I hear your idea."

"And I don't know you, but I know you curse frequently, and I know enough to know you won't like it."

Emmeline folded her arms, raised an eyebrow. "So...?"

Nicholas pushed a frustrated sigh. "The man said, he was glad I got my wife under control."

Emmeline's hands flew into the air and back to the table. "To which you said..."

"I should probably offer a lie, but you seem like a lady who prefers truth. I said feisty can be more interesting."

Emmeline propped her elbows on the table, covered her eyes with her palms. "Please, oh please let me be in 2022 again when

I move my hands." She slowly slid them aside. The new world was still before her. "Alright, what's your idea?", she uttered in exasperation.

"As improper as this may sound, there is a cabin, my cabin, or at least it used to be mine, on the west side of town. It still stands. I walked there when I first came from the train depot. There's a lock on it I didn't recognize, but I am sure I can find a way in."

"A cabin, from 1898? I can imagine that's pure comfort." She couldn't contain her snark.

"Miss, I am a single man, but I still enjoy warmth and cleanliness."

"Please stop calling me Miss. It sounds silly. Emmeline is fine."

Emmeline's brain was sending alarms at his suggestion, yet her breathing slowed. The words hadn't been spoken. They were too absurd. But there it was. Time travel, and not one but two time shifts. Now she was considering staying in a fifty-year-old cabin or one hundred years, depending on what year you were tracking from. But that had nothing on the level of crazy as staying with some guy born more than a century before her, ages before the #MeToo movement. There was a flash of regret for scoffing at the Jujitsu PE class offered in college. She set aside her go-to logic, which had finally resurfaced. Her gut was vetting this guy without alarms. Even though her head usually ruled, her mom annoyingly urged her to trust her gut more, particularly in the oddest of situations.

This qualified. "Okay, I'll check it out."

Chapter 3

The Cabin

Nicholas gestured west as he began walking. "Miss, can I carry your case for you?"

Not wanting to let go of her only possession or her independence, "No, I got it. And the name's Emmeline." The crisp fresh air filled her lungs causing a quick shiver. "I gotta say, I don't make scenes. Certainly, never in public."

Nicholas shrugged, focused on a passing car. There was awe in his tone. "These automobiles are most incredible. Ours are nothing like these. I wonder what else has changed?"

"So much has changed with machines but not sure if people have kept pace. To me, these look heavy and uncomfortable. You called them automobiles back then?"

"For a while they were called mechanical wagons, but automobile became the standard. Is it still the same in your day?"

Emmeline shifted the suitcase from one hand to the other. Nicholas slowed and moved behind to her other side. "Please let me share the load for a bit. It's not that much farther."

The streetlight shed just enough light for Emmeline to catch the hue of blue in his teal eyes. "Thank you, it was getting heavy. We tend to say cars not automobiles." There was a wave of blonde hair that had fallen across his forehead. A reflexive head flick put it back in place.

As they reached the edge of town, the light from the streetlamps faded. Emmeline pulled out her phone, knowing the flashlight feature would still work.

"A telephone that has a lantern. Fascinating." Soon Nicholas directed them right to a more isolated part of town. Emmeline knew she should feel uneasy, but she didn't. She believed his gentlemanly behavior.

His body startled as he walked to a sign. "Well, that's a surprise."

Emmeline shined her light toward it. It read "N. Jones historical site".

"I missed that in my panicked state."

The cabin was tucked back into the woods. They paused out by the chain. Pointing toward it, Emmeline asked, "You're saying this was *your* place?" The rough sided pine cabin cued up a cute, but rustic, Airbnb or Hipcamp experience from her day. Not the dilapidated shack with holes she expected.

With a curl of his lips into the first partial smile either of them had broken, "Yes, it is, was. Nice of someone to do the repairs while I was gone."

Mirroring the small smile, "Heh. Sarcasm spans the centuries I see." Emmeline enjoyed the moment of levity.

Her finger touched the words on the sign. "Is your last name Jones? Is this place named after you? N. Jones?"

"Maybe. It's a very common surname. If it is me, I was a stand-up guy."

They re-confirmed the door was locked. "Museum curators aren't likely to put a key under a doormat, but one never knows unless they try." Asking Nicholas to step aside, she trained the phone's light onto the stoop, bent down, and waved it to each side. Emmeline noticed a long key, too short for a skeleton key, but much like an old one she found wedged behind a drawer in her sister's house. This one was hanging on a nail behind the bush. After reaching for it, she stood beaming, key in hand.

Nicholas returned the smile. "The last thing I wanted to do right now was climb in through a window. Being arrested for trespassing is better than false entry."

Emmeline unlocked the door and pushed it open. She had expected to see her breath. Instead, warm air rolled around her.

"The temperature surprises me," Nicholas remarked as he entered. "Someone had to be here recently for it to be so comfortable." Walking to the wood-burning stove his hand hovered over it. "No fire has burned here recently."

"I think there's a different heat source." On one wall, a small iron heating device hung in the corner. There was a rectangle wooden table in the center of the cabin with a bench on one side and a wooden chair on the other. One wide single bed was against a wall. A pitcher sat on a shelf above a hand water pump.

Nicholas set down the suitcase and slid the gun from his shoulder. She saw he'd hidden it under his coat. Emmeline moved to the bench and dropped to it. The gravity of the day overcoming her. Her back leaned against the table and a loud sigh attempted to release the weight from her chest.

Emmeline glanced back as Nicholas ran his fingers along the smooth arc of the chair. "I hope you like my craftsmanship."

Nicholas looked at her as if waiting for a compliment. Emmeline spoke flatly. "Whatever. I'm sure it's fine work, but I'm not much of a judge. It's good to be somewhere 1938 isn't staring me in the face. If I wasn't a realist, I could pretend to be in some reality show challenge." Emmeline pressed her hands to her face and rubbed. "Drinking a glass of wine at my sister's house and ordering food delivery is what I'm supposed to be doing."

Nicholas cocked his head. "Part of me can imagine I have come home since some items are truly my own."

"At least that sign outside indicates you are real. Part of me is still wondering if I've gone off the deep end."

"Deep end of what?"

"Somehow gone crazy, become delusional. Nothing is how I know it."

Nicholas's eyes were soft, reflecting understanding. He pulled out the chair and sat down across from her. "The magnitude of this is hard to comprehend, however we'd be unlikely to conjure the same delusion. I conclude we are where we see ourselves to be."

Rampant emotions controlled Emmeline's body. Her breathing was slow, relaxed one moment, while the next her fingers tingled, and her skin hummed. One moment she felt her rational self, the next trepidation reared. Emmeline's heart palpated deep in her chest. She had no control over what her body chose to do. It decided how long the panic lasted. When a deep breath was finally allowed, she gripped the edge of the table and spat, "I have to figure this out!" With defeat she laid her head on folded arms. "How soon will someone come back here and wonder what the hell we're doing squatting in this cabin?"

Nicholas's tone remained calm. "Let's go back to the beginning. We both arrived here at nearly the same time. We both came around the building."

She muffled words into her arms. "You mean the train station."

"Yes. We both walked out of our own times into a different era. It's absurd."

The offer of problem-solving comforted Emmeline. She leaned her chin on her arms. "I fell asleep on the train sometime near the end of the ride. When I woke and looked around everyone was gone. Did you notice anything unusual in your walk?"

"Not until I was near the train depot." They grew quiet.

Emmeline lifted her head from her arms to see Nicholas digging his hands through his blonde hair. She snatched control and reason back from her body. "There isn't much we can do tonight. We would draw attention casually hanging around the train station this late. Attention isn't something we need."

They agreed to stay. Emmeline's stomach was still flipping and unsettled. "I've got nothing left to puke, but my stomach is rolling."

Nicholas reached for the flask again. "I don't know if this will settle your stomach, but it calms me." He surveyed the room. "I am hungry. There would be food supplies in my day."

"I have health bars and some beef jerky. My sister and I never liked the same brands, so I learned to bring my own. Jerky is always good for road trips." She handed the bag to Nicholas. As he gave a nod and small smile, she admired his broad lips.

Reaching in for a piece, he scanned the words on the bag. "What does organic mean? Grass fed beef sounds a bit obvious."

"Not as obvious in my day, my time, as yours. Organic fed natural food, not raised with any pesticides or growth hormones." Nicholas's left eyebrow raised, accompanied by a slight head shake. "Given your tone, nothing good was in those words. This jerky tastes good." He pointed. "What are those blocks?"

She sensed a curiosity in him. "Health bars...a snack that has a bunch of good, healthy ingredients covered in chocolate. Wanna try one?" Emmeline held it out.

"Seems I can trust you after the jerky." Taking it from her, his warm fingers touched Emmeline's, momentarily warming her own cold fingertips. He chewed slowly, with pauses, like it was an experiment. He nodded; his lips curled up. "Surprising groups of flavors." Circling his hand holding the health bar, "So we will stay here for the night. What about after that?"

Forcefully, Emmeline replied, "We have got to figure out how to get back to our own times. My family must be off the rails with worry. Yours must be too."

Time travel rules rolled around in her head even though no one really had a clue. It was all projection. But since she had now traveled through time, had her travel changed anything in her own life? Everything from Nicholas's past may be untouched because it's over, it's happened. The unknowns were for her own future.

"I don't have family in these parts and most people from town will figure I wanted to be alone or went off somewhere. I doubt I will be missed." Emmeline assumed from the statement, Nicholas was not a social butterfly.

She jumped topics. "So, you used coins to pay for the beers. Do you have more of those?" She continued without waiting for an answer, "One reason for visiting my sister was going through the coins my dad had, researching their value." Emmeline recalled she had pulled out a book of coins just before she fell asleep on the train. She shoved them in her case before she hurried off. "It's going to sound odd, but did you have your money out for any reason coming out of the canyon?"

"I might have had my hands in my pockets, but most of my money is in my satchel."

He pulled a few coins from his pocket: one silver dollar, a quarter, and a nickel. "Just these."

Her fingers warmed again at the roughness of his palm as she reached for them. Breathing stopped for a moment when their eyes met. Emmeline opened her suitcase and pulled out the coin books. The top one was the silver dollars her dad had collected over the years.

He hoisted one book and raised and lowered it twice. "No wonder your case weighed so much."

"I wasn't expecting to trudge all over town with them."

"My dad and I used to go through coins we'd saved over the year and sift through them searching for any treasured ones which might be that rare, valuable one. Never found one to make us rich, but I miss sitting, our shoulders touching, passing the magnifying glass back and forth to distinguish an S from another letter. My sister and I were planning to research if any value had changed. She let it slip she'd contacted buyers on her own. I was pissed."

Her eyes fixed on the dates of Nicholas's coins. She recognized a Barber quarter, a prized coin in her day. Excitement coursed through her with holding one in her hand. There was a pang wishing she could show her dad. A silver dollar from 1879 was next.

Holding it up, her eyes were wide, "The date on this one matches a year I have! What that means about why we are here—still no idea."

Nicholas's voice lifted. "They could be what triggered us coming here. Tomorrow we can take the coins with us to the station and follow the tracks."

"Tomorrow? We need to try it now! I can't stay here. Things are no good for women in this era. I just graduated from college and want a job."

Nicholas replied, "Even though I do like what's been done to this place, I would be considered a squatter."

"Hardly the time for humor," she sneered as she grabbed the coin and rounded the table toward the door.

Nicholas reached out touching her arm, "Wait. I want to leave too, but we don't need police wondering why we are at the station so late. You said so ten minutes ago. Besides it's too dark to walk much beyond the station."

Confusion filled Emmeline. She wanted to go right then but knew his words had logic. Emmeline huffed and returned to the coins. She pulled out everything from before 1938. These coins were her adult security blanket and a link to her father. The prospect of giving any up tugged at her heart, but she needed to be ready. Her eyes held focus on the coins, but her thoughts were focused on the other reason for her confusion. She knew her heart skipping as Nicholas's fingers touched her arm was not from fear.

Nicholas's voice jolted Emmeline from her thoughts. "Today has been exhausting. I need sleep. The lady gets the bed. I am used to my bedroll. If you have night clothes, I can hang a blanket over the beam for your privacy."

Emmeline's head cocked to the side. "Normally I would've questioned your intentions, but early on I could see you were more stunned by this strangeness than I was. I figured you wouldn't leap into predator mode. Anyhow, it would be good to get out of this dress."

Nicholas grabbed the blanket at the end of the bed and flipped it over the beam. "You have no worries. I am unmarried at my age for a reason. Women usually scare me."

"I guess I time traveled with the right man then. Are you going to be warm enough on the floor; not that I have any alternative to offer you. It's still on the cool side."

"I am inside four walls; better than the lean-to I usually build when out hunting. Whatever that heat system is, it is comfortable for me."

Emmeline flipped through the case for her pajamas. She skirted behind the blanket and quickly switched out of the dress. She climbed onto the mattress finding it soft but not lumpy, appreciating the curator's updates. Sleeping on a mattress from the 1800s sounded nasty.

Emmeline assumed Nicholas was still sitting at the table. She peeked around the blanket to see him standing in front of the window peering out into the darkness. He had removed his flannel shirt. It was impossible not to notice his V-back shape through the tighter under shirt. She spoke in a soft voice. "I'm going to sleep."

Nicholas turned, showing furrowed brows, but he gave a tight-lipped half smile. His gaze slid to her legging pajamas. "Interesting night clothes. Polar bears? Your short dress was eye-catching too. I have run into the occasional woman in pants. Nothing like these and not the short dress. Isn't it scandalous?"

She held in a scoff as she thought of what he'd think of a thong bathing suit bottom or festival tops. "That dress was nothing compared to short in 2022. But everything must be blowing your mind. For me, I can pretend I'm just in a period reenactment; for you it's being in a sci-fi movie."

"Ok, I passed by 'mind blowing' because I could understand what that meant, but sci-fi?"

"It means science fiction. It's a term for stories people write about what the future will look like."

"This is most definitely sci-fi then. Good night, Miss...good night, Emmeline. I hope you sleep well. Tomorrow, we need to find our way out of here."

Emmeline tucked the sheet around her shoulders. Its softness surprised her. The woolen blanket scratched her chin, but its weight anchored her body. Her eyelids closed only to bring a scene of her missing person face on fliers around town. She knew the police wouldn't list her as missing for at least a day. It'd been less than twelve hours, but for her mom and Hannah, hours would feel like days. Opening her eyes, she searched for outlines in the cabin. With no sounds to use for distraction, she listened to the silence.

Later Emmeline woke with a gasp. She dreamt she was in her apartment streaming *The Witcher* when a commercial popped up advertising a job for a secretary that enjoyed serving coffee and running errands for the male lawyers. Her chest was thumping.

She scanned the darkness in terror when she remembered where she was. There was a rustling as the stranger called Nicholas rolled over on the floor. She barely made out his shape on the floor. The breath lodged in her throat, rushed out. She was not living this nightmare alone. Emmeline didn't know when but somewhere in the darkness sleep returned.

Chapter 4

Day Two

E mmeline woke wrapped in warmth from the added blanket spread over her. A moan slipped from her throat as she oriented, once again, to not just the place, but the time. Her gaze slid throughout the cabin, taking in the wooden walls, the table, the chair. Nicholas moved past the window. When he stepped inside, he was cheery and very blonde.

"The outhouse is locked, so I dug a hole away from the cabin so you can relieve yourself if needed. If you just kick snow over it, it won't be noticed. I will hide our tracks leading to the cabin. Someone could get suspicious." He plucked the blanket from the bed and draped it back over the beam.

"Thanks for that...putting the blanket on me last night. Did I look as if I needed it? I'm shocked I managed to sleep at all, but I did."

"You were moving around. I thought the temperature might be the reason."

Emmeline suspected even if he was afraid of women, they probably weren't afraid of him. His demeanor was gentle, he was considerate, and he was definitely a ten.

Her feet touched the cold plank flooring. She lifted her suitcase to the bed and easily located clean underwear in her neatly organized clothes. She would wonder many things about this era, and his, but her mind was stuck on underwear and if it was customary in 1898. Maybe underwear wasn't even a thing. She changed behind the blanket while Nicholas sat at the table. The dress wasn't practical for all the walking they may do. It was a risk, but jeans were a better choice than leggings. Her coat would cover much of them and her sweater would blend in. She chose her low lace-up boots and hoped they wouldn't be around long enough to care if her clothes turned heads.

As she was dressing, Nicholas said, "There's no need to change on my account. My clothes, even my toothbrush didn't make it to this century."

Even though people find her practice odd she responded, "I am one of these people who always travel with more than one toothbrush. I know people who have a different one for every week."

"Sounds like someone who is either strange or wealthy."

"I'll presume you're not calling me strange since I only travel with one extra. Maybe prepared is more the word. Hey, I'm going out to use that hole. Hopefully, there aren't any coyotes or people wandering the woods."

"Quite sure you won't interest a coyote, but seeing a woman squatting in the woods would stop most men."

"Guess some things never change."

Nicholas had plunged a stick into the snow so she could find the hole. She squatted hovering over it and wiped with her last tissue. Stinging cheeks made her think she'd dehydrate before she'd do this on a regular basis. Shaking off a shiver as she came through the door, "It is COLD out there. Did I mention I'm not a huge camper?"

"Judging by the sun, it is 8:30 am. The sun won't provide warmth for hours. Did you kick snow over the hole?"

Emmeline nodded. "Yep."

They brushed their teeth with the remaining water in her bottle and spit outside. They opted to not use the pump, uncertain how long it'd been since water passed through it.

Emmeline fell into her beloved planning mode. "Let's pull out your newest coins so we can find somewhere to eat breakfast if a trip to the station doesn't get us the hell out of here." Nicholas's eyebrows raised. She said, "Swearing is really not a concern in my day." Meeting his gaze squarely, "Even for women."

"Good to know. It is unseemly in my time, but it appears to be a favorite part of your vocabulary."

"Sometimes nothing works as well."

"I am eager to try our plan but those blocks of food from last night were insufficient to curb my appetite. I am famished. I need to eat, then go."

"Are you fucking serious?" Emmeline chided.

Nicholas flashed another startled look but said, "Food may be available everywhere in your day but that is not what I will return to. I need to eat."

Emmeline ticked through possible reactions in her mind. She could go on her own, but wondered if they arrived in this time together if they needed to leave that way. It was her own stomach rumbling that led to, "Okay, but let's be quick."

She gathered her pre-1938 coins into a small, zippered pouch she kept in the bottom of her purse and put it in her coat pocket. "Breakfast can't cost much. What did a breakfast cost in your day?"

"About twenty cents."

Emmeline's eyes widened. "I don't know anything I can get for twenty cents."

They ensured the cabin appeared as it had when they came in. It took the most work to make the bedsheet taut. This was more a museum than a living space.

Nicholas grabbed his rifle. She said, "I barely saw that yesterday. Nicholas, a rifle slung over your shoulder might not be the wisest thing in this era."

"People weren't expected to walk into a restaurant in my day carrying one either. Remember, eating in an establishment wasn't my plan for the day."

"Does that thing come apart? It could go in my case." Emmeline flashed a smile. "I'm sure you want to carry my bag anyway." As he slid the rifle off his shoulder, he chuckled and made some remark about the wiles of women being unchanged. Nicholas had in short order, shown himself to be open minded. She accepted the wiles remark as friendly banter and smiled.

Chapter 5

That First Taste

The streets were quiet, which is exactly what both had hoped for. Emmeline saw only one man glare at her jeans. She rather liked shaking his patriarchy tree. They picked the restaurant with the fewest people. It was where Juicy's stood in her era. It was a small café with muslin curtains covering the lower section of windows. Emmeline acknowledged everything in 2022 is oversized. These straight, dark wood booths were narrow and suited for two, not four people. Emmeline was happy to see any wood besides pine. They sat away from the counter where other patrons were eating and chatting with the server.

Even in 1938 they had ample money for a good breakfast. The scent of sausage sizzling enticed her to order biscuits and gravy with two eggs over easy. Nicholas ordered pancakes, eggs, toast, bacon, and a steak.

Emmeline chuckled. "Seriously, you can eat all of that?"

"I have no doubt."

Emmeline ate a few bites. She giggled a quiet squeal. "I know I'm starving but this food is incredible." The eggs had large orange yolks and perfectly peppered milk and sausage gravy smothered the biscuits.

Emmeline sensed Nicholas watching her. His chin was resting on his fist, as he smirked. "Am I eating fast?", she asked.

"No, but you are looking very serious about your meal."

"I call it savoring. I'm eating similar named food as in my day, but it doesn't taste the same. This is amazing!" She pointed her fork at the gravy. "This gravy rivals any hangover biscuits and gravy I've ever tasted." She squeezed the fork on the oozing bread. "And this toast! It's slathered in real butter, not just dabbed in the middle. Whoever dabs butter is no bread connoisseur."

"It does taste great, but it looks much more, hmmm, organized than my day. I would say the taste is similar. What would make your food so different?"

"Not sure. I don't eat much fast food, but I buy pre-packaged, heat-and-serve."

"Fast food? What's that?"

"Places like a restaurant, but you can order your food from your car. They hand it through a window, and you drive off, eating on your way to wherever you're going. Most of them are processed foods. I suppose my microwave meals are too, processed, I mean."

"Not sure what that word with wave is or if what you are describing sounds worth savoring. Your look of contentment with this food must be satisfying to the cook."

Nicholas's expression shifted from frivolous to worried. He tracked his fingers into his hair, holding it off his forehead. "Although this is educational, and the food delicious, I am in agreement we need to solve the mystery of returning to our own time."

Reality replaced Emmeline's food orgasm. "It's got to be the silver dollars, but it could've happened at any point between the Grizzly Creek area and the train station."

Nicholas peered under the table at her boots with a heel, "It is nearly a two mile stretch and it's a trail."

"Oh! Walking wouldn't be my choice, even if I had the right shoes. Anyway, I was on the train, not a trail. Wonder if they rent cars in these days or have taxis, buses? We could get close."

"Bigger cities have cabs even in my day. I doubt they look the same, but we can likely get a ride."

"I haven't seen a phone booth, not sure if they were around then...yet... now. Let's find the library."

The waitress dressed in a crisp white belted dress and a hair net gave them directions as they paid. She beamed, possibly pleased by Nicholas's tip and his looks.

"Tipping was customary in the 1800's?"

"It's a long-standing practice among some."

As they walked, Emmeline questioned, "I know you read the menu and food ingredients and I don't mean to be insulting, but can you ... read?"

She heard his incredulous tone, "Yes. You know there are universities in my day, right?"

She threw her hands up. "I confess I don't know how widespread literacy was in your time. I didn't want to embarrass you at the library."

"Je suis allé à l'école. Je peut lire et écrire," Nicholas said in French.

Emmeline conceded. "Okay okay, you are clearly an educated hunter and I hope you didn't just insult me."

His head flicked. "I have been too impressed with the modern woman to have any insults."

"Considering I am basically the only modern woman you've met; I will consider myself complimented."

"Please do."

Emmeline was curious what other surprises this guy may hold.

Chapter 6

The Library

E ntering the library, Emmeline saw heavy wooden furniture. Thick spindle backed chairs were warmly tucked against the thick rectangle tables. The era didn't have plastic, and no one wanted the noise of metal scraping across a library floor. World and local maps lined the walls. File cabinets stood under the maps. Nicholas found a table while Emmeline asked for a telephone directory. She returned to the table with two, remarking she hadn't seen one in years.

Nicholas's gaze was fixed on the phonebook. He leaned into it and fanned through the pages, randomly stopping. She whispered, "I get all the information might astound you, but remember what we are looking for."

It didn't take Emmeline long to find taxis in the yellow pages under T. She'd never used a phone book but was glad for that elementary lesson in alphabetizing. The town had one cab, a DeSoto. "Not sure how far the taxi travels, but hopefully the couple miles we need." She gestured out the window. "That road is completely different from the one I am used to."

"It did not exist for me," Nicholas said without lifting his eyes.

Emmeline began searching other information. Her parents embraced searches from their phones. There was something about this paper version that even though cumbersome, was refreshing. "While we are here, we should look up a coin collector. See what they're worth." She paused. "Nicholas, I know I may need to use mine too, but I'm not ready to give up my father's coins. Do you mind if we only get yours assessed?"

Nicholas glanced from his scouring the phone book. "I understand. My coins are money to live on. Hopefully, we won't need to resort to that. We will be happily in our own eras before then."

● ● ●

Silence shrouded the ride back. Anticipation turned to hopelessness. At the onset, they shook hands, exchanged polite remarks, expecting to walk through a fog or something to their own eras. That didn't happen. Nothing did. They had pulled out their coins and concentrated on them, as they stood by the road. A gust, or some altered foreboding condition was expected, but never occurred.

At their request, the driver stopped several times along their way back, and they mimicked their same process at each point. He watched them the first two times, likely considering them odd birds. After that, he returned to his newspaper at each stop.

Emmeline longed for the familiar and the hotel across from the train station was the closest to that. They collapsed into lobby chairs. For Emmeline, yesterday's panic and disbelief had given way to a mental scrambling to understand and inner turmoil over what to do next. "I believe we're in 1938, but I sure don't want to hang around."

Emmeline leaned her head against the plush high back chair as her mind scrolled through their obstacles. Money was finite. They had nowhere to stay, and no way to make more money. Then there was the looming issue of being nearly strangers. With each added obstacle, Emmeline's fingers tightened on the arm of the chair. They needed a plan, so they didn't call attention to themselves. They couldn't wander like vagabonds.

"Right now, people may think we are vacationing, but Nicholas, your clothes look like you slept in them."

"Because I did when I was hunting." Nicholas leaned in. "We need to find a place to stay. Has the means of doing that changed in the forty years?"

Ideas ping-ponged in Emmeline's mind. "We could stay a night here, or we can return to the library to look up other places. Returning to the cabin is too risky. I guess we see what's available here. I was told $2.50 yesterday."

Approaching the desk, Emmeline asked the clerk if they had rooms available. Only one remained. That solved her personal dilemma of asking for one room or two.

Returning to what was feeling like their spot in the lobby, "They only have one room remaining; it's still 2.50."

Nicholas nodded, "Considering the time of day, it makes sense to take it, but we cannot afford that for long. What if he asks about our relationship?"

"I could say we are brother and sister on limited cash flow, or I could say we are married. I predict he won't ask."

"Your lack of concern about the perception of being in one room, is still surprising. Considered improper in my time. It leads to a reputation as a..."

She cut him off. "It's very different in the future. No one cares who shares a room." Emmeline added, "Bet he won't question me."

Emmeline was up at the desk. She gestured back to Nicholas. "We arrived yesterday by train. We weren't very comfortable last night. My husband isn't feeling well, and a night here would be wonderful."

The clerk looked over at Nicholas. He said, "The only room left has 2 beds. Is that alright?"

She hid her inner relief. "We'll make that work. Just happy to get a good rest."

"Will you need the bellhop to carry your bags?"

"No, we packed light. We're exploring the area. We're considering relocating."

When she returned, Nicholas asked, "How did it go?"

"We're all set. Got the right clerk. Maybe a bit curious but he didn't ask questions. Your gentleman's behavior has brought you luck. You get to sleep in a bed. There's two of them."

Nicholas stood, grabbing Emmeline's suitcase. "Eager to try the twentieth century bed. See if there are improvements. We won't have to worry about people overhearing anything that may be hard to explain away."

The room overlooked the train station. They didn't need reminding of the predicament, but the reminder glared back.

Emmeline plopped down on the edge of the bed and stared out the window.

Nicholas sat in the one chair by a small round table, rubbing his stomach. "Food is a priority right now. We need to see if any of my money may be worth more. I like to eat. Where should we go?"

"There must be a grocery store. People buy food somewhere."

"Grocery store?" he asked. "Like a general store?"

Emmeline explained. "Same idea, but larger. For decades we've had stores with mostly food in them and you go buy boxes, cans, fresh food there."

"Food in boxes? What kind of food?"

Emmeline named a few, stating that in 2022 most food was either in a box, a can, or frozen.

"That hardly seems like a good advancement. Food should be natural from your own garden or a neighbor's."

"In my day, we eat more based on convenience and speed. I admit it doesn't lead to the healthiest lives—especially with the additives.

Emmeline checked with the desk clerk and discovered a store was around the corner. She put on her coat. "I'll go unless you're curious to see how one looks."

"I am curious about all of it, even what words like additives mean." Nicholas put on his coat.

"We need to clean your clothes. Thank goodness you didn't have luck on your hunt. Blood-stained pants would have been a definite ick."

He glanced down, brushing away nothing visible. He straightened and said, "This is your second remark. Do you always judge a person's fashion? Do I smell?"

"No! Sorry. I'm just too concerned about blending in. Let's go see what 1938 has to offer."

Chapter 7

Good Food

E mmeline smiled walking into the grocery. Near the door were bins of potatoes, carrots, late season apples, and beets. Farther in, rows of boxes stretched, and the aisles had pyramids of cans. It was like walking into a rural locals-only market. She wandered, perusing the choices. Nicholas still stood near the door, with wonderment in his eyes.

She went back for him. "You look like you just walked into a candy store."

He nodded, his eyes still scanning. "What *hasn't* changed in these forty years?"

Emmeline pointed toward the aisles. "Let's see what looks good."

Her eyes landed on the Corn Flakes box. "This is familiar. Have you heard of Corn Flakes? I know they're old. Not my favorite, but I know how they'll taste."

Nicholas didn't answer. He kept walking, head turning both ways, eyes moving up and down. Emmeline grabbed peanut butter, in a tin can, not a jar. It looked odd, but it would keep.

The canned ham was too big. Her eyes widened at the size of the chocolate bar. She scooped up two at only a nickel each.

"You are picking items up and placing them in the basket. Is that alright?"

"Yes, I'm even used to cashing myself out. What looks good to you?"

Nicholas no longer expected to understand every word. He stopped at the fresh fruit and vegetables. "I am not used to seeing so many. That bacon was incredible this morning. I would love more of that."

She chuckled. "I witnessed your love of bacon at breakfast. Remember, we can only get things that don't need cooking or to be kept cold. Better to look for items in boxes, like this cereal."

Emmeline marveled at the inexpensive breakfast. But here, several days of food was even less than their one restaurant meal. They had settled on bread, local cheese, peanut butter, apples, carrots, and two individual bottles of milk. She was eager to drink it. Corn Flakes and Velveeta cheese were left on the shelf.

Along the way back to the hotel they talked about the differences in growing food, production, and storage. Nicholas still seemed astounded. "It seems good to be able to store food longer. The electric refrigerator vs icebox is pure genius."

Emmeline explained how packaging had burgeoned by the late 1900s. She wasn't sure why but now there was packaging within packaging. Food was extensively stored in plastic. Plastic was a great resource for holding freshness, not so great in other ways. She stopped when they reached the hotel.

Once in the room, they spread the food on the table. Emmeline kept talking about packaging pollution becoming so accepted. No one could give up the convenience. She noticed Nicholas reading each of the containers.

She asked, "Are you even listening?"

Nicholas's head turned towards her while his eyes stayed on the words. He then looked directly at her. "I understand everything is very different in your time." He ran his hand down the assortment of food. "This is different enough for me. I have been listening to most of it. Do you always lecture on this way?"

Her face heated. She had droned on, but the rambling was for her own benefit. The reasoning distracted her from the time-travel mess. "I guess I was lecturing. It's dawned on me this might be where my era's love affair with convenience began."

Nicholas asked, "Why do people in your time need things to be so easy, so immediate?"

"I never said immediate, but it is true we don't like to wait long for anything. Our lifestyles just keep accelerating. Both men and women work full time. After work, parents are running their kids to activities." She gestured toward her phone on the table. "Everyone has a phone, as well as other devices. We are always glued to them. We spend time multi-tasking, trying to do two or three things at a time." She broke off. "I'm doing it again, aren't I?"

Nicholas opened a bottle of milk and passed the other to Emmeline. "It is apparent what you see in 1938 is prompting reflection."

Emmeline had seen the play Hamilton and remembered the characters in deep debates. Yet, Nicholas's ability to analyze the issues still surprised her. His furrowed brow while digesting her answers accentuated his attractiveness. An intellectual man always sucked her in. She knew they existed in her era, but she hadn't met many. He'd be someone she would date in her own day. He was not that backwoods, crazed guy coming from the train station two days ago. Speaking French was impressive too. Maybe she was the uneducated one on this trip.

Emmeline's attention jerked to her bottle of milk. Licking her lips "This milk is so creamy! Yum!"

Nicholas took a final chug from his. "Tastes like I remember."

Holding the up the bottle, Emmeline said, "Just one more thing, these bottles. It's rare to get milk in bottles anymore. It's mostly plastic or cardboard.

"You keep speaking of plastic. What is that?"

"Don't think you want me to start in on anything else. That lecture, as you put it, would be even longer."

Nicholas smirked. "Then I won't ask why both the man and woman work jobs, either. Besides, we must get back to setting a plan. There must be more we aren't connecting."

Emmeline agreed. "That librarian was nice when I asked for a phone book. We could go back. For one, she may know places to rent; someplace we can quietly figure out how the hell we got here and what we do to get back." She paused. "Since this was the last room they had, we should plan one more night here in case we don't find anything else. Better than having it gone."

Emmeline's shoulders relaxed knowing they had the room another day. Some pressure was removed. Living life an hour at a time was not comfortable. Yet, with setting even a short term plan, her heart skipped a beat. A plan acknowledged the horrifying idea they might be stuck awhile in 1938. Better to have a plan and not need it.

Emmeline watched Nicholas while they nibbled. Thank goodness she wasn't navigating this on her own. As if reading her mind, Nicholas looked at her. "I haven't felt this comfortable with a woman before. I find you so easy to talk to. Maybe it's because you aren't expecting me to lead the way in all the decisions. You aren't batting your lashes, hoping I want to court you. I can merely relax and be myself."

"I'm comfortable too. You haven't seemed appalled by the changes you are encountering. You don't act shocked by things I say or do."

"I can assure you that your demeanor and language have surprised me, but not in a bad way. Maybe it's the delight one finds in a spirited horse."

Emmeline gasped. "Seriously? Did you just compare me to a horse? You don't want to do that again."

Emmeline yanked her pajamas from her suitcase and stalked off to the bathroom. She brushed her teeth and left the one Nicholas had borrowed on the sink with the toothpaste. She stared in the mirror seeing her emotionally exhausted self. *"What the fuck happened? Who the hell am I in 1938? Things look similar but nothing is the same. No credit cards. No microwaves. Women can vote, but that's about it. Loving vintage isn't the same as living vintage. There are few job options for a woman in my field. Emmeline you gotta figure this out."*

When she returned, Nicholas was leaning forward elbows on his knees, chin resting on his folded hands. His eyes shifted to Emmeline emerging from the bathroom. "Women in pants really is a style in your time, isn't it?"

Chuckling, "Oh yeah, in the 1970s, women spent a good deal of time making whatever the hell I want to wear—or not wear, acceptable."

Emmeline pointed at his shirt. "Not to offend you, but tomorrow we should find you something other than your mountain man clothes...soon people will know you are coming before you enter the room." Bringing his shirt up to his nose, he took a long whiff. He looked up and winked. "No idea what you're talking about."

She laughed. "Your clothes smell fine. I don't know 1898 or 1938 style for men but based on what I've seen during these two days, you will have to decide which era you dress for."

"When in Rome, do as the Romans," he replied. Knowing her own rigid nature, Emmeline liked his flexibility.

Nicholas stood. "Unless you are used to seeing a man you barely know in the buff, I will need to sleep one more night in these long johns."

Disappearing behind the bathroom door he yelled, "This toothbrush for me?"

"Yep!" The next moment she knew the comfort he mentioned was real. She heard a very noisy, long fart. He peeked out the door. "Sorry, in case you were wondering, we do fart in my era."

She vigorously shook her head no. "That might be the LAST thing I was wondering about, but I will be sure to share that common practice when I return to the twenty-first century."

"Glad to dispel another misconception about the manners of my era."

Emmeline wondered about his upbringing. Not only did he speak two languages, but he had a great vocabulary. Her impression of 1898 was skewed.

Emmeline sat on the bed, rubbing her stomach. The nausea reared again, but her head reminded her to hold faith this mystery would be solved. This room was a haven. The antique furniture, or what would become antique, could be in any twenty-first century B&B. For this minute, she pretended it was a weekend away.

Chapter 8

The Snare

When Nicholas came out, he crawled into his bed, laying on his back. Emmeline pulled back her covers and slid under the sheet.

She propped up on her elbow, facing him. "So, what is your question about both women and men in a family working?"

"What do you mean by both working?"

"They both leave the house and go to their jobs. Well, maybe they work their job from home, but they both get paid for their work."

"Women have always worked...in the home, or on the farm. Why did they start going to jobs?"

"They wanted to do more than cook, clean, and take care of the children. Then there's always the financial reason. Twenty-first century living is expensive."

Nicholas lay looking at the ceiling. "Women always seemed satisfied with those things in my day."

"Every woman? Or was that the only option they had?"

"Women could be educated, but once married that was the expectation."

Emmeline couldn't help going on defense. "That expectation was likely established by men. That was the problem. Even in this 1930s era, women were allowed very limited roles, not making room for the woman who wanted more."

Returning a defensive tone, "You think I am arguing a point? I am only explaining. You asked me. Believe me, there are men who want intelligent wives."

"Yeah, they want intelligence but not ambition."

"I said I wasn't comfortable with many women. You asked me a question. I answered." He huffed and exhaled. "You seem to bring up topics that give you reason to pounce like a cougar."

"First a horse, now a cougar. Stop with the metaphors!"

Nicholas shook his head and returned to staring at the ceiling. Emmeline plopped back onto the bed. She brushed her hand over the chenille bedspread, the variation from smooth to bumpy calming her system. The silence stretched between them.

Nicholas couldn't know which concepts had become offensive. She needed to give him more grace. Emmeline groaned and swung her legs to sit on the bed. "Let's try this again."

"Try what?"

"I will be lighter. Let's call it a game."

"Based on my brief experience, this sounds risky."

"I will keep it friendly. Tell me one thing that might surprise me the most about your era, one thing I would like and one thing I would hate."

Flipping to an elbow, "I will if you do the same. I need to think a moment, as you don't seem easily surprised."

She said, "Start with what I would like the most."

"That might be easy. You would like that women can vote in 1898 Colorado and have for the past five years."

"Can people of color vote?"

"Clarify what you mean?"

"Can black women vote?"

"Colored women? Yes."

"We don't use that term anymore, but you're right, I do like that. What about Native Americans?" Seeing his confusion, and remembering his era, "You know, Indians."

He repeated in an astonished tone, "Indians? Nooooo."

Her body tensed. "Why do you say it like that?"

He just stared at her. Emmeline didn't realize she was being very much that cougar.

Finally, Nicholas said, "Well they aren't considered citizens."

She sat taller, and challenged him, "What are they considered?"

Shrugging, "A bother to some, a worry to others, while others want to make them into white people, but to a few they are friends."

Pushing more, "What do *you* consider the Native Americans to be?"

Putting his hands up as if raising the white flag, "Look, I know we are speaking from different eras. I know what native means and I know what Americans mean. That makes this no simple discussion. We need to move on with this thing you call a game."

Emmeline forced her back to relax against a pillow. Nicholas was very articulate.

"Okay, I know something less controversial you would hate. You would hate the long dresses woman wear and the corsets. You wouldn't be wearing your pants very often."

He rushed onto the next subject, "Something of a surprise...H.G. Wells just wrote _The Time Machine._" One corner of his mouth curled up and his eyes twinkled. "Which seems rather pertinent at this moment."

Looking off, Emmeline said, "You're right. It is surprising. I knew it was written a long time ago but would have assumed it was the 1920s."

Nicholas slapped his hands together. "Alright, your turn and don't treat me like I am some backwoods pinhead."

"Ha! I don't think I have been doing that! But okay, what would you hate about 2022? Congestion. People, cars, busyness, crowds, so maybe the activity."

"How busy, how crowded?"

"If you like the Hanging Lake area, you can't even go there without a permit now and it can take months to get."

"I would hate that. Crowds are not something I seek. Even today...well my era 1890s, Denver is too busy for me. Continue. What would surprise me?"

"I think it would surprise you, since it still does me, that not only have people walked on the moon, but some people also live in space for over six months. The big thing is that people...rich but ordinary people have taken rides in spaceships, rockets just for fun."

Nicholas's head jerked to attention. "The moon! Rocketships! They achieved it!" Flashing a large grin. "Incredible! What else have people accomplished?"

"Ahh, so much has happened. We fly in an airplane at least several times a year to get somewhere faster. There are televisions, computers."

Astonishment glistened across Nicholas's face. "People have always dreamed of flying. People of my day are working on it. And you say everyone flies. Maybe that's what I heard in the sky two days ago."

Emmeline nodded. "I did see an airport, a place to keep planes, listed in the yellow pages."

"A place for planes. I would love to see it, but those last two you named—what do they do?"

"The tainted answer is they make our lives more complicated while marketed as making them easier."

"What about your thing, your telephone you kept pulling out of your pocket and looking at yesterday?"

"That's called a cell phone. It has morphed into a combination of computer and television."

"You're back to those two words," Nicholas said.

"They are devices that essentially control our lives. You know, we'll be up all night if I get started. We can keep going tomorrow along with the other topics we started."

Nicholas's eyebrows squished together. "What other topic?"

"You would like it to be forgotten," she said rolling her eyes while moving to her back, "I think I'm tired enough to sleep now. I hope my mind doesn't circle in the horror my family must be experiencing. There are Missing Person posters with my face, all over by now. I've watched enough missing persons shows to know my mom or sister may be suspects. I wish I could let them know I'm safe."

His head turned to Emmeline. "I hope my brain dreams of our way out of here or we wake having returned to our respective times." She saw worry in his eyes as he said, "Good night."

Chapter 9

Day Three

E mmeline's eyes opened, immediately studying Nicholas who was turned on his side facing the bathroom. Her eyes lingered on his broad shoulders and the muscular definition of his arm resting on his hip. She was crazy to be attracted to this guy. She had to stay focused. This was a nightmare. Granted Nicholas made it easier to bear, but still a nightmare.

Nicholas rolled on to his back and stretched his arms long above his head, tensing those defined arms. He groaned one of those first sounds of the day. His floppy blonde hair was in disarray, well like, he'd slept on it. She struggled to regain her usual self-control over her thoughts. He turned his head toward Emmeline and slowly he smiled. Her watching had been obvious.

Abruptly sitting, she asked, "Are you hungry? We have some food that would work for breakfast. How about a peanut butter sandwich?"

Nodding vigorously, Nicholas said, "Yes. That was a delightful surprise yesterday."

She planned the day as she made sandwiches. "Maybe a coin store should be first on our list, then we will know what money we have to work with."

Responding, "Good idea but I need to hold some money, so I have it when I get back to 1898. Newer coins won't be any good and could cause new problems."

"Me, I get to just pull out my credit card. Then we need to find a clothing store. It'd be fun to have an authentic 30s dress for my return."

He smirked. "And give up your pants?"

She dismissed him with a wave of the hand.

His light mood flipped like a switch. Nicholas had turned away and his shoulders slumped. She asked, "What just happened?"

"Reality struck. I have moments where I am flooded with terror and the next moment, I trust we will figure it out or fleetingly I think, it's not horrible here."

Gazing downward, she nodded a slow "Yeahh." Emmeline dealt with panic quietly. People rarely saw it. Time travel qualified as a time she'd let herself freak out.

Turning back to her, he said, "I am glad this didn't happen to me—by myself. I would have hidden in the woods initially, but it wouldn't work forever. Another person makes this easier—you make it easier."

"I know exactly what you mean. Other than the day in the bar, my paralyzing moments have come at night. Any shitty situation is made better with company." Emmeline saw his head flick. "I will do my best to minimize my swearing, but I don't hold out hope for that either.

●●●

They were first through the library door. A wooden cabinet loaded with small drawers caught her eye. The front of each drawer displayed letters of the alphabet. She opened the drawer to see a series of cards with topics and book names. The system was unfamiliar, but Emmeline surmised they were a rudimentary version of her Google. The librarian approached her to ask if she needed help. She told her they were enamored with the town and would be staying awhile.

Emmeline made her way to the table with a list of places to rent and shops to buy what they needed. The Curio, a shop on 10th St. sounded like a pawn shop but the librarian thought the owner may deal in coins too. Nicholas had found a map of the town and noted, "There's so much more here, more streets than forty years ago.

"That's what I meant last night. Things keep expanding and getting more crowded." List in hand, Emmeline continued in a whisper. "People haven't asked many questions. With my dark hair, we don't look like brother and sister. I think they assume we are married. What do you think of that?"

"I might be from a stricter time than you, but many situations make strange bedfellows. We can pretend to be whatever makes sense for what I hope to be a short time."

Emmeline checked the list and located places on the map. She found the Curio shop location. She worked through the rentals. There was a boarding house, an apartment, and a cabin. "Nicholas, look at this!"

He shifted behind her to see exactly where she pointed. Emmeline could feel the warmth of his breath on the back of her head. "Find something interesting?"

"The cabin we stayed in; YOUR cabin is for rent!"

"It is?!"

"The note just says historical cabin, but based on location, it must be yours. Plus, it's the cheapest. It's probably why they updated the bed and the heating system. It's more than a museum."

Emmeline approached the tall, slender librarian once more. "Since I keep asking you questions, I think I should know your name."

The red headed woman wore her hair in a bun. "My name is Marjorie." She beamed at being acknowledged.

"Nice to meet you. I'm Emmeline. My husband, seated at the table, is Nicholas."

Emmeline pointed to the list. "We walked around yesterday and passed a historical park in memory of N. Jones. I think it's the same cabin. It looked cozy. How do we rent it?"

Her tone was enthusiastic. "For now, that's me! It typically draws no renters in the winter. You may want to check the other places first. It's very rustic."

"We're fine with rustic, and the price is right."

"Then I can show it to you over my lunch at noon."

Emmeline said, "Perfect. We have some errands and will be back at noon."

Chapter 10

Old Coins

A bell jingled as they entered The Curio. A man in his thirties with a scar along a cheek sat behind a case. He adjusted his wire-rimmed glasses as he greeted Emmeline and Nicholas. "Welcome. Browse around. I have many treasures."

As Emmeline navigated toward a wooden tree stand holding hats, she wondered about the scar. She listened as Nicholas approached the owner. "I have some old coins. I am curious if their worth is beyond face value." Emmeline kept an eye on the counter between glances of a hat in the mirror. Nicholas checked to be sure his silver dollar matching the year of Emmeline's was securely in his pocket. He dumped twenty coins from his drawstring pouch onto the counter. The man spread them out and lifted his magnifying glass. As he scrutinized them, he reached for his valuating book. He muttered sounds. "Hmmmmm," and "Oh!" as he bit down a smile and glanced repeatedly from coin to book.

He moved his glasses to his head. "You have very nice coins. All beyond face value, but a few of these are quite rare. Where did you get these?"

Nicholas punted smoothly. "I found them when clearing out my grandfather's house. They were in this pouch under a mattress."

"Your grandfather must have known there was value to keep it under a mattress."

Nicholas shrugged. "I doubt it. I found several meaningless items stashed away. Some were simply sentimental."

His smooth delivery impressed Emmeline. Emmeline averted attention several times with made up stories during the past few days. Nicholas doing so raised curiosity. Did he have a practice of lying or could he think quickly on his feet?

Of the coins laid out, five were from the 1880s and one from 1870. Still peering down, closely inspecting each one, the man quietly spoke. "You could receive a nice sum for these. I could take the lot off your hands."

"Thank you, but I am not interested in selling any more than necessary. Can you tell me what each may be worth?"

The merchant issued a flat tone, "I see." He arranged them in a line from least valuable to most. He examined and re-examined the most valuable with the magnifying glass. He looked at Nicholas with a forced smile. "You must have several thousand dollars in your possession. I don't hold that kind of cash but if you came back, I could help you out." Emmeline stopped wandering the small store and joined Nicholas at the counter in case he needed backup.

Nicholas shifted feet on the creaky floor. "We only need some cash to get us by. We found ourselves suddenly without money for our trip."

The merchant showed no interest in their story. He held a stony expression as his eyes ran along the coins. "I can only estimate but I believe this last coin could be worth three-hundred dollars."

Nicholas barked a quick laugh, "I could live a year on that amount."

The proprietor replied, "Then you live very frugally, sir, but yes, it is a nice amount."

In 2022, Emmeline could only stay a couple nights in a reasonable hotel for three-hundred dollars. Nicholas picked up the coins beginning with the most valuable. The merchant's face grew sullen as he watched each coin drop into the pouch. To Emmeline, his expression darkened beyond losing a sale. Nicholas handed over the five that would get them by in the foreseeable future.

The merchant said, "My name is Herman Jameson. Who do I have the pleasure of working with?"

"I am Nicholas, and this is my wife Emmeline. I must say, you know a good deal about coins. How did you become interested?"

Jameson blinked twice. "Just a hobby that developed into more." He quickly added, "I need to get cash from the safe. I will be right back."

While gathering up the coins for exchange, he invited them to browse, indicating there may be an item or two on which to spend their money. Pointing to the vintage jewelry as he turned away, "Perhaps a new trinket for your wife."

Emmeline's eyes met Nicholas's. Her eyes widened hearing the term spoken by a stranger. Nicholas flicked his eyebrows and smiled. Emmeline would resent the assumption in her day, but right now, the term eased risk of suspicion. She repeated his earlier words. "When in Rome."

Emmeline wandered the store, pausing again at the clothes. She was a sucker for vintage hats, but these were vintage to her vintage. It reminded her of familiar consignment stores. Cluttered, full of someone else's treasures that outgrew them physically or emotionally. Some of these clothes were more costume attire. There was a dropped waist dress with beaded fringe and one with a scooped neck, and a handkerchief hem. Much of what she saw, she considered flapper style. On the other side of the store, the man returned, and handed Nicholas a hefty stack of bills, a few coins, and some other small item. She guessed Nicholas found a treasure of his own.

Once outside, Emmeline scanned Nicholas up and down, saying, "Next stop, new clothes." Emmeline knew Nicholas was trying to imply an insult when he chuckled and mimicked the same up-down scan. However, they both knew who was winning that contest.

Nicholas opened the department store door. "It's best if we stick together. You probably have better judgement about appropriate dress for this charade." He gestured his hand head-to-toe. "But I am keeping all of this for when I return."

They walked past the home furnishings to the men's clothing in the back. It was all there, from socks to shirts, pants, suits, even boxers. Emmeline knew this was a time of most men wearing hats, but she was excited eyeing the ties. They were an expected item for so many occasions in her dad's era. He often wore them to work. Now, in 2022, they weren't even necessary for a wedding unless you were a groomsman. She assumed Nicholas was not the tie kind, but she'd already misjudged him several times in three days. It didn't matter. She wasn't about to put on a girdle the salesperson would likely suggest.

Nicholas wandered aimlessly. The salesman approached Emmeline. "Are you shopping for new clothes for your husband?"

"We need your most comfortable clothes."

The salesman sized up Nicholas' 5'11, broad frame and brought over a pair of pleated high-waisted pants, a belt, an argyle sweater, and a polo shirt. Emmeline nodded approvingly and Nicholas gestured toward the flannel shirts. The salesman suggested something different from his current attire may be nice. However, grasping the customer type he was dealing with, the salesman grabbed a pair of Levi's and carried it all back to a dressing room.

Emmeline followed. "If you want to come out for an opinion, I'll be here."

Naturally he emerged in the jeans and polo shirt first. The salesman had nailed his size. Emmeline could make out his lean muscular legs and the short sleeve shirt revealed his taut forearms.

Emmeline was focused only on his physique but said, "You look great!"

He smiled at her with genuine enthusiasm. He took a muscular arm stance and laughed. "One sold," he said as he turned back into the dressing room. Coming out with the sweater and pants, he gave a slight bow.

"Get out of the way, Ryan Gosling." She exclaimed, swiping the air.

"By your expression, I assume that's approval."

The salesman, interested in a sale said, "Sir, you are ready for a fine restaurant in Glenwood Springs."

Turning to the salesman, Emmeline asked if Nicholas could wear the jeans out and bag up the old clothes since he'd traveled several days in them. The salesman returned with an empty bag but then asked about socks etc. She nodded yes, and once he was all set and checked out, they were directed back toward the front of the store for the women's clothes.

Emmeline had noticed a comfortable pair of pants on the mannequin in the window. She made a beeline for those. Coming up behind her, Nicholas gibed, "Pants, but of course."

"Someone has to start the trend toward women being comfortable. I will find a skirt, too."

The saleswoman suggested that, of course, she wanted a slip. Emmeline had no intention of spending money on such a ridiculous item to go with a lined skirt.

She politely said, "I have one that will work nicely." Then the woman asked about the nylons and a garter belt. Even though Emmeline knew them as a lingerie item in Victoria's Secret, they would provide some warmth.

Emmeline couldn't pass up the navy cuffed wide-legged pants that buttoned up the side. However, she walked out in a burnt orange pleated skirt with a tight cream sweater.

The clerk turned to Nicholas when Emmeline said she was ready to check out. She pushed down her surly remark. Her adult-self recognized it was merely a sign of the times. The total was meager, and she now had three outfits appropriate for the era. She hoped she would need no more.

Chapter 11

Making the Best of It

E mmeline was pleased they had shopped without appearing out of place. They were ready for the next big task; getting into that place to stay. They found Marjorie still behind her desk. Marjorie smiled at Nicholas, noticing his fresh clothes and their bags from Toeller department store. "You made some purchases, I see. So was the Curio fruitful?"

Nodding, Nicholas said, "I wish everything my grandfather hid was of such value."

Marjorie concurred, "Yes, every old person thinks they have an entire house of valuables."

Emmeline nodded, "We are ready to check out...to see the cabin." Only they knew, they already had.

"The heat remains on low, but I can show you how to adjust it, and it'll be toasty warm within a few hours."

Gazing at Nicholas, Emmeline assured Marjorie, "We are both use to roughing it. I have been on campouts and Nicholas hunts, so we'll be comfortable."

Enjoying the pretending, Nicholas added, "Emmeline is one hearty lady. She even enjoys sleeping on the ground."

Emmeline squinted her eyes suspiciously, wondering if he was considering changing up sleeping arrangements. Jokingly to nip the idea, she retorted, "Sleeping on a wooden floor is not my preference, dear."

Ignoring Marjorie's confused look, Nicholas jabbed back. "That's only a consideration for the nights you snore."

Emmeline flashed a sweetly fake smile. "We both know that never happens."

Marjorie cleared her throat. "I can step away in about thirty minutes."

"Great. We will meet you there after I grab my bag at the hotel. They are holding it for us."

Once outdoors, Emmeline admitted, "That was kind of fun."

Nicholas tossed back his head with a laugh. "If we must be here, we may as well try to have fun."

Even after grabbing the suitcase, they still arrived a few minutes before Marjorie. They made sure their previous footprints were erased.

Reviewing the outhouse Nicholas said, "This is in the same place as years ago, but I hope not everything is as it was, if you know what I mean?"

"Anything will beat squatting in the woods, exposed to frigid air. God, I can't wait to get back to my flush toilet and take a hot shower in my very own bathroom."

Marjorie was prompt. She located the key in its hiding spot. Opening the door she said, "I do apologize. We usually have a single man choosing to stay in this cabin. It is rustic."

Emmeline went through motions of scanning the cabin. "We can make do nicely. I see the heater. Is there a cooking place?" Emmeline knew there was an old wood-burning stove with a burner on top. That had not been updated. Marjorie explained most of the men who stayed took their meals in town, but there was wood out back. Since it was his, Nicholas would know how to get it cranking.

They paid Marjorie for three days, a mere $2.50. That price inspired them to make do. Marjorie showed them how to operate the heater and primed the water pump to make sure it wasn't frozen.

When she left, she unlocked the outhouse, which also had a hidden key. Nicholas checked it out as soon as Marjorie was out of sight. Returning with an armful of wood, he reported the privy had been shored up and had a fresh hole. Emmeline laughed. "Nothing like petrified poop."

He set about making a fire, while Emmeline pumped water into a pitcher from a shelf. After setting out the remaining food, Emmeline made a trip to the grocery, returning with some items she hoped would suffice. "If I had to time-travel, I'm glad it was at least during the paper bag revolution. I don't know what you used but lugging even one bag three blocks in the cold made me miss my car."

The temperature had risen at least ten degrees, a candle flickered, and a fire crackled. A cast-iron skillet and pot were out on the wood-burner. Nicholas slouched in the chair holding the coin from his pocket. "Now that we are settled for a couple days, we need to get back to what the heck happened to us and how we un-do it."

"Absolutely. In my calm moments I can enjoy this as a reenactment. But I miss my coffee maker, my door-dash meals. I miss the independence I get from my car."

Nicholas pulled a folded flyer from his shirt pocket. It told of a meeting the next night on the other side of town. He unfolded it and rubbed his chin. "Have you ever heard of Edgar Cayce?"

"No, who's that?

"I haven't either, but from this flyer I think he's a psychic. His understudy will be in town tomorrow, offering readings. Maybe he could give us some answers."

Emmeline tilted her head. "I am a bit surprised by your openness to the topic."

He mirrored her head tilt. "Soothsaying isn't a new concept. My grandmother seemed to have a gift for knowing something may happen before it did."

"Interesting. I never knew my grandmother, but my mother would talk about her doing the same. I don't usually put much stock in it but my sister, Hannah, and I have shared dreams more than once." Her head drooped. "The dreamworld seems to be one of the few places we connect."

"If nothing we try on our own tomorrow works, I say we attend. We could get an inspiration."

"Maybe. But let's go over it all one more time. We walked from the station about the same time. It doesn't seem to be the Grizzly Creek connection. I didn't notice anything until I stepped off the train, but I had been asleep. The same-year coin seems the stronger link. But there must be something else."

Emmeline stopped talking and pondered what all changed in this time travel escapade. She peered at Nicholas. "It's a random thought, but how old are you?"

"I am 25, why do you ask now?"

"I know this is changing topics, but has it occurred to you that if this was your cabin in 1898, that was only 40 years ago by 1938 standards. You are very possibly still alive...somewhere. If you aren't alive, you might have died relatively young."

Nicholas scratched his head. "I calculate I would be sixty-five. For my era, I have likely died. It is often the people with a more comfortable lifestyle that live long."

Emmeline scooted forward on the bench. "I agree the priority is to get back to 1898 but it could be cool finding out what happened to you. God, I could really use Google right now! If you have died, then if...when you get back, you could avoid it."

"Hmmmm, I am not sure I *want* to know how I die."

"Now that I'm thinking about it, I can't let go. Why is this cabin memorialized? It's like you did something notable for the area."

"I find it hard to believe my simple life became anything notable."

Emmeline sat straight up. "Now that I'm thinking about what happened to you, I wonder about *my* family. My sister's house has been in our family for a hundred years! So, whoever lives there is probably a relative. That is a mind-blowing thought."

"Mind...blowing. Another term from a different century, but it is surely astounding to consider."

"There must be phrases from your time that imply something big without the use of grand vocabulary."

With eyes twinkling Nicholas countered, "We don't have to speak so simply to be understood. Maybe intelligence didn't keep progressing."

Emmeline twitched her brows. "There are many who would agree with that statement."

Nicholas rubbed his stomach. "I am hungry. Who's the better chef?

"If you can show me how someone opens a can in 1898, I can take a crack at it." Pulling out a substantial knife, he aptly worked his way around the lid of Dinty Moore beef stew. "How different can it be to open a can?"

●●●

While eating, Emmeline said, "Should we discuss sleeping arrangements, your 1898 impressions about Indigenous People, or our plan for tomorrow?"

"I anticipate I know the sleeping arrangements. I will avoid the second topic, and the last seems mind, what is it, blowing?"

They ate slowly, enjoying even the canned stew. Emmeline pushed down a rising awareness of liking this man across the table. "In my century, we are always in a hurry, eating during lunch or in our cars. I heard a man speak about how being attentive to the eating process can have a healing effect. Like what we are doing now. Eating slowly, among friends, or having pleasing candlelight. This is relaxing. You're good company Nicholas."

"As are you—most of the time," Nicholas said with a wink. Emmeline admitted to herself her intensity was too often a buzzkill.

"Based on how frequently you looked at your tiny telephone that first day, it does seem you are always waiting for something else."

"There's so much else. Podcasts, texts, gaming, zooming, memes. Sorry for the spew of words. Like I said, we thrive on multi-tasking."

His lips scrunched to one side, "Other than some fascinating advancements, your era doesn't seem so appealing."

"There are problems, but I can't imagine staying here as a woman. It's a grand time for men, not women. I don't mean to make it sound horrible. I love having so many options when it comes to careers, food, shopping."

Nicholas stood. "I think it's a grand time to bring in more wood."

●●●

Emmeline went to use the outhouse before it got dark. In the last of the sun, she could just make out etchings on the wall. A tree, a bear, and a paw print.

"Was that you who spent time drawing in the outhouse?" She laughed. "Did you get bored?"

His face flushed. "It might seem odd, but they provided atmosphere when I first built it."

She smiled. The similarities of people across time warmed her. The comfort from touches of making a house a home is unchanged. Her mom did the same. The knick-knacks, wall hangings, and squishy pillows all offered stability. In that moment she hoped she could soon touch all those items she'd poked fun at for being old. Her mind slid to her own apartment. Would she ever breathe in the scent of the lavender candle in her bathroom? Would she sleep again on her memory foam mattress?

When Emmeline came out of her nostalgia, she noticed Nicholas had lit a lantern and used the extra blanket Marjorie left to create the private area again. They lingered at the table awhile longer. They agreed their time in 1938 stretched beyond the three days it had been. "There's a bond that forms when people go through traumatic events together," Emmeline reflected.

"Yes, it happens in wartime, during disasters. You bond rapidly and in a manner that resonates forever."

"That might be why families are so bonded even if not friends. They have seen struggles and the worst of each other over the years."

Nicholas stood to get his flask and a small pouch from his coat pocket. He handed the pouch to Emmeline. "I thought if we are going to pretend to be a couple, to be married, this would help us look more convincing."

Emmeline's eyebrows shot up as she tugged the draw strings and slipped out a rose gold band with a small garnet. "When did you do this?"

"I picked it out while you were trying on hats in the curio shop. I hope it fits. I was only estimating."

It was silly, yet quite sweet. It was pragmatic, but thoughtful. "I'm not sure what I think of this. It makes sense and could be a sweet memento when we return to our separate eras. I will need to think of something for you to remember me by."

"You are pretty memorable on your own." Emmeline held his lingering gaze, then tucked away the stirring she'd rather deny. He was right. This experience, this fiasco, will forever change them. She liked this guy. Even if he accepted her style and language, it was absurd to have thoughts that it could be anything. 1898 and 2022 might work for a day or two out of necessity. Clashes can't be far away.

Chapter 12

Night Four

It was warmer in the cabin than it had been that first night when they were in a state of utter shock about time traveling. They changed clothes from their own sides of the blanket. Nicholas changed into a different pair of long johns he'd bought at the department store, and she stayed with her polar bears. When Emmeline came around the blanket, he ran an imaginary line down her pajamas and said, "Based on the past two days, I presume it is not unseemly to walk around in them.

"Not at all. There was a trend for teenagers to show up at grocery stores in their pajamas." But what she really thought, was even though thin, she didn't have the ripped muscle tone that his revealed.

Nicholas guffawed. "Night clothes worn outside the house. Your era isn't overly appealing, but it is entertaining."

"Happy to provide levity. Hey, it isn't necessary to close the blanket between us. After all, we spent the past two nights at the hotel in full view, with only a few feet between."

Nicholas pushed back the blanket. "I am very comfortable sleeping anywhere by myself. But waking up and seeing another person makes this easier to bear."

Emmeline settled in the bed, and after blowing out the lantern, Nicholas sprawled on the floor. "Nicholas, I feel guilty since this was your bed. If we are still here, I can try the floor tomorrow." Those words, still here tomorrow, created a moment of question and that question was if she held a sliver of hope they could remain together.

While on her back, she turned her head and reviewed the plan. "Let's go back to the train station tomorrow. We think it's the coin, but maybe some specific activity needs to be happening. Then if that doesn't work, we go see the understudy in hopes of new insight."

"If we strike out again, let's find the museum. You have made me curious about my future past," Nicholas said.

"Maybe you gifted the cabin or did something honorable that made the town want to memorialize you."

He still couldn't fathom the word remarkable was paired with Nicholas Jones. "I lead a pretty simple life."

"At least it was simple until 1898." Emmeline ended the conversation stating she hoped he would be warm enough and to grab the blanket or turn the heat higher if not. He nodded, saying goodnight, and turned to his side so he was facing away from her.

With the waxing moon shining, Emmeline could see his outline in the dark. Her eyes rested on him for a bit, and she wondered if he might be wishing that this could somehow continue. When his breathing became rhythmic, she turned toward the wall and willed herself to sleep.

Chapter 13

Finding Nicholas's History

The familiarity and silence of the library soothed Emmeline, particularly following another failed attempt to return to their own times. They dropped heavily to the chairs, engulfed by defeat. "I really thought this would be the one," Emmeline whispered.

Marjorie appeared at their table. "You don't look happy. Was the cabin truly comfortable enough for you? I wouldn't like it."

Emmeline shifted out of her slump for show purposes only. "It stayed cozy, but the outhouse was very frosty," feigning a shiver.

Marjorie glimpsed the ring on Emmeline's hand. She pointed. "Your ring! I love rose gold. This one is simple, but beautiful."

Unsure how to respond, Emmeline chose a partial truth. "Nicholas surprised me last night. We were spontaneous in our marriage and the original didn't fit very well. I didn't wear it often."

There was no questioning her statement. "What brings you back this morning?"

Emmeline told her they wanted to know the cabin's history, and why the cabin had been preserved.

Marjorie asked, "What is your surname? I notice your husband shares the same first name as the man that owned the cabin."

Emmeline opened her mouth to give her own last name but caught herself. Glad that Nicholas's last name was common, she said, "Jones."

Looking surprised, Marjorie said, "You must be wondering if he's related."

Nicholas spoke up. "I don't know any relations that lived in Glenwood Springs."

Marjorie directed them to the local history museum. "I do know Mr. Nicholas Jones was instrumental in helping the town fight the influenza pandemic of 1918."

Emmeline pushed down her desire to commiserate since her own world was just emerging from its own pandemic.

She resonated with Marjorie's next words. "It was horrible. So many died, and it left many survivors wondering why they had been spared. I was raised by an aunt in Denver because both of my parents died within weeks of each other."

Emmeline let out a small gasp. "That's so tragic. You must have been pretty young."

"I was." Marjorie looked past Emmeline to Nicholas and mused. "Maybe he's related in some way. He resembles pictures."

Emmeline attempted to deflect the comment. "Maybe, but I know I have one of those faces people think looks like their cousin or friend. It's probably that." She turned toward Nicholas. "Thanks once again, Marjorie. We'll check out the museum."

They had considered a haircut for Nicholas to help him blend into the 1938 style, but after Marjorie's statement of his looking similar, they agreed the longer hair and start of a beard were wiser right now. They didn't want him recognized as the original owner of the cabin.

They strolled admiring the housing architecture on their way to the museum. Nicholas said, "I am not sure if I am more curious or apprehensive about what I will discover."

Emmeline touched his shoulder. "I get it. At least it sounds like you were one of the good guys."

●●●

Admission was free to the museum and empty of patrons. There were exhibits on Doc Holliday, Kid Curry, and photos of the filming of the *Great Train Robbery*. It was strange to be viewing history from more than a century ago discussed as recent. Doc Holliday, a famous gambler and wanted man, arranged for the Colorado governor to deny his extradition. Before dying at age 36 from tuberculosis, he'd been a dentist. Emmeline was curious why the governor would protect him. Part of the silent film, *The Great Train Robbery* was filmed in Colorado, but it became renowned for cutting edge film techniques.

They finally came across a small section about Nicholas. They stood close but read each placard silently. Flushing, Nicholas shook his head and rubbed his jaw. "I don't know what I should feel. Pride? Sorrow because I am dead. Or do I henceforth strut like a peacock?"

"It *is* quite impressive. I sensed you're a good man, but this certainly confirms that impression." She smiled up at him. "It must be humbling to see such kind words written about yourself."

These photographs were of a man nearly twenty years older. The hair was shorter, with strands of gray. Nicholas struck a proud profile pose but spoke softly. "I age quite nicely, don't I?"

"Even if you do say so yourself," Emmeline had fun saying it even though he didn't understand the quip.

Throughout the afternoon, Nicholas showed growing comfort with his notoriety. He referenced himself with the most complimentary remarks, laughing out loud each time.

"If you are quite done lavishing your ego with compliments, how about if we spend some time figuring out what else influenced our jumping time periods."

With a sideways glance Nicholas remarked, "I do enjoy our banter. I know I said it before, but you are very easy to be with." Emmeline turned her head away. She wondered if he too, could be second-guessing the rightness of going their separate ways.

They repeated the only things they knew to do. Hold their coins inside the train station. Hold their coins standing near their tracks. Walking from the back of the station to the front. Nothing worked. They plodded along the tracks with their silver dollars in hand. Their shared defeat showed as they slogged to the cabin. They slumped down on the stoop letting the cold cement permeate their clothes, instilling a discomfort besides melancholy.

They sat with their own thoughts. Nicholas stood. "The chill has overridden my disappointment, and now I'm hungry." He extended a hand to help Emmeline up. His grasp distracted her disappointment.

Nicholas opened the Lays potato chips Emmeline had bought. He surveyed each chip before munching it. "I know you said you grew up on Lays, but I have never tasted such thin, crunchy potatoes.

She took the bag from him and chuckled. "Please try to focus on the task at hand."

Nicholas faked a protest. "Wait, you're stealing from one of the most gener...."

"Oh stop," doing her best to sound disgusted instead of amused. "You weren't traveling by train. How long does it take you to walk by foot from the creek area?"

"Getting back takes about 20 minutes by foot. I moved at a good pace."

Chiming in, Emmeline asked, "What were you thinking about?"

"I was remembering a Christmas when I was fifteen. I received a new pair of shoes and a book. It wasn't what I received. It was the last Christmas with my parents. That memory pops up during most holidays."

"Wow! I was thinking about my dad, too. One year he gave me a couple of old coins for Christmas. It started my coin collecting with him. My father has also passed away."

"But your mother is still alive?"

"Yeah, but my sister has always been closer to her than I am. I find her too flighty. She describes me as intense, serious. Don't get me wrong, we love each other. We just aren't connected as Dad and I were."

He lowered the chip from his mouth. "We were both thinking about our parents and a specific Christmas. Maybe there's a connection there! We were both reminiscing about a time which felt good. Nostalgia. Maybe that's what has been missing. The emotion paired with the event. Not the place as much as the emotion."

"Oh my God! Yes! Let's try it!"

Each holding their coin, they stayed seated in the cabin with their eyes closed, calling up their Christmas memory. They agreed to focus on it for one minute. Emmeline peeked one eye open. Nicholas was watching her with a contemplative gaze. "Did you focus for the full minute?" she asked.

"I am sure I did, but alas, here we are. We should try this at the train station."

Emmeline's heart pounded with new hope as she set a swift pace. Nicholas trailed behind. "You don't seem in a hurry to get back to your era," she said, as she outpaced him.

"I was pondering. Whatever brought us here didn't bring any others that we know of. Why? Was it only the thought? Or was it the time of day paired with the thought? Maybe, the place and thought? Our coins and our thought? We are flailing around, throwing darts blindly at the dart board."

Emmeline slowed her pace to his. "My father used to describe me with the word tenacity. I won't let discouragement take over. We have got to figure this out. I can't stay here in 1938." Even as she spoke, 'I can't stay,' the slightest of doubt crept in.

The Taylor house in its original splendor came into view. This home to a former senator, was apartments in her day. Glenwood was as charming in 1938 as it was in 2022. Possibly more so with fewer people and cars. She was never a big city lover even though she lived in a sweet Denver neighborhood with homes from the mid 1800s. Emmeline halted as the red sandstone station came into view. She was afraid to fail again, while on the edge about it working.

●●●

Once they were inside the station, an attendant approached and asked if they needed assistance. He suggested Emmeline might be more comfortable in the women's waiting room away from the men. A heavy smoke and cigar smell lingered in the air, but Emmeline said she hoped it was alright if they sat a moment. "We won't be long. I need a minute out of the chill."

Nicholas leaned his head sideways towards her. "You don't think so, but you embellish very well."

"Time travel has made me a quicker thinker," she chuckled.

Moving toward a wall, they stood side by side, shoulders touching, their fingers wrapped around the coins. With eyes open to minimize looking odd, they each connected with their Christmas memory.

Not a thing changed. Nothing. Emmeline dropped her head. She rubbed her forehead and released a low, disappointed sigh. Nicholas nudged her gently with his elbow. She met his forlorn teal eyes. He slowly shook his head and spoke with a dulled tone. "Not a thing has changed. Let's walk outside."

Just before reaching the door, Nicholas touched her sleeve. "If it works this time, I want you to know you made this outrageous event better than I would have ever expected."

She gently touched his fingers. "Same."

Emmeline shoved a vision of success into her mind. She saw Hannah opening her front door. For this attempt, they concentrated their gaze on the ground. Emmeline squeezed her coin so tightly there would be an imprint.

A moment later, she lifted her lids to see a man in a suit and tie pass by. It was his derby hat that told her it wasn't 2022. She thumped her head back against the wall. "Arrrggh! I hope you see 1938, because I don't want to do this alone."

Turning to Emmeline, Nicholas swallowed hard. "We are still here—together." His voice was low and thick.

They didn't move. They didn't speak. They stood silently. Emmeline questioned if a faith or belief factor might impact this working or not. She had seen movies with seances falling flat because there was a skeptic in the group.

Apparently reading her mind, Nicholas asked, "What are we doing wrong?"

Frustrated with the absurdity of their circumstance, she said, "How would we know? I am basing my experience with time travel on movies, and you on a couple of books and your imagination."

"I guess we see the understudy tonight," Nicholas said.

"Yep. Nicholas, have you ever had a reading?"

"Never, have you?"

"A couple, which is why I ask. I'd love to believe we will get something out of it, but too often they speak in generalities. At best, we will have to unravel some clues, or it will serve absolutely no purpose."

Nicholas swallowed hard again. "You need to keep that tenacity strong. If we don't get information from the understudy, a different reality will be upon us. When little money remains, we may be faced with trusting someone about who we are."

Shaking her head to release the failures, "You're right. Tenacity. Tenacity. I won't think past today. My mom would say we have to hold the belief tonight will work out."

She put her coin back in her coat pocket and buttoned it. She shoved her hands through her hair and flung them down. "Okay. Shake it off. That's hours away. Let's go to a movie. In the dark, no one will see the helplessness on our faces." She explained movies to him as they walked.

●●●

The Lady Vanishes was on the marquee. "Ha! How appropriate is this? Not sure what it's about but if the lady vanished, we might get a fresh idea."

Emmeline asked for two tickets from the woman in the booth. Nicholas put fifty cents through the small opening. Emmeline inhaled deeply. At least the delightful aroma of popcorn was the same. They stopped by a poster display of a movie called The Law of Texas, a western. She told Nicholas, "I'd be curious what you'd think of Hollywood's version of the 1800s."

He quirked his eyebrows up. "History is often rewritten."

They selected seats in the balcony, hoping for fewer people. The silence and the darkness of the theater was like a fitful night's sleep for Emmeline. Her brain generated every single thing that may go wrong for them. Her glassy stare didn't see the black and white movement. The movie she watched was of a mother's terror over a missing daughter. The sister was frantically calling anyone she'd known since childhood, asking if they'd seen her sister.

Nicholas leaned forward, elbows on his knees as he continued to pull buttered popcorn from the bag and push it into his mouth. If she hadn't noticed his mesmerized actions, she would have escaped her own mind and run from the theater. Instead, she sat letting conversations with her mom loop in her head. That ceased only when her mind stumbled on to being discovered as frauds in 1938.

They sat still through the credits. When the lights went up, Emmeline turned to him. "That didn't help our situation at all. I didn't see a moment of it. All I saw was my mom's and sister's sobs. They must be going nuts trying to figure out why I didn't show up, though I did."

Nicholas didn't respond to her remark. His eyes were round and his mouth open. Seeing his amazement she realized, he hadn't experienced the slow progression of movie magic with frames jerking by or the melodramatic, heavy make-upped silent ones. He went right to the realistic black and white film.

Excitedly, he said, "That was astonishing! I know you explained it, but it had to be seen. Plus, I had only heard of popcorn. It's delicious!"

"I'll give you a pass for ignoring my heart rending words."

Chapter 14

The Understudy

E mmeline had never walked so much in any four-day period. Luckily the snow didn't develop, and the winter weather was in the thirties. The hall where the readings were taking place was on the far north side of town. Emmeline was surprised to see nearly twenty people milling around as they entered. They weren't sure how things would run, but the hall had rows of wooden folding chairs. It was chapel sized with smooth sided pine wood interior and small windows on opposite walls. There was a lectern off to the side implying it was a building used for meetings. Cayce's understudy was Edmund Girard. Wearing small rectangular glasses, he looked to be in his late thirties. He had a dark goatee and a short hair style parted on the side.

Mr. Girard circulated the room then shook hands with people who approached the table for tea and a cookie. His lips held a gracious smile while his eyes lingered when he introduced himself to each person. Emmeline thought his eyes absorbed the worries people held, and his genuine smile showed pleasure for each person's interest. The mannerisms were more inviting than unnerving.

At about five minutes past six, he asked everyone to have a seat. Mr. Girard sat at the front where there were two empty chairs beside him. For a few moments, he watched everyone get settled. He reintroduced himself and offered background regarding his experience, his purpose, and how the evening would progress. He indicated readings would be public but last varying lengths of time.

Mr. Girard guessed some people likely came out of curiosity and were only there to observe. "Can I have a show of hands of the brave souls who want to participate in a reading?" He nodded to each and offered his warm smile. He began with a man who attended alone. He shuffled to the front with shoulders slumped. None of their words were audible, but the man pushed a sigh and returned to his chair with a straighter posture.

Next, he selected a woman seated with a man. He did not want to participate, saying he was only there to provide a safety net. She sat in the chair closest to Girard. "Is it alright if I take your hand. It improves the connection."

She nodded, and he shifted his eyes off to the side. He grasped her hand lightly. When she began to speak, he held a finger, signaling for her to stop. After nearly a minute, his eyes turned to hers. This exchange was spoken so his words could be heard. He stated she had no children at this time but would soon find herself with twins. With a clear line of sight to the woman's husband, Emmeline saw his head drop, and he wiped an eye.

The woman let out a brief squeal of excitement and quickly tempered it with a blush as she related, she had been hoping for a child, but had not been blessed. They had come for any insight. Girard asked her husband to please take a chair beside her. This time, the man agreed. Girard scooted his chair in front of them, leaned in and softly spoke to them. They chuckled and nodded. Then holding hands, returned to their chairs, not letting go.

Girard slowly scanned the room. His gaze landed on Emmeline and shifted for a moment between her and Nicholas. "Would you both like to come up?"

Nicholas and Emmeline nodded to each other and went up to the front. He reached his hand out to Nicholas, seeking another handshake. Nicholas reciprocated and Girard's other hand rested on their grasp. His eyes shone as if very pleased to see Nicholas, almost as if he knew him. He gave a slight nod and released his hand. He turned to Emmeline and a puzzled expression came over his face. She glanced sideways at Nicholas but said to Girard, "Am I a mystery?"

With a wag of his head, "No, not a mystery, but I get a sense you are quite intuitive yourself and I know you two are new to here."

"Yes, we arrived about four days ago," Nicholas replied.

Returning to Nicholas, "I get a sense you have traveled a distance, and there is, or there will be, discord about whether to remain or find your way back." Emmeline noted Girard had not said new to this area, since technically, Nicholas wasn't. He specifically had said 'new to here', not visiting, but here.

Emmeline inhaled. This man had already come closer to the truth than expected. "I, we, hoped you might give us insight on how to make that decision, how to accomplish the return."

She didn't know if he was speaking metaphorically or if Girard had more knowledge that their distance traveled was not in miles, but years.

He spoke with a knowing tone. "Sometimes the best decisions are ones of the heart."

"Well, that's not so much my style. I usually work more from my head."

"Madame, a shift may be required to resolve your dilemma."

Following the meeting, Girard stood at the door, much like a minister might stand at the church steps thanking people for attending. As Nicholas and Emmeline passed, he asked if they would wait a few minutes. He had another thought to share with them. They stepped aside. After the final farewells, he turned to them with a shiver, suggesting they step inside where it was warmer. Girard asked if they would meet him tomorrow at one o'clock for lunch. He was staying at the Hotel Colorado and lunch was his treat. He stated he would like the evening to roll his thoughts around.

● ● ●

Emmeline caught Nicholas's pensive expression as they sauntered toward the cabin. Speaking first Emmeline said, "I wonder what Girard meant by discord? It seemed related to our return."

Nicholas had his own point of reflection. "He looked at me as if he knew me. He appears somewhere in his thirties. I suppose he could have been alive when I am...was."

Banking off that remark, Emmeline added, "Did you notice he said he could tell we were new here, not visiting, not new to the area?"

"Yes. He was carefully selecting his words."

Emmeline pulled her coat collar tighter and put on her mittens. "Thank goodness for oil heat in the cabin. The temperature really dropped. Were you able to keep the cabin warm in 1898?"

"Yes, it's just one room. The wood burner was sufficient."

Neither felt tired when they got back. Thoughts swirled in Emmeline's head. Some were spoken. She knew there were others kept to herself. Grabbing a piece of bread, Emmeline gave a sigh of pleasure while chewing the first bite. "People in 1938 slay bread making. I only know how to buy it, nothing about baking, but I wonder what they do to create this liveliness in a slice of bread."

"You can't bake a loaf of bread? I can do that."

"So? I have no need. I can buy it anytime. Admittedly—not like this."

Minutes of silence passed at the table as they sat with their thoughts. Emmeline shook her head and said, "All we can do now is wait until tomorrow in hopes Girard has something constructive to add. The follow my heart remark didn't do much."

Emmeline propped her elbows on the table. Her hands folded together. "However, now that a couple days have passed and the emotion has subsided, let's return to topic of the Native Americans." Emmeline had no insight that she was reverting to her pattern of striking a challenge out of safety.

Nicholas's face flashed with irritation. "I feel like an animal knowing he's about to be snared by a trap."

"No, no, let's approach it from a what has changed angle. I really am curious, since I only think I know the history of your era."

"I will only agree if we approach it from a general perspective of what is happening in each era. I am not doing it if it's all perceived as my opinion."

Nodding agreement, Emmeline said, "I will start with what I perceive was your era's thinking."

Nicholas huffed. "You have an advantage of knowing if things have changed, while I only know what experiences have happened up to a point. I highly doubt this is a good idea, at least for me."

"I promise, I will be logical. My perception is by the late 1890s most Native Indians have been sentenced to..." Checking his expression and her own word choice, Emmeline switched to, "Most Native Indians have been placed on reservations."

"They were assigned land. They were expected to learn to farm."

"You know the assigned land was often not farmable? Nor were they farmers. Would you expect city people to be instantaneous farmers?"

Nicholas leaned in, his lips tight. "You may believe your words are logical, but I can see you preparing the pounce. How about if you just tell me everything my era did wrong and get this over with?"

"I will. There were so many things. They weren't considered humans by many. You killed their food source. The government tricked and broke agreements with them. Then there was the Sand Creek Massacre."

"Don't lump me, my family into everyone when much of it was the government. Chivington was reviled for his actions at Sand Creek. Yes, many were afraid of the Indians. Many demanded actions out of fear. Fear spreads like prairie fire, whether factual or not. There must be something in your time that happened at the hands of your government without your knowledge or control." Nicholas stood. "I am done. I am going to bed."

The abruptness surprised Emmeline, even though his tone should have tipped her off. He'd been so even keeled. "Salty," she said under her breath. She watched him head to the outhouse, the door slamming. She knew, based on previous life experiences, she was the cause of the conversation going south.

Chapter 15

Night Five

Nicholas had come back in and heaved the blanket over the beam. "Greed. Is nothing in your day pursued out of greed, out of power? What was boasted as Manifest Destiny had a heavy overlay of greed."

Emmeline swallowed seeing a muscle bulge in his set jaw. She changed her clothes. Pausing as she sat on the bed, Emmeline offered an olive branch. "Nicholas, it's not right I should get the bed each night while you sleep on the hard floor."

To her surprise, and maybe with a smidge of vengefulness, Nicholas approached the edge of the bed and said, "I'm happy to make a switch for a night. You like equality for all. We can start here."

She hadn't considered he'd accept so readily. They held the other's steely gaze, and Nicholas stepped aside as she stood up, plopped onto the floor, and brusquely flipped the blanket over her shoulders. It wasn't that she felt chivalry was necessary, but she was irritated feeling he had paid her back. When she peeked, he was in bed, turned toward the wall. His breathing deepened. The edge of satisfaction had served as a sleep tonic.

She questioned what compelled her to push topics she knew stirred agitation. It wasn't as if it was a new trait, or one people enjoyed about her in 2022 either. Rearranging her body several times on the pad didn't bring her sleep. Was it her need for control? A safety mechanism?

Several of the evening's comments circled. The average person wasn't to blame for all the bad that happened. There was plenty wrong in her own timeline that she wouldn't want to be blamed for. And greed was still rampant. Control guided too many actions. His words rang true, and she knew it. Her mind settled and her lips broke into a small smile. She hadn't met many people who could debate her so well. Who put her own biases into view. She rather liked it.

●●●

Emerging slowly from sleep before daylight, Emmeline noted the floor had not been as uncomfortable as she anticipated. As she roused a bit more, her eyes jerked open. She was NOT on the floor; she was in the bed, lying on her side, facing the sleeping pad. Nicholas wasn't on it either. Her eyes searched the dark room but didn't see him anywhere else. She recognized his breathing behind her. Silently she rolled over, seeing his back with the blanket pulled only to his waist. She wasn't sure which emotion was stronger, shock, curiosity, or pleasure of the warmth. She lay there sorting that out with no intention of springing from bed in alarm or fake outrage. That was not what she was experiencing. Daylight peeked through the window as she watched his shoulder rise and fall. His elbow poked hers as he rolled onto his back.

He jolted awake, giving her a sideways glance. Then he jerked his face toward the ceiling.

He uttered, "My apologies. This is, must be very indecent from your perspective."

"Well, no. I must say I'm curious. Indecent is not a word I'd use, nor am I outraged."

"You were tossing around on the floor. I watched you for a while and debated how guilty I felt for taking the bed in contrast to the comfort I felt being in it. Sleeping comfortably on the floor is an acquired skill." He paused, turning his head toward her, "It was more gentlemanly to move, so I tried to wake you, but you didn't stir. I picked you up and laid you where you are now. Nothing more happened. I am not a man who would disgrace you."

"Either you are quite progressive for the late 1800s, or as was obvious last night, I have misperceptions. It's only been a few days, but I find you trustworthy. Many guys from my era wouldn't have such concern for me."

"My not being comfortable with women is changing. I had intended to move to the floor, but when you didn't wake, I slipped back into bed, anticipating I would be up before you."

No words came to mind. She felt her comfortable smile and gazed at the ceiling. Somewhere between cozy and still believing she should be uncomfortable, she stood, suggesting she make coffee. As she was slipping out, he took her hand. She sat at the edge of the bed, admiring his calloused fingers that told her he knew how to live off the land.

He gently said, "First, you don't know how to start a fire. It's important you are assured this is both very out of character, and extremely out of era for me."

Turning her head toward him, "This isn't out of character for my era, and I'm finding it sweet." Pushing aside this new inner conflict, and some remaining guilt, she said they needed to plan the day. She slipped away and began pumping some water and setting out food.

"I have an idea! Let's buy bathing suits and go to the hot springs. I can't wear the one I brought without getting arrested. The warm water will soothe our worries. Oh, I bet we can clean up in the bathhouse. This hunting cabin experience is already growing old."

"Bathing must be a considerable pleasure, not a necessity in your era. The hot springs have been around for a long time, but I haven't experienced them. You have mentioned that suit before. I am intrigued." Her back turned to him, she smiled. It had been a while since she'd intrigued a guy.

The store kept a small display of bathing suits for tourists who stumbled on the hot springs. They had an hour to soak before needing to change and meet Girard for lunch.

Emmeline moved with a slow pensive float. Her hands glided back and forth rippling the water. "Sorry, I pushed the issue last night. I can't even stop when a person is clearly uncomfortable."

"Your passion for the topic was clear. I regret my behavior as well. I did some thinking about it while you were tossing on the floor. I have never mistreated any.... Native Americans but I have seen my fair share of mocking and mistreatment." Floating around a bit, Nicholas continued. "People are influenced by the newspaper stories and many lost families in some of the attacks."

"I am quite sure every single Native American family lost people." She sighed. "Sorry, I think I made that point last night."

Puffing out air, Nicholas concurred. "Oh yes, emphatically.

He provided a definitive end to the conversation by kicking an enormous wave of water at Emmeline. "This is amazing. I can't believe I never took the time. It'd be perfect after a few days in the woods." Nicholas smiled at the azure sky and blissfully floated in circles.

"It's always renewing. And thanks for saying you thought about it. Probably the best way to shut up my type."

"Lucky for you, I think about things. It'd be good to keep in mind, I don't get pushed around either."

"Believe me, you made that clear too." Emmeline continued while paddling her feet. "I am surprised you cared that I was tossing on the floor. I might have reveled in it."

"You are also lucky I may flare but don't hold on to it."

"Last words, I swear. I reflected too."

"We will save that for another day. If Girard can enlighten us, it won't matter.

Chapter 16

New Developments

T hey arrived at the Hotel Colorado dining room just as Mr. Girard was coming down the stairs. He walked with a spring and his mood was gleeful as he asked for a table away from others. They were seated in a corner. They chatted about visiting the hot springs and other niceties about the town. When there was a pause, Mr. Girard, who insisted they call him Edmund, brought up the reason he wanted to meet with them.

He was vague but indicated Nicholas looked like someone he knew in his youth. He was further convinced after he visited the history museum that morning. Nicholas could be a relative, but he didn't think so. His gaze rested on Emmeline. "I sense a knowing about you that is not of 1938."

Nicholas and Emmeline exchanged a nervous glance unsure how to respond. Emmeline blurted her gut response, "You are the gifted one. What do you think it is?"

Edmund ignored the challenge. "I think you two arrived here at the same time but didn't travel together. If that's correct, the ring you are wearing is only to squelch suspicions." As she slid her hand to her lap, he leaned back in his chair and glanced from Nicholas to Emmeline, back to Nicholas.

Nicholas spoke first. "Let's order some food. This seems like a discussion for full stomachs."

"That's a grand idea."

To continue deflecting, Emmeline added. "Edmund, how did you come to develop your abilities or get into this line of work?"

"Everyone has more intuition than they believe they do. Some of it can be developed by bringing out the skill the person already has."

Emmeline nodded agreement. "Nicholas and I were talking before we met you. We have family members who seemed to know about events or people, as if they sensed things."

They ordered lunch and enjoyed a glass of Bordeaux. Edmund thought it might help them be more comfortable with the topic. Her described intuition trusted Edmund but she sipped the wine slowly. She worried she could say too much.

Edmund started, "Nicholas, I went to the historical museum today. Even though the photos showed a man older and more kept, the soul of the photo was you."

"What inspired you to go?" Nicholas asked.

Edmund explained curiosity spurred him, but he couldn't ignore a familiarity when they shook hands the previous night. He looked intently at Nicholas as he explained, it was in fact a feeling of re-connecting with someone he had once admired. Edmund shared he had last been through this area during the pandemic of 1918. The flu was killing so many, visitors were not welcomed. Someone intervened when a group recognized him as a stranger in the town and aggressively confronted him. People seemed to know the confident man and immediately backed off. The man offered me a place to stay for the night even though it was only a tent set up near his cabin. He suggested it would be wise to move on in the morning. The man was gone when I awoke, so I never had a chance to thank him."

Nicholas's hand was on his chest. He stared into his wine. Responding with a cautious tone, "I somehow remember that night. Oddly, I did not remember it when I saw the exhibit, nor before you said it. How is it possible to recall something that hasn't happened?"

Emmeline's eyes flashed to him. Edmund sat back in his chair. His eyes warmed. He slowly smiled. "So, it is you." Edmund held an admiring gaze on Nicholas and said, "It has happened in my timeline. How do we know what latched on or remains of memories?"

They sat sorting out what the reality of this moment meant. Emmeline shifted in her chair, avoiding eye contact. Her muscles stiffened. Their table was in a corner, but other tables were not far away. They liked her suggestion to finish their wine and go to the cabin so they could speak more freely.

● ● ●

Approaching the cabin, Edmund pointed to where the tent had been in 1918 and remarked he was glad it had been summer. He asked, "Did you have the tent for other visitors?"

That's what the information said in the museum. "It served as a respite to many wayward travelers. The cabin was farther out of town, then. Eventually townspeople began steering them in my direction. It removed the visitor from seeming a threat to the townspeople."

Emmeline's heart warmed with admiration. She knew how angry people had become during her own pandemic; how divisive responses were. It took courage and compassion to stand up for people who needed help.

Cradled by warmth as they stepped inside, Nicholas said he would boil water for tea. Emmeline suggested opening the bottle of wine they had purchased. It received a resounding yes. Nicholas motioned for the others to sit down. "Sorry I don't have another chair. I rarely entertain." He went out and came back with a stump from the log pile. He turned it on end and perched. They drank wine from tin cups, not glass, but manners were not the focus.

"Emmeline." Edmund turned toward her. "I am curious about your story."

"My story wasn't in the museum."

"You carry yourself as a confident woman, not tethered by norms."

"Norms are overrated. Many more things should be acceptable than are."

"What I am implying is you do not feel like a woman who was born shortly after the turn of the century."

"I was born just before the millennia changed but you are right in questioning which millennia that was." Emmeline took a drink of wine, her mouth dry from revealing even that much. It was both terrifying and relieving. He was their first hope for finding the answer of returning to their own times. She took the plunge, "I am from the year 2022. Eighty plus years in the future."

With that, Edmund's head went back, and marvel carried on his word, "Incredible!" There was no doubt. "I don't know which questions to ask first."

Emmeline interceded. "We are risking telling you this only because we hope you can steer us toward our return." She paused. "We have been here five days. Given the intensity, it seems longer, like months."

He looked to both Nicholas and Emmeline, "I can only try to help you find the link. Even though I believe time to be non-linear, I have never encountered your kind of traveler before."

Nicholas joined in. "We believe we have some of the connections but there must be something we're missing."

Edmund scooted to the edge of the chair; his face beamed. "I am sure this is pressing on both of your minds. However, I have questions particularly for you Emmeline. I am so curious about the future, your future. We have cars but do yours fly? We have airplanes, but how have they changed? Are people more open-minded, accepting? Have they solved hunger?"

She inhaled before beginning. Emmeline was more interested in how he could help but didn't want to alienate him. She explained the technological changes, then elaborated on shifts in social norms. There was general acceptance of homosexuality and far more opportunities for women; a recognition that people of color and indigenous people deserved to have their atrocities told and be accepted with equal rights. Even though progress had been made, there was still too much room allowed for hate and complicity. She ended with her opinion that people were less connected socially even though technology purported to keep them joined.

Edmund's gaze fell to his hands folded on the table. They gave him time. It was a tremendous amount of information to digest. After a few minutes of quiet, Emmeline said, "Edmund, do you think you can help us?"

"It's intriguing you came from two different times to the same moment. Tell me what you believe brought you here."

Nicholas took over. "We both have a coin from 1879. We assume we were each touching that coin at some similar place in our travels. Even though I wasn't on the train, we both emerged from the area by the train station. When we went back again, holding and focusing on the coin, nothing happened. Oh, but first we returned to the Grizzly Creek area, believing that might be the common place. That didn't work either. We have made numerous failed attempts."

"I see." Edmund said thoughtfully. "It is my experience when energies merge, it is often the emotion that is a strong driver. Think back, what were each of you thinking about or contemplating when you were touching the coins?"

Nicholas said, "We considered that. We were both recalling a Christmas memory with our parents. That wasn't the answer."

Emmeline added, "Maybe we should go deeper."

She and Nicholas sat and reflected one more time on that day. Emmeline connected to an aloneness. "My sister and I are bonded as sisters and of course share the same background. We have good times, but my dad was that go-to person. He was more my cheerleader than my mom. When he died, loneliness was heavy."

Nicholas leaned in, forearms on his legs. "I too was thinking about my sense of aloneness." Emmeline's eyes shot to Nicholas.

Edmund captured the gaze of compassion between them as Nicholas paused. Emmeline didn't know about Nicholas, but her loneliness had not hovered the past few days. Given the circumstances, it should be immense.

Then Nicholas gave a voice to her very thought. "Odd though, it hasn't been hanging over my head the past few days."

Still gazing at Nicholas, Emmeline said, "We had talked about the loneliness brought up by an event but not general aloneness. I thought that too."

Edmund asked where in their travels they thought they were when they were experiencing those emotions.

Nicholas jerked his lips sideways and breathed in deeply. "Being alone is a bit pervasive in my life, at least it was in 1898. I don't know if that shifted in later years or not."

Nodding, Emmeline indicated, "I know it's been a couple years since I lost my dad, but I have felt an absence I find hard to shake. It set me adrift. I dozed in the final minutes of the trip but didn't notice anything around me change before that time."

Edmund wasn't sure how to proceed. He proposed along with the coin, it wasn't the place but perhaps the deeper emotion beyond a memory. There could be yet another item, or some random occurrence they wouldn't have noticed.

Emmeline struggled with her conflicting emotions. Which was stronger, the sense of being stuck, or her emerging fondness for Nicholas? Restlessness cascaded over her. What would happen if they were here much longer? She may not be close to her sister and mother, but she ached for them knowing the anguish they were living.

After Edmund left, Emmeline pumped water into the pitcher. Nicholas stood watching out the window. Emmeline knew he found solace among the trees. Their eyes fixed on each other as they sat back at the table. Emmeline only said, "I feel confused about all this, Nicholas. I am usually sure of everything."

"This sense of comfort is novel for me, Emmeline. It gives me hope. Hope that I won't always be alone.

Instead of leaning into the warmth she found in his words, she leaned away. "But I still need to get back to my real life."

The water in Nicholas's cup circled slowly as he rolled it around. Emmeline let her mind take a moment to picture a future if she remained in 1938. Her era was inclusive of people, this one was not. As a woman in 2022, she could pursue whatever opportunity she chose. Sure a few women attended college in 1938 but in her era, more women attended than men. What would she do with her business and management degree? She'd be bored as a phone operator, and she'd hate the constraints of being some man's secretary. Besides, she'd never used a typewriter. Her mind drifted back to the comfort of waking next to Nicholas that morning. Her psyche offered no opposing argument.

Emmeline discovered Nicholas had been pondering similar things. "I don't know how I'd make a living here. Particularly one that would support a wife— if I had one. I can't drive an automobile. Not sure if I could hunt."

Emmeline squelched the provider pressure. "Even though most women didn't work outside the home, I'm sure some did. It'd suck to live in a world where I couldn't. I've seen some women driving around town. I could teach you to drive." Emmeline doubted her statement since she could only drive an automatic and these cars were stick-shift.

"This is all conjecture anyway. We are still in agreement returning to our own times is best," Nicholas said.

They opted for another day at the cabin, taking time to find longer-term lodging. Their money would run out and Nicholas didn't want to trade more coins needing them for his return to 1898. Emmeline wanted to avoid it unless it was for survival.

She pursed her lips and stared off toward the wall. "Even talking out loud about a longer stay feels like we're admitting defeat."

"You speak of being a planner, Emmeline. That's what this is. I worry if we trade in too many coins, it could call attention. That man at the curio shop, Jameson, seemed a little too helpful."

"Well, he's a coin guy. Of course, he's interested."

"Maybe, but something felt wrong," Nicholas said doubtfully. "With the current money from the coins, we have enough for another week unless we find a way to live on less than we already are."

Chapter 17

Night Dreams

After a logic-filled conversation about sleeping arrangements, they agreed they were comfortable being in one bed. Once in bed the decision extended beyond logic. Emmeline said, "I find this consoling. It should feel uncomfortable, but it doesn't."

The bed was an oversized single bed. Nicholas chuckled. "We are each at the farthest edges of this meant-for one bed. But yes, it is most agreeable."

Something awakened in Emmeline when she saw the softness of Nicholas's eyes as he said goodnight.

Emmeline slipped into a sound sleep. The sharing of dreams with her sister occurred most often in times of stress. It happened when their father died and when Hannah went through her divorce. Compelled to share it with the other, they discovered they had converged in the dream state. This time, Emmeline found herself at Hannah's bedside. It was only blocks from where she was physically, at this moment, except it was 2022. She saw Hannah's phone on the nightstand. Her laptop sat open on the straight backed chair that had pants draped over the back. A family photo from before her dad had died was on the dresser. Emmeline resisted caressing these items that were decades from where she was. She needed to talk. Hannah was a side sleeper, but her dark hair splayed across the pillow as Emmeline touched her shoulder and she rolled onto her back. There was no sign of waking.

Emmeline cut to the chase in case the dream ended. "Hannah, I am okay. It will be hard to believe, but somehow, I went through a time portal and came out in the year 1938. I'm trying to figure out how the hell I get back. When I came out of the train station, everything was different. If being in 1938 isn't crazy enough, a man somehow came through the same time portal, but he's from 1898. So, I'm not alone. You have probably been through my apartment a thousand times scouring for clues to what happened but look in the shoe rack behind my lonely pair of fuck-me heels; you'll find a small bag. There's a bracelet in it...remember the one with blue stones you loaned me to wear to Prom? I told you I'd lost it, but I loved it so much I kept it. When I got older, I didn't know how to confess it without admitting I'd been a little shit. Really, I was going to surprise you with it at some point. Surprise! Oh, one last thing— that guy from 1898 is definitely a ten."

Chapter 18

Hannah

Hannah woke with a jolt, eyes wide. "Emme."

Hannah scanned the room, but no one was there. She was alone. Beads of grief escaped down her face. She curled into a ball to capture the residual emotion of the dream. It was still vivid in her head; she knew beyond a doubt, Emme had been at the edge of the bed. She struggled to recall her words. Emme said she was safe; she'd arrived in Glenwood but, she was in 1938! Remembering the cute guy, she smiled, really wanting Emme to find someone. The bracelet flashed in her mind. The covers flung back, she threw on some clothes, grabbed her keys, and dashed out the door. Realizing it was ridiculous to make the three-hour drive to Denver, she sat in her car and dialed her mom.

Her words rushed out. "Mom, I need you to head to Emme's apartment and just believe the bizarre story I am going to tell you."

"Whoa, Hannah. Is there news about Emme? Tell me what you know!"

Still speaking with a panicked speed, Hannah said, "Mom, please, grab Emme's apartment key and get in the car."

"I'm moving, but why? Is she at her apartment?" Agnes asked.

"No, well, I don't think so. If you're walking to your car, put me on speaker and I'll explain."

"I'm getting in the car now. For God's sake, tell me what's going on!"

"You know how Emme and I have shared dreams a few times, well it happened last night. This is INSANE, but she says she's in the year 1938 and to help me believe her, she told me to look for something."

"You're right, Hannah. That is insane."

"I know it sounds that way, but we have to check. I need to know."

"What will I be looking for?"

"I'll tell you when you arrive. It's something in the back of her closet. I want you to tell me what you see so I don't influence it. Mom, drive carefully. I'll just hang on so you can focus."

"Any chance of focus playing a part in this drive went out the window when you said Emme. My angels better take the wheel for these fifteen minutes."

Agnes ran to the door and opened it. "Ahhh, even after a month, there's a whiff of Emme's candles."

"Mom, turn your phone to camera, so I can see what you find. Good. Now go to her bedroom closet and pull out her pair of fuck-me heels."

"Her what?"

"Her only pair of black high heels."

Holding them up to the camera, there was urgency in her voice, "What am I looking for, Hannah?"

"Go the back of the cubby."

The shoes dropped from sight as her mom peered in the back. Wedged in the back was a small purple jewelry bag. Holding the phone in one hand so Hannah could see, she yanked it out. Hannah's stomach was churning, afraid to have it be what Emme had said and more afraid it was not.

"Hurry, Mom, show me what's inside."

Her mom had propped the phone when she crouched on the floor and pulled on the drawstring, dumping the contents into her palm. She held a bracelet to the camera, "Isn't this your old bracelet?"

"That little shit is alive, but she stole my bracelet!" Hannah smiled as more tears slid down her cheeks. She stared at it through the phone, then laid her head on the steering wheel and wondered what she should do next. The pounds of pressure she'd been carrying on her chest the past weeks lifted, and she took her first deep breath. "So, Emme is 'here' in Glenwood Springs, yet not here."

"What the hell is going on, Hannah? What does this bracelet mean?"

"Don't ask me how, but somehow Emme has time-traveled to Glenwood Springs, just not 2022. She is stuck in the year 1938."

"What the hell! Why does this bracelet tell you that?"

"Emme told me in the dream, she was with some man who is from 1898 and they are both stuck not knowing how to return. In high school, Emma said she lost that bracelet during the prom. In the dream, she confessed she loved it and didn't want to return it. Guilt made her hide it, I guess."

"That doesn't sound like our steadfast, honest Emme."

"Exactly, which is why it's even more believable."

Agnes's phone leaned on a low shelf with the camera on. Hannah saw her mom huddled on the floor, knees drawn to her chest, hands covering her mouth. Disbelief covered her face. Agnes startled when Hannah said, "Mom. Are you okay? It's a shit ton to take in."

Agnes picked up her phone and switch off the camera. "This is so far-fetched. But I prefer it to every other possibility my mind has conjured. What do we do now?"

"I don't know, Mom. Breathing for the first time in a month is my start."

●●●

Emmeline woke and turned her head toward Nicholas. He was looking at her and a corner of his mouth slid back into a half smile. "You must have been dreaming well. You were murmuring to yourself."

Emmeline sighed. "I was able to talk to Hannah. I let her know I was alright. She's probably somewhere between ecstatic and pissed off if she's followed my words."

"You're really able to communicate with her in a dream?"

"Yeah, but it just happens; we can't control it. We've tried to make it happen but just like this time travel shit, we have no control."

"Why do you think she will take it seriously, and how will she know it was real?"

"I told her where to find a bracelet I had borrowed in high school, then basically stole from her. If she finds it, it will seal the deal. I never told anyone I kept it."

Nicholas sat up against the wall. "Maybe we need to go to your sister's, err, your great-great grandmother's house and make up a story about why we are knocking on her door. Maybe seeing her will help us in some way. It may at least feel comforting to look upon a blood relation."

"This place works, but something with more conveniences would be nice, like a bathroom. Let's just tell my great-great grandmother we were told she might rent rooms. I would love to get a glimpse inside the house. The outside is much fresher in this timeline."

After breakfast, they walked to the house. Emmeline stood in front of the gate feeling ridiculous to be considering this. "I don't even know her name. I have the family history written somewhere, but this goes farther back than I can remember. Why would someone think she rents rooms? Just because it was a thing women did in It's a Wonderful Life? This woman is likely to have a family."

Nicholas nudged her gently. "Even after these few days, I have given up asking what all your references mean. But if it is about looking odd, we look odder standing here than going up to the house." They opened the gate and crossed the stoop, while staring at the door. After they lightly knocked, a young girl about ten-years old opened the door.

"Oh! Hello. My name is Emmeline, and this is my.... husband, Nicholas. Is your mom home?" Emmeline couldn't take her eyes from the girl she knew must be a relative.

"Yes ma'am, she is in the kitchen." She left, leaving the door more ajar than her mother would appreciate, given the temperature.

A plump woman with dark hair and a streak of gray at the crown, came to the door. After introducing themselves to her and pretending to read the words on a piece of paper in her hand, Emmeline said they were visiting in the area, and someone had indicated she may be renting rooms or know another who does. Surprisingly she smiled, wiped her hands on her apron and stepped out onto the steps. As she pointed two houses down, she said the person had given the wrong address. She hadn't talked with her in the past week but was pretty sure Mrs. Miles had a room available.

Emmeline admired the woman, seeing something familiar in her face. It was the heavy lips and long nose. She asked her name if she didn't mind sharing it. Emmeline's brain lit up at hearing it was Agnes. The woman smiled when Emmeline said that Agnes was also her mother's name. She didn't know Emmeline's mother considered her name old-fashion and hated it. Thanking the woman, they exchanged goodbyes. Agnes wished them luck and stepped back inside.

Nicholas and Emmeline walked back through the gate and started down the street. "My mother never told me specifics, only that she had been named after someone in the family. If she said more, I likely tuned out."

Nicholas stopped them, saying they needed to know what price they could afford, and what was included in the stay. Agreeing on a cost, they knocked on Mrs. Miles's door. In the moment waiting for an answer, Emmeline thought Hannah may know the 2022 owners of this house. Soon, a child about six opened the door. The little girl was quickly pushed sideways by a younger boy. They giggled and jostled to be the one in front. Their faces sobered in politeness once the order was decided. Hearing the activity, Mrs. Miles came to the door apologizing for her enthusiastic greeters. Nicholas introduced themselves and indicated that Agnes Nolan from down the way had told them there might be a room for rent.

There was but the cost was higher than they'd hoped. Asking if it was negotiable, Mrs. Miles turned to Emmeline. She said she could reduce the rent in exchange for help with preparing meals, dishwashing, or child watching. Irritation rose. Mrs. Miles didn't give Nicholas a glance talking household chores. Yes, it was different times, but this slapped across her face. The woman had no idea kitchen chores and baby-sitting ranked low on Emmeline's list of pleasurable tasks. Her interest was presumed. She didn't dislike children; she just didn't consider them. Her only kitchen skill was with the microwave. Desperate times called for desperate measures.

"Sure, I can help in the kitchen. Childcare might be good practice," Emmeline said with faked enthusiasm. They settled on a cost, and told her they would return after letting Miss Marjorie, the librarian, know they were out of the cabin.

Her eyebrows raising, Mrs. Miles said, "This will be like the Taj Mahal compared to that old cabin."

●●●

They chatted with Marjorie at the library about the plan. Marjorie told them Helen's husband had been a foreman in a mine, but he died tragically during an accident a few years earlier. Offering the house for boarding provided a sustained form of income. Emmeline and Nicholas would discover people rented there for a comfortable place to stay, but raved about the food they were served.

Walking back to the cabin, Nicholas said, "We are on to the next phase of whatever this is called...nightmare, adventure, chance meeting."

"Hmm. It doesn't feel the nightmare it did a few days ago."

While tidying the cabin, their heads jerked at the sound of a knock at the door. It was Edmund. He apologized for coming unannounced, but he didn't know how long they'd be here. "I plan to remain in Glenwood a while longer. I have not stopped thinking about the oddity of your predicament. I want to learn more about your era, Emmeline, and am happy to assist however I can. When working an assignment for Edgar, I receive ample compensation. When exploring my own threads, I must use my own reserves. A place such as this would be perfect."

"We've checked out, so it's open," Emmeline said. "But are you sure? There might be something at Mrs. Miles's boarding house. Besides, isn't this quite a step down from Hotel Colorado?"

Edmund cocked his chin. "It is a bit rustic, but it will be quite calming. Sensing and filtering people's energy can drain my own. This will be a place of respite."

Emmeline said, "I hope we aren't part of that draining. It's a relief to have another who knows our truth."

● ● ●

Mrs. Miles welcomed them and showed them to their room. She hoped they were alright with the double bed. "When my husband died, I moved the children down to my space. I needed the single beds." Emmeline chastised herself for being pleased there was just one.

It was a spacious and pleasing room with one small bureau and a floral area rug covering much of the plank floor. Emmeline embraced the room, seeing the long window extended close to the floor. On a sturdy three-legged table, there was a shallow bowl with violets floating in the water. Noticing an old writing desk, Emmeline slipped over and pulled on the fold-down section. A soothing energy arced from her hand up her arm. She held the connection but covered what she felt with words. "Oooh, I love little nooks for treasure items."

"I am not sure what it is about the desk but it's a favored piece of furniture for most who stay in this room."

The window gave a view of the street. Emmeline looked forward to watching passersby and scurrying creatures. It quieted her mind, and it took a break from never-ending plans.

"Thank you so much. This is very homey. You've done a wonderful job of decorating." Giving a satisfied smile, Mrs. Miles closed the door as she left them to settle in.

Nicholas flung Emmeline's bag onto the bed. "I promise I will continue to be the gentleman."

"I could take care of myself if there were other ideas." Emmeline knew it was a feeble attempt to hide her genuine thought, she was increasingly attracted to this man. "Besides we're still focused on getting out of here."

Recovering from a fleeting look of disappointment, he said, "Yes, we are. No point taking something somewhere it can't be fully realized." Oddly, she resented his quick agreement.

They headed downstairs. As they entered the sitting room, she traced the carved spirals of the dark molding. Heavy, tied back curtains framed each side. Mrs. Miles soon appeared. The squeaky steps must have alerted her. "Why don't I show you around, so you know the common areas?"

"Mrs. Miles, let me know how I can help around the house to offset our rent." Emmeline surprised herself over and over. She wasn't one to stretch the truth or embellish it.

"Please call me Helen. After all, you will see my dirty dishes. I will give you a day to settle in and then we can discuss what's next." They followed her as she stepped into each room. "The sitting room, the dining area, and this living room with the radio are yours to enjoy." Emmeline heard big band music coming quietly from the radio.

The backyard was small and narrow with a sidewalk leading to a carriage house in the back corner. This house was a labyrinth of rooms. She would welcome her return to the wide-open great rooms of the twenty-first century. These were cozy yet confining. They moved to a small south-facing room off the kitchen, full of heavily foliaged plants. Even though it was winter, there were a few plants bearing fruit. A small green pear hung from one, and three large red tomatoes weighted down the branches of an otherwise sturdy plant. Emmeline didn't own a plant or know how to care for one.

Next, she showed them the kitchen, explaining that guests weren't to linger in this area. "Emmeline, you will of course be welcomed once we sort out chores." Emmeline's thoughts drifted off as she stepped further into the kitchen. It was warm from the oven's heat and a meaty aroma filled her senses. The white oversized enamel sink was offset with a row of black tiles running along the front of the counter tops. The sparkling black and white speckled linoleum flooring continued the pattern. Mint green cupboards and the green and white gingham wallpaper softened the room. The counters were cozy with baskets of breads and eggs.

This kitchen carried a flair of calm activity, a stark difference to her own. The microwave was her kitchen staple. She re-heated her take-out for three minutes and boiled her tea water for two. Frozen sausage and veggie pizza was the only action her stove got. Emmeline's mind returned as Helen listed the sunroom, her living quarters, and the main floor bathroom as private.

Asking if other guests were staying, Helen indicated all rooms were full. One guest was passing through. Another was at work, but both would join them for dinner. Beef roast from the butcher's was served, along with roasted carrots and potatoes. Mentioning they appeared fresh, she said that they hold up in the root cellar if she leaves the tips on. "I like to bring out the freshest for a new guest's first meal."

Helen liked knowing where her food came from. She was no fan of many items showing up in the grocery stores. "I recognize necessity is the mother of invention, but it's not healthy putting everything in a can. The frozen foods I read about aren't natural. I grow what I can, then put up fresh fruit and vegetables that keep all winter. Mr. Williams, the butcher, can tell me exactly whose cow this meat came from. I like that. City folk probably don't have that option, but it will be a problem someday, mark my words."

Emmeline wanted to tell her how correct many would find her predictions, but she couldn't.

● ● ●

Helen watched Emmeline fumble through drawers after being asked to sift the flour for the chocolate cake being served for dessert. Emmeline felt her face heat. She knew what flour was but had no idea what sifting meant. Helen leaned down and pulled the flour bin from a lower cupboard. Then she pulled the sifter from a shelf. "The measuring cups are in the drawer in front of you."

Setting the sifter in a large bowl, she explained, "Put one cup of flour into this, and crank. Repeat that for three cups." Emmeline didn't understand why it was necessary but wasn't inclined to show her lack of twentieth century culinary skills more than she had to. She performed her task slowly, unsure what she should do next. Awkwardness left her body and her neck unknotted when Helen instructed each step after moving a smaller bowl with the butter, sugar, and eggs to the counter. "I presume this is your first cake?"

"Obvious, isn't it?"

"What is your favorite thing to prepare?"

"We're not rich or anything but my mother hired a young widow to do most of the cooking." A tinge of guilt accompanied the lie, but Emmeline was growing accustomed to making things up as she went along.

Helen offered a kind smile. "From now on, I will know to assign tasks like peeling the potatoes."

"I hope you aren't regretting your cutting the cost of our stay."

"No, it's nice to have someone in the kitchen with me. Have Ruth and Richard been behaving when you play?"

"Oh yes. They're very easy to hang out with." Emmeline caught Helen's eyes narrowing in confusion. "They're so polite and play quietly with their toys. It still feels odd being called Miss Emmeline."

"Good to hear there's no arguing and they mind their manners."

"They barely speak unless I ask a question."

"They are never to bother an adult."

Emmeline and Helen fell into a routine in the kitchen, and she finally had to confess the laundry was a mystery also.

Emmeline sat on the floor as Richard played with Lincoln Logs. She built a house then pretended one log was a rocket ship that flew to the moon. He giggled. "You're silly, Miss Emmeline."

She couldn't help slipping in possibilities after Ruth's only future vision was being a housewife or a mother. There was no leaving that alone after Richard said he wanted to be an engineer. One day playing dolls with Ruth, Emmeline made her doll a doctor and Ruth's a patient. "Miss Emmeline, you can't be a doctor. You have to be the nurse."

"My doll is smart enough to be a doctor. Maybe someday she can be."

Weeks passed. Emmeline still longed to walk out of 1938 and back to 2022, but for snippets of time there was something romantic, something simple about these days.

Chapter 19

Out of Nowhere

E mmeline sat at the writing desk, swiveling on the chair. She flipped the desk cover and her eyes darted to a small book poking from one of the larger cubbies. A cherub-looking angel graced the cover. How did the book get there? Glancing around as if checking for someone, she picked it up. Fanning through the book, she stopped at a page holding a small slip of paper with familiar writing.

"I did some research and discovered Susan Downing's house down the street used to be a boarding house. I am hoping you ended up there. Emme, the relief of knowing you are okay is indescribable. Mom may be sleeping for the first time since you disappeared. Yep, she is believing this too.

See you soon—fingers crossed. Tell the Ten hi.

Love, the thief's sister, Hannah." Beneath the writing was a small stick figure girl with crazy curly hair; it was Hannah's signature sign-off.

Emmeline's heart pounded, throbbing up into her throat. She read the note over and over. Angels were one of the few illogical beliefs her entire family had fully embraced. Going back to the inside of the book, she noted the publish date, 1940.

She slid down in the chair staring at the book, but no longer seeing it. She mouthed, "What the fuck." Her brain grappled with discovering a book from a future year but considered an antique in her own time. Emmeline knew her sister's handwriting. It was always a blend of print and cursive. The stick figure drawing convinced her. The ante of bizarre possibilities was raised.

Nicholas knocked and opened the door. Her eyes remained fixed on the book. "If someone hears you knock before walking into your own room, they might suspect something."

"What, that I am polite?"

"You know what I mean—about us."

Seeing Emmeline's dazed expression, he placed his hand on her shoulder. "You look as if you've seen a ghost. What is that?"

She handed the book to him. He too fanned through pages and asked, "Do you believe in angels?"

"Yes, but that's not the surprise." She passed the slip of paper.

He read it, turned it over, and slid the paper through his fingers. He gazed out the window for a few seconds. "This paper quality feels different than paper does, even now."

"That's hardly what I was focusing on. Since it's written on 'my today's-2022 paper', it feels normal to me." Her head jerked up. "But you do know, that's not the point, right?"

"So, your sister somehow got this note inside this book?"

"Better than that. She got the note AND book into <u>this</u> room, at this time!"

Nicholas huffed, "Just when I think I am grasping what has happened to us, more comes along."

Emmeline nodded. "I am with you on that one. This book is from 1940. Which means it hasn't been written. I'll keep it out of sight, along with most of my belongings."

Her head was still cluttered with possibilities. "If we can communicate across time, then there must be a way to travel back through it."

"Based on our failures leaving here, communication and objects may move across time better than our bodies."

Nicholas stood motionless at the window. His voice carried sadness. "I was lonely in my time. I haven't felt that recently. Has the thought of staying here entered your mind?" He turned to her with a hopeful gaze.

Laying her head back on the chair and closing her eyes, Emmeline listed her thoughts. "I feel the comfortableness. I'm sure it stems from you. This era has multitudes of advancements for you. The limitations this era holds for women and others are in my face. Plus, I know the history that's about to occur. It's not good. I have family worried about me and a career to begin. Women in this time don't have careers, they have jobs—working for men."

Nicholas was silent. Emmeline opened her eyes but stared ahead. "Nicholas, there are so many reasons to go back...". Lifting her head to meet his eyes, "...and only one reason to stay."

Chapter 20

News

For days Emmeline dragged her suitcase from under the bed to check the angel book. She tenderly touched all the items she had to hide. Her cell phone, credit card, cash, driver's license showing who she really was, and her favorite bathing suit. The return note she had written was still resting in the book beside Hannah's with no response. On impulse Emmeline removed the book and slid it to the back of the writer's desk considering placement may be important.

One week passed, then another. Her vigilance slowed, but for three days Emmeline had seen the number five everywhere she went. 10:05, 11:55, $5.00. Emmeline thumbed through the pages of the angel book to check its significance. The number five read, "A significant change is occurring...." It continued onto the next page, but as she turned it, there was a small piece of paper wedged into the book's spine.

It read, *"It's been months. I haven't heard back from you. I don't know if my note got through, or if you found it. Got some hard news. Mom's sick. She was diagnosed with Stage 4 cancer. Currently undergoing treatment. She wishes you could find your way home."*

Emmeline stared until her body quaked and tears spilled forth. Digging an embroidered hanky from her pocket she soaked it with tears. The immediacy and intensity of her body's response surprised her. Emmeline's usual control was fracturing. Something unexplored was waking.

She paced the room, while her hand was turning white from squeezing the note tightly. She scolded herself out loud. "What the hell am I doing? I'm allowing myself to be lulled into this Hallmark fantasy. Deluding myself that I can continue this ruse without the truth being discovered. I'm not meant to be here. I've got to find the way back!"

Hurriedly tossing the book on the bed, she scribbled a note for Nicholas, who was out looking for work. The note said she was running an errand and would return before dinner. Poking her head into the kitchen, she told Helen, "I am going out, but I will be back to help cook."

Emmeline headed to Nicholas's former cabin. She didn't know if Edmund would be there, but when smoke spiraled from the chimney, her hopes rose. Maybe he was still the tenant. Emmeline pounded on the door. Opening it and meeting her frantic eyes, Edmund asked, "What's happened? The worry is seething from you."

"My mom has cancer, and it sounds really bad, really advanced."

Edmund's brows furrowed. "Emmeline, how would you know such information?"

She told him about the book appearing and about the notes inside from her sister. "I know most would think I am deranged, but you might believe me. I can't talk about this to anyone but Nicholas. Have you given more thought about how we get back? It was ridiculous to be lulled into a comfortableness or an idea that I am meant to stay here."

With gleaming eyes Edmund gushed, "That is quite exciting don't you think?

"Exciting? My mother dying is exciting?"

Edmund looked down and cleared his throat, as if to squelch excitement. "Forgive me. Naturally, I am very sorry about your mother. That news is most terrifying. However, this doesn't sound deranged. People claim to heal remotely. You got here, why not a piece of paper?"

A lilt returned to his voice. "You want to try again?"

Her tone was emphatic. "What? Yes! Of course I do! I need to figure this out. I'm not sure Nicholas wants to go back to his time. There's something he likes better here. I am *not* meant to stay. I don't know what triggered the time travel, but I need to go home."

Edmund sat on the bench, "I have been thinking about you and Nicholas without pause. I am particularly interested in some things you said about your era. If we can determine the event, might you allow me to return to your time with you? I wouldn't remain with you, but for me to learn to live in your time. Some things you said made me believe the twenty-first century is more suited for me."

Immersed in her own worry and fear, Emmeline didn't take time to ask why he would want to go forward. In her despair, she would have agreed to anything but only responded with, "Sure."

"Excellent! Most excellent. I should have thought of this when we met. Have you ever been hypnotized?"

"Never felt I could be. I always considered myself too controlling to allow myself to fall under another's control."

"That's apparently a fallacy that has traveled into the next century. You don't lose control of your faculties; you remain in charge of which stored memories you access in your unconscious. I cannot have you do anything out of character."

Still skeptical, Emmeline asked, "What will hypnosis feel like?"

As if explaining a medical procedure, he related how the process would start, words he would say, and the deep level of relaxation she would feel. He then assured her she would know she was completely herself. "We can accomplish much in an hour."

She doubted its viability but agreed out of desperation. "I'll try anything."

●●●

Edmund counted backward from twenty. She sensed the hard chair softening and molding to her body, encasing her in comfort. Edmund spent a few minutes asking her questions about her life events before time travel. "Tell me one of your fondest memories with your father."

She recounted a time they had walked back to the river near their house. Weaving through the trees on a trail, she could again smell the dry dirt mixing with the pine needle scent. She was ten or so, but they still held hands and alternated squeezes. Safety and joy swelled in her heart. She squeezed his hand tighter. She flicked her finger over the bump on his knuckle. She'd forgotten that. She wasn't merely remembering the day or watching it as in a movie. She was there holding her father's hand. The emotion was now.

"It's time to say goodbye to him.

Her voice quivered. "I don't want to leave."

"We have a purpose and need to move on. Take a moment to say goodbye." Edmund paused, giving her time. "Now come forward to the day you traveled by train to see your sister."

With the same precision, she could see it all, feel it all again. She felt the rolling jostle as the train passed the towering rock walls of Glenwood Canyon. "I'm going through my dad's coin collection and feeling worried Hannah will want to sell them all. They're my strongest connection to him." Emmeline turned her head. "There was a nice woman who asked me about the book in my lap."

"Tell me about that conversation."

"I thought the woman would be annoying, but she was very kind and understood my sadness about my dad. The woman went to get a snack, and I needed to pee."

Edmund told her to move ahead to the moments beyond relieving herself. Walking back to her seat from the bathroom, she spotted a nickel on the floor in the aisle. Looking ahead, hoping the woman had returned, she absentmindedly picked it up, registered it as old, and slipped it in her pocket.

Emmeline abruptly stopped speaking. Edmund asked, "Emmeline. What is happening? You were relaxed and now you are pressing your hands into your legs."

Emmeline didn't speak as she watched her hypnotized self, looking around the train. "I dozed off, the train stopped. It's empty. Everyone got off." Her voice escalated as she explained the train was different, older. She watched herself shove her father's coins into her travel bag, throw on her coat and hurry to get off the train.

Edmund said, "This must be significant."

"Yes! I forgot about finding the nickel, and even though I knew I had dozed; I didn't notice the changes on the train. It wasn't until getting to the front of the station. Something happened after I picked up that coin!"

As Edmund was saying the words to bring Emmeline out of her hypnotized state, there was a knock at the door. He ignored it until finished, but the knock thudded harder. Emmeline remained seated, floating out of her body like she'd had a deep tissue massage. She turned her head to the door. Nicholas spoke a brief hello to Edmund as his eyes landed on Emmeline.

Without asking to come in, he edged past Edmund and came to stand in front of her. Still foggy, Emmeline saw more than just worry. His eyes were wild, fearful. "Are you okay Emmeline?"

"Nicholas, why are you here? How did you find me?"

"I saw your note, then the crumpled one from Hannah. I am so sorry about your mother. I had a hunch you might try to find Edmund."

Emmeline flicked her eyelids several times, trying to reorient herself. "I have to get home, Nicholas. Mom's situation has slammed me with how out of place I am. I knew Edmund was the only one who might be able to help." Emmeline ignored his worried face, "I did come across something."

"Oh really," Nicholas flatly stated, his tone void of inflection or curiosity. There was no excitement.

"Before you time-traveled, when you were heading back to town, did you by chance notice or pick up a nickel?"

Nicholas shifted his feet before he spoke. "Yes, a way back from the train station but we already tried a coin. It didn't make a difference."

Emmeline's words rushed out. "We tried the silver dollar. It may be the wrong coin. What did you do with your nickel?"

"I am not sure. It may be at that shop where I exchanged money," Nicholas maintained his flat tone.

Emmeline spoke firmly. "I've got to get to the house, check for the nickel. It's still in a pocket or in my purse. Let's hope yours wasn't seen as valuable or it wasn't in your pouch for exchange."

Nicholas lowered his eyes to the floor. "I had said, I am becoming quite content here."

Edmund interjected, "No one believes time travel is truly possible. Projected requirements are obscure. If the nickel is instrumental, Emmeline, I imagine you only need your single coin. It may allow anyone nearby to travel too. As I said earlier, I am hoping I can fit through the gap with you."

Nicholas's eyes widened darting between Edmund and Emmeline. Jealously dripped from his words. "What?! You two would return together? When did that come about? What *is* that about?"

Emmeline snapped, "It's not any*thing*, Nicholas. I am quite sure I can return in any fashion I choose. Edmund believes he is more suited for the thinking of the twenty-first century than the twentieth."

Nicholas glared at Edmund, his hands bunching to fists. "Why do you want to go forward?"

Edmund reddened. "I am not prepared to discuss that at this moment, but I do believe the way I prefer to live my life fits another time better than the current."

Edmund raised his hands in a truce, "I told Emmeline I have no intention to remain with her. I would expect nothing in return." Nicholas's shoulders hung as he turned back to Emmeline, his expression sliding from anger to sadness.

In her haste, Emmeline hadn't questioned Edmund. "We need to be sure I even have a coin, but then I will need to understand your reasons. I know I immediately said yes, but I barely know you." Edmund gave a single nod of acknowledgment.

Emmeline saw disappointment on both of their faces. She presumed Nicholas anticipated losing her. Edmund worried a different future was slipping away.

Chapter 21

Return Trip

C limbing steps two at a time, Emmeline shouted to Helen that she would be right back. Helen emerged from the kitchen just in time to witness her taking the top two steps with her skirt hiked up. Emmeline hoped Helen would presume she had a bathroom emergency.

Flinging the door open and dropping to her knees, she anxiously pulled her suitcase from under the bed. She dumped the contents of her purse. The worn nickel bounced on the bed, and she tossed aside the purse. Emmeline reached for the nickel, holding it like treasured gold. Turning it over, she could just make out the faded numbers-1890. She didn't look up but felt Nicholas' penetrating gaze as he walked through the door.

Both sitting on the bed, Nicholas stared at her hand. He gently slid his index finger over the coin and her palm. His eyes drooping, he breathed a defeated sigh. "The gravity of this moment, what you believe this coin means, is a weight pressing on my chest."

She finally met his eyes and found a gentle tone. "Nicholas, I understand you want there to be something between us. I feel something too. But how real can it be? We're two people from very different worlds stumbling our way through another. Even if it's genuine, we've known each other for a matter of weeks. There are people who need me, people I've known all my life."

Placing the coin in the zipper compartment of her purse, she slid it into the suitcase and eased the case back under the bed. "I have to get downstairs. Let's take a walk after dinner." Glancing back as she walked out the door, she tightened her lips in a grimace when she saw him despondently staring down at his hands.

●●●

The weather was warm for early December as they walked comfortably through the neighborhood. Garland wrapped lamp posts, and a few houses had candles lighting their windows. They stood shoulder to shoulder on Grand Street, admiring the lights and ornaments on the town's mammoth Christmas tree, but the distance between them was wide. The decorations were pretty, but the silence was thick. They wandered, filling the void by glancing at the homes. There were many craftsman bungalows, smaller than the storied homes like the boarding house.

Nicholas broke the silence. "I got a job today but the excitement of it vanished when I got back to the room."

Emmeline winced having not thought to ask. "Oh! What is it?"

"At the butcher. He wants to grow the business and will need help quartering meat and waiting on customers. Given my hunting background, I was perfect for the job. Apparently not everyone is seeking frozen meat at the grocery stores."

"That's wonderful! It didn't take you long."

As they continued, Emmeline was frustrated with the renewed silence and burst through it. Her thoughts spewed. "Nicholas, we have to talk about my return. Yes, I have mixed feelings. I must admit, I wonder if we're imagining a bond because of what we've been through?"

"I cannot speak for you, but I am not imagining what I feel."

"I do care about you, but I can't let it take precedence over my family, seeing my mom before...before it's too late. I need to get back to my real life." She threw her hands into the air and said, "It just makes sense for me to go."

"You have said you were close to your father, but not close to your mother or sister," Nicholas pointed out quietly.

"That's true. I never have been, but still, it isn't an obligation I feel right now. It's something about family I feel pulled to do. I can't explain it exactly."

Nicholas remained quiet, so Emmeline pushed on. "Nicholas, I don't know what's more real right now. Of course, I'll miss you. Would you want to come to 2022 with me? We could go together."

Nicholas lightly grasped her elbow, stopping them. Emmeline knew he searched her face for any emotion beyond conviction. "I don't think it's practical for me to go forward that far. Too much has changed in your day. Frankly, it doesn't sound appealing."

Emmeline's guilt surged when she saw Nicholas watching a couple sitting on a bench. They were laughing and holding hands. She knew he wanted a different outcome than the one she was proposing. She had to do this. To shed the guilt, she inhaled, getting a whiff of tomorrow's baking bread mixed with the sweetness of pastries. Nicholas swept his hand taking in the street. "I am finding this a good change, but I don't know what it will feel like without you in it. You may be a primary reason it is so inviting."

"I know the history about to transpire and it may not be safe for you here." Her tone became exasperated. "Sure, if you stay, we know you survived the Spanish flu and lived through WWI. Another war is coming, an even worse one. I can't remember exactly when it starts but we read about horrendous things abroad already. I hate the thought of you being dragged into it or even worse, dying."

Shrugging, he began walking again. "The world seems to be at war somewhere all the time. I am not sure it's a reason to avoid being where *or when* you want to be."

Nicholas was speaking as someone who didn't watch horrific events on real-time broadcasts. He was not exposed to it on every social media platform. Although he had experienced war, it wasn't in one's face to the extent she was accustomed. "There is truth in your words. There have been only isolated decades without a war somewhere."

Emmeline pressed her palm to her forehead. "Nicholas, I'm still confused. I knew you were tossing around the idea of staying, but I am shocked you really want to. There's so much about this era we know nothing about. It's absurd. We could end up in an insane asylum if anything was discovered...or a science lab."

"Both are highly unlikely. People pass through these western towns unnoticed all the time."

Emmeline huffed a sigh. "Are you at least interested in helping me figure out what more I need to know to have this work?"

Setting his eyes on the horizon, Nicholas spoke quietly. "I will help you find the location, but that is all." He turned his head as if watching a passing car. "My heart is obviously in a different place than yours. I do have to begin work tomorrow, but more than anything, I refuse to watch you pass through whatever will take you away."

He kicked a frozen snow clump across the sidewalk, as his pleading eyes met hers. "Have you considered you can't be sure you'll return to your original time? You could end up alone in a much worse place or time."

Emmeline flung her hands out and scoffed. She was irritated by the boundary Nicholas placed on helping her. She stiffened; her voice was terse. "I get you don't want to buy me a first-class ticket out of town, but we have been in this craziness together for weeks. Are you hoping that scaring me will change my mind?"

Nicholas shrugged his shoulders. "Maybe I am not as benevolent of a person as the cabin's history made me sound." He walked on. "Let's talk about what we tell Helen. We could say your mother is very ill, and you must return to take care of her."

Some of Emmeline's irritation receded. "That's believable. It wouldn't feel like a complete lie. We can tell her I will return when I'm able—when my mother is well enough." Glancing sideways at him, she said, "I feel guilty you'd be stuck figuring out what to say when I don't return."

Nicholas reached for Emmeline's hand and stopped. Her cheeks warmed when she saw him swallow hard and hesitate, searching for words. He said, "It appears we are both steadfast on what we want. I know I don't want to keep arguing."

Pulling her in closer, he wrapped one arm around Emmeline's back, and placed his other hand on her waist. Nicholas guided her to his chest.

She pressed her hand to his chest, her heart pounding. She caught a whiff of the spicy aftershave he now wore. Fleetingly, she thought about the year plus since she'd been close with a guy. He kissed her forehead. Her frustration with him dissipated more quickly than she wanted. Turning her head up, he immediately pressed his lips to hers. Emmeline slid her arms around his waist, bringing him more firmly against her.

Lips lingered after the kiss. Slowly, they opened their eyes.

Emmeline's lips curled slightly at the edges. "I guess you really aren't going to help me do this."

Nicholas's hands fingered through her hair. His gaze slid over every inch of her face. His voice cracked as he began to speak. "I will leave no doubt as to why I won't participate. I would regret if you didn't know how much I have come to care for you. Using your words. My brain understands why you need to go. My heart hopes for failure."

Emmeline placed her hands on either side of Nicholas's face and dipped his head towards her for another kiss. "And I want there to be no doubt this isn't easy, but I am sure for now, it's right." She clutched his hand as they made their way back toward the house.

Repercussions in every time-travel book Emmeline had ever read were rising like flags. "Have you considered that if you don't return to your time, you may mess with your hero-hood of helping the town during the Spanish flu and helping Edmund?"

"If there are rules for time travel, I don't know them. It could be what is written is written, what has been impacted will be impacted, even if it is by another individual."

"My mom was healthy as could be a few weeks back when I left 2022. Given my sister's notes, and the severity of the stage of cancer, I wonder if time passes more rapidly in 2022 than we experience here in 1938. If it does, after I travel, many more days will have passed for me, while you are working even one day at the butcher."

Nicholas nodded. "If we stay in this 1938, we don't know what the impact will be. But if we part, we may follow different timelines."

He squeezed her hand and held firmly. "I know how I am feeling. I do know I want you here. I also know I embrace this era differently than the time I was born into. We can regret any decision made day to day, and this decision is no different." His eyebrows flicked. "Maybe your return will result in thinking it was a bad choice."

"Anything is possible, but my logical side doesn't expect to regret it. Not to sound cruel Nicholas, I do believe once I am back, my feelings will fade. These weeks will feel like a dream. You will be the best part of that dream. A part I'll be sad to wake from."

● ● ●

After returning to the room, Emmeline asked Nicholas to check the pockets of the pants he wore the first day. His pockets were empty. They had been washed and he didn't recall what pocket money he used to pay for their drinks the first day or which coins had been exchanged for current-day currency. He found a few nickels among the coins in the pants he was wearing.

Emmeline reached for them, and Nicholas closed his hand to a fist. She said, "You don't even want me to find the right one, do you? I'm doing this. I can travel with my own coin. We don't need to know which is yours."

Nicholas took Emmeline's hand and emptied the coins into hers. "Fine. Here. *You* find the correct nickel."

Two were minted in 1890. Not an unusual coin for his day, as it was for Emmeline. They couldn't know which was the right one. Emmeline folded them both into a piece of paper and put them into her suitcase.

Tired from the evening's tension, they sat in the chairs they had placed by the window. Emmeline stared into the darkness. Her pulse accelerated as she relived the kiss. As if reading her thoughts, Nicholas reached for her hand, interweaved their fingers, resting them on the arm of his chair. She relaxed into the roughness and strength, enjoying the security of his grasp. It was a new feeling, welcoming the safety. She relaxed into it knowing she would miss it.

Chapter 22

The Discovery

Emmeline waited for Nicholas to leave for work before returning to the cabin to see Edmund. He sat on the bench and offered the chair to Emmeline. They drank a cup of Postum, a coffee-like drink of the day. They talked about the unusual warm streak.

Emmeline became antsy with small talk when bigger conversations loomed. She dinged her spoon on the cup, over stirring her coffee. Her head jerked up. "Edmund. During these past weeks, I have been tuning into my heart and gut more than ever. They each tell me to trust you. But you have to understand I have led with my head all my life. I need to hear your motivation for going forward."

Edmund stared into his cup. Emmeline watched. She chose her words so she didn't sound challenging. "You are asking to leave this time behind. Nicholas and I didn't choose this. You might be romanticizing what you'll find in 2022."

Edmund spoke softly and cautiously. "I didn't choose this life either. You talked about the acceptance in your era...for the unusual."

Emmeline leaned in. "Do you mean because of your psychic and visionary abilities?"

"No, that is not it. That would be so easy. Visionaries are part of every culture since the beginning of time."

Emmeline's gaze followed him as he went to the window. He looked out and his fingers drummed the sill. He nervously adjusted and readjusted his glasses.

He was edgy but her impatience grew. "Hey Edmund. Whatever it is, it's ok. It's not a test. I just need to know why."

He walked to the door and peered out as if there'd been a noise. He closed the door and when he turned, his fingers pressed against his lips and his breathing was shallow. His hand dropped like a weight to his side. "Who I am is currently illegal. I have friends in jail who did not hide who they were well enough."

"Edmund. I am getting the picture. You don't have to be scared with me."

He returned to the table. His hand rubbing the back of his head. His eyes raised to meet Emmeline's. He pushed out the words, "I am homosexual."

"Oh, Edmund, I am so sorry you have had to hide who you are. You should know that is a non-issue for me. In 2022 pretty much everyone knows someone who's gay...homosexual."

"It is comforting to hear another say the word without disgust in their voice."

"Oh, believe me, there are people who still despise gay...homosexual people, even in 2022."

"But can people legally and safely acknowledge who they are?"

"Mostly, yes. Some parts of the country are more accepting than others. You would need to be aware of that when picking a place to live. But yes, in most cases, people can 'come out' safely.

"Come out. What does that mean, exactly?"

"It means you can come out as your authentic person. It's what we say when someone tells their friends or family they are gay—homosexual." Edmund nodded and his lips curled up.

"But what about your family, Edmund?"

He seemed childlike as his arms hugged himself and rocked back and forth. "I have rarely spoken of my family since leaving home. It's hard to share and hard to relive it."

Emmeline extended a hand across the table and brushed it across his arm. "I'm so sorry. You don't have to share anything traumatic. I just wondered if you needed to say goodbye."

Edmund inhaled, raising his shoulders, and breathed out a long sigh. Emmeline guessed he was releasing a lifetime of pain. A lifetime of stories he'd told to hide the truth.

"I was raised in a very religious family. I was young and careless. My parents discovered my secret. They loved me too much to report me to the law but wanted me to denounce that life. They said I could learn to fall in love with a woman. One night, I overheard them talking about a psychiatrist who claimed to use hypnosis as means of eliminating my desires."

"There are still people who believe conversion therapy can be successful, but it's not a sanctioned practice, thank God. Where are your parents now?"

Tears brimmed Edmund's eyes. "My mother died from pneumonia. My father blamed me. Said I had broken her heart—her worry for me had weakened her. I tried to convince myself it was his grief talking, but my guilt was immense."

Emmeline couldn't imagine what it felt like to be rejected so viciously. She never doubted her parents wanting the best for her. "Ugh. That's so wrong. Even with that crap, don't you want some closure?"

"I closed that door years ago. He despised who I was. He wanted nothing to do with me. I knew it was my mother who had tempered his actions. I began moving around a good deal and eventually stumbled on training by Edgar."

Emmeline rubbed her hands over her eyes and sat silently. "Edmund, I get why you need to leave this behind. You may need to go more than I do. But I'm worried only one of us can travel."

"I know you are aching for your mother. It should be you." Emmeline's head agreed with him. Her heart was wondering if she could really leave him in such peril.

Chapter 23

Tough Choices

E mmeline drew from genuine worry when telling Helen about needing to care for her mother. Nicholas had just gotten a good job, so it sounded authentic he would remain behind. Emmeline had no plan to return to 1938 but played that she would.

Travel was delayed giving Edmund time to get up to speed with essentials of the twenty-first century. Meanwhile, doubts bubbled into Emmeline's mind. Were her feelings for Nicholas real or a fantasy? Would he just fade into her future-past? How would traveling play out? What if she ended up in some war-torn country or some alternate Handmaiden existence, not Glenwood Springs?

Emmeline wasn't sure if Nicholas was creating moments she'd miss or if he was being himself—the boyfriend other girls talked about. No matter, she welcomed and cursed his increased romantic efforts to dissuade her from leaving. That first kiss was only the beginning. When they sat by their window after dinner, Nicholas's fingers gently brushed over her hand sending sensual shivers through her. His breath tickled her ear as he whispered

146

comments in the movie theater. Emmeline's heart fluttered when she saw him come up the sidewalk from work. Light kisses set her aflame. Emmeline reminded herself she had already lost one parent. Being there for her mom was paramount. A truth was waking in her. She would miss Nicholas more than she wanted to admit.

●●●

With a sideways glance, Emmeline saw Nicholas watching as she laid her travel clothes over a chair. He was sipping whiskey he had bought on his way home from work. It was not completely out of character, but she knew tonight it was dulling the pain of tomorrow.

While folding some items into the suitcase, her heart jumped; the two travel nickels were gone. Her gaze shot to him. "What happened to your 1890 nickels?"

"I gave them to Edmund. I don't need them."

A warm glow flowed through her in awe of this man sitting in front of her. "Nicholas, that was so kind and selfless. But why?"

"I double-checked his reasons for going with you. If what you say about your century is right, he should leave. Plus, he may help you to remember me."

Emmeline sighed as she tilted her head back. Control over her emotions frayed further with every moment. Her voice shook. "I'm scared of missing out on what could be. I'm scared travel will go wonky. I'm scared I will forget 1938."

His eyes fixed on her. "Then stay. You have prepared Edmund well. He can do this on his own."

"But I'm also scared of not seeing Mom. I'm confused, but I need to be there for her."

Emmeline pulled a chair close to Nicholas's and sat. Taking his hand, she traced a heart into his palm. He closed his eyes and his lips curled slightly at the edges. Placing her fingertips lightly on his chin, she turned his face to hers. Leaning in, she kissed the curled sides of his lips.

She shifted her position from the chair to his lap. She kissed each eyebrow, each ear. Emmeline took the glass of whiskey. Taking a sip, she held the whiskey in her mouth. Placing her lips on his, she infused the warm liquid through his.

Swiftly Nicholas scooped her into his arms and stood effortlessly. Carrying her over to the bed, he laid her down. He lifted himself over and lay beside her. Shivers woke every cell in her body as he slid his fingers up then down her arm. They both knew sleep would be restless, and for the moment, decided to soothe the edges another way.

His fingers slid from her arm to untuck her fitted blouse and began small spirals up her stomach, unbuttoning her blouse one button at a time. With each one, his fingers spiraled up her skin to the next. She fleetingly wondered if this nineteenth century man had visited the upstairs of many saloons.

Her blouse unbuttoned, he slipped each side from her chest. He leaned in to kiss her stomach at her waistline. He jerked back when he saw the tattoo of angel wings framing her bellybutton.

She murmured, "Just one more example of differences in the twenty-first century."

"This is common for women in 2022?" he asked in a surprised tone.

Emmeline chuckled. "Yes, quite common. More people my age *have* tattoos than don't. By the way, I am not believing for a minute that you are a virgin."

His head jerked up. "Oh, I never said I was a virgin. I said I wasn't comfortable talking with women."

"Obviously, my mistake," she whispered as her eyes closed, hoping he would return to the task at hand.

His hand skimmed down over her skirt to her knee then slipped underneath, following the line of her garter belt up to her panties. He pressed. "Hmmmm nice." Nicholas moaned when he felt her wetness. His hand slid back, unhooking the front garter on her right leg and moved over, unhooking the other.

She cupped her hand on his shoulder and whispered, "Come up here." He growled in disappointment but glided up beside her. She ran her hand down his thigh to his knee, and back moving between his legs. Emmeline gave a little chuckle. "Life is so easy for men."

Nicholas's eyes floated open. "Why is that?

"Zippers." As she pulled his down, she added, "They're so much quicker than buttons and hooks." Emmeline pushed him to his back and rolled on top of him. "You're only half done with the garter."

He yanked her skirt exposing the back garter clasps. He rubbed the back of her thighs and unclasped each one. Emmeline, for the first time, recognized the sexiness of that archaic piece of equipment.

She dropped her mouth to his. The kisses were urgent. Breathing was intense and they took in short sips of air between long pressing kisses. Nicholas held tightly to her flesh. Emmeline wrapped her fingers in his curls. Both spoke of never forgetting this moment.

Chapter 24

The Day is Upon Us

They lay entwined all night, both sleeping lightly. Emmeline would wake to hear Nicholas's steady breathing and let her breathing match his. Other times she could see the outline of his face, his eyes watching her. They'd kiss throughout these moments and then doze.

Emmeline woke facing the wall. The early morning light was filtering in, and she lay looking at the maroon flowered wallpaper. She had a few extra minutes. Instead of relaxing, panic rose in her throat. Stumbling into time travel was one thing. By doing it on purpose, was she messing with what was meant to be? She focused on Nicholas's warm body draping hers and asked herself how long she would hold the memory of Nicholas's touch, of his handsome face.

Nicholas's arm tightened around her waist, pressing her closer. He whispered, "I will resist what I wish to do. I must accept your need to be with your mother. It no longer feels right for me to change your mind."

Emmeline kissed the back of his hand. "I need to do this; it's not without regret. If today works, I wonder if it then means I could return to you."

Nicholas nuzzled his face into her hair and took an inhale. "If wishing you back can make it happen, then we will see each other again."

Nicholas rolled onto his back. With a sigh, he pushed himself to a seated position. "The time is near. You should probably clean up and head to the station."

She rolled to a kneeling position. She kissed his forehead and slipped over him before he stopped her. Carrying her clothes to the bathroom, she stared at her reflection in the mirror. The tingling sensation in her fingers and tight chest was anxiety sliding its way through every inch of her body. Scenes of seeing her mom, walking away from Nicholas, and walking into a post-apocalyptic world, all swirled and collided in her head. In these six weeks, she had shifted from panic in new surroundings to comfortableness. She knew in her heart the reason for the comfort. But her practical nature would reorient to her familiar world just as it had always adjusted.

Nicholas was gone when she came out of the bathroom. He had probably gone down to breakfast, but she had no interest. The butterflies in her stomach were all she could digest.

Moments later, he entered holding a small bouquet of flowers. He stroked the garnet ring on her finger with one hand and said, "You do have this, but the florist said these sweet pea flowers offer safe travels."

She spoke with misty eyes. "Thank you." She groaned. "It's time for me to go."

He had no tears, but his shoulders slumped as he placed his forehead on hers. Emmeline asked, "Are you sure you won't walk me to the station?"

Tightening his lips, he shook his head. "I need to go to work."

Nicholas got to the door, then swung around. Upon her in one broad step, he locked his arms around her waist. Her back arched as she hungrily kissed him. His lips slid to her ear. "I have fallen in love with you Emme."

His arms dropped from her waist. Her chest heaved as she watched him go from her life. Motionless, she stared at the wooden door. She walked to the desk, removed her garnet ring, and folded it in a jotted note. Reaching for her suitcase, she uttered, "I might be crazy."

● ● ●

As Emmeline approached the train station, Edmund was arriving grinning from ear to ear. "Look at you in your pleated pants and overcoat ready for a fantastic voyage," she said.

As his grin grew larger yet, he said, "An opportunity to not hide any longer is fantastic! I could hardly sleep."

They had agreed to meet at the station since neither Emmeline nor Nicholas was sure of the exact point where the 'transfer' had occurred. They would follow the tracks if the building with the nickel wasn't the trigger.

Walking around the station, Edmund caught Emmeline's elbow, keeping her from slipping on some ice. Finding a spot without other passengers, Edmund said, "We don't know, but it may be helpful if we share the same mindset. You said you were thinking of your father and feeling alone. Try to recapture that emotion. I will be thinking of my own loneliness."

"Okay." She initially focused on her dad. She was surprised when her mom's face slipped in and her dad's faded. They stood with their backs against the wall. Seeking security, she let her shoulder touch Edmund's. Their eyes met and they nodded, as if preparing for a leap. A moment later Emmeline opened her eyes to see Edmund watching an approaching train.

"It's not the train you described from your time," he said.

Emmeline spoke with resignation. "No. Let's try the front."

The road was still dirt. They saw the same old front of the Hotel Denver. Emmeline had turned on her phone just before leaving the room. She peeked at it in her pocket, checking for anything, hoping for something. Her heart sank. No service, no glowing date.

"It still didn't work."

No more proof was needed. They were still in 1938. The next step was walking east, paralleling the tracks. Emmeline's shoulders had drooped, and Edmund's smile had dulled as they reached destination two. "We must remain hopeful," Edmund said.

At that moment a car drove by. They jumped away to avoid being splattered by slush. Turning to look at Edmund, Emmeline found herself alone. Her head turned both ways in search of his overcoat. She took a few strides toward town. He was gone.

"Oh no, oh God, where'd he go?" she said aloud.

Emmeline's attention flipped to the cars whizzing by on the freeway. She noticed the fluorescent green of the early summer mountain leaves as her eyes lifted to watch a jet pass over head. Her head followed as a Tesla rolled past. Suddenly, her heart raced in worry for Edmund. They had planned for this possibility. He had cash and names of people who could help him. His business was meeting people and reading situations. She assured herself he'd be alright. She sensed dampness on her leg and noticed the splatter spots. 1938 splatter marks?

Pulling out her phone, her heart climbed to her throat. There were bars and a circling icon searching for service. "Holy shit." It was June 4, 2023—six months later.

Chapter 25

Re-connecting

Emmeline danced herself across 7th street and squealed, 'Woo-hoo!' She didn't care what the people of Glenwood may think. She laughed as a man crossed the street talking out loud. For the past six weeks it would have implied a deranged person. In 2023, they were wearing earbuds, talking on their phone. Exhilaration continued as she saw jet contrails crisscrossing the sky.

Passing by the side of the Hotel Denver on Blake Avenue, she figured anyone could text Hannah using her phone, but Hannah would recognize her voice. Emmeline knew her phone was turned off the past six weeks, but she was still relieved when she tapped Hannah's number, the call went through. The phone rang once.

Emmeline heard a cautious voice. "Hello?"

Her words were strained. "Hi -----Hannah. It's Emme."

There was silence. Then Hannah's volume exploded. "Oh my God, I can't believe this is happening! Where are you?"

A swallow clunked in her throat. "I am only a few blocks from your house. I am coming up Blake from the train station."

Emmeline was sure now that she had returned to her era. Her heart pounding interrupted her breathing. She had barely hung up the phone when she spotted Hannah coming toward her in a full-out sprint. They met, flinging their arms around each other. Emmeline squeezed her sister saying, "I can't believe it worked this time."

"This is unbelievable! Wait till Mom finds out!" Hannah said.

Emmeline was acutely aware of the value of all family, not just the favored.

Calming their breath, they walked arm in arm. The words, "How is she?" rushed from Emmeline's mouth.

"Not great but holding her own right now. You're going to make her day!"

Emmeline stopped as they passed the old boarding house where Nicholas might be right now. Where they had lain entangled only the night before. She gave an awkward little wave to the past and to whoever might live there now. With a shallow sigh, she wished she could exist in both worlds. Hannah didn't notice.

Walking into the house, Emmeline asked, "What's the real story on Mom?"

Hannah elaborated on a not-good prognosis. "She'll be thrilled knowing you're safe. There is still uneasiness that you were kidnapped."

Emmeline took a deep-chested sigh. "I was hoping the twenty-first century carried more chance for a cure. Was there a wide search for me that will need explaining?"

Before Hannah could answer, Emmeline glanced at her ringing phone. She answered in case by any miracle it was Edmund. "Naturally, my first call turns out to be a telemarketer."

No matter who it was, hearing the Sign of the Times ringtone was comforting, reassuring. "Ahhh. How I missed Harry Styles." She clicked it off as she blew her cheeks out. "Is it really June 4th, 2023?"

Hannah nodded, confused.

Emmeline said, "When I got your note about Mom, I wondered if time was advancing differently in the two eras. She was completely healthy when I left six weeks ago. I was still in Glenwood Springs. How can the exact location pass time so differently?"

Hannah shook her head. "I'm still grappling with time travel being real. I have no idea of its details." Cocking her head, "Uhm. You know you have been gone much longer, right?"

Before Emmeline could process further, Hannah exploded with questions. "Did that ripped guy come with you? You really should call Mom. What's his name? Your clothes look new vintage. Did you guys hook up?"

"Those questions can wait. Call Mom. Tell her I'm back. It'll lighten the shock if you prep her. I don't want to make her crash. Then hand me your phone."

"Hey! You didn't take that into account for me! I almost fainted when your name popped up on the screen!"

Emmeline scrunched her nose. "You aren't old. Your body can take it."

Hannah called. "Mom, I have news about Emme." She sucked in a breath. "Get ready. She's standing here in my living room."

Emmeline teared up hearing sobbing through the phone. She seized it from Hannah. "Mom, it's really me. I figured things out. I'm here, really." The sobbing continued as machines dinged in the background. "Mom, where are you.... are you in the hospital?" Hannah hadn't shared that.

There was a loud sniffle. "Hold on." Her mom blew her nose. "Yes, I was admitted after I suffered a small stroke. I think my system is so depleted, it weakened everything. They are running more tests and scans. Honey, I can't believe I am talking to you."

After a new round of sobbing stopped, her mom said, "The nurses say the stroke caused me to be more emotional, but this crying is justified. When can I see you?"

She switched Hannah's phone to speaker. "Mom, why don't I come tomorrow morning? It'd be so late if I left now."

Emmeline's hands were trembling. This was real. She wasn't too late to fix things, to make up for being so flippant with her mom. "I love you, Mom. I'm sorry I never said it much. I'm so sorry if I made you feel second-rate to Dad."

Her mom spoke softly. "Oh Emme, I understood your grief and the relationship you had with your father. I may have been a little jealous at times. But I knew it didn't diminish my own place, my value in the family." Her sudden laughter lightened the mood. "Anyway, Hannah was always my favorite."

With a burst of laughter, Emmeline said, "I KNEW it!" The joke released tension. "I will get a train tomorrow."

Hannah leaned into the phone, glaring at Emmeline. "Oh no. I will drive you. Not letting anything wonky happen on that train again. Besides, I am not letting you out of my sight!"

"Hopefully we can drive by my place so I can get rid of my suitcase and change into something else."

Hannah flicked a look at Emmeline as her hand sprang to her mouth. She muffled a "Ruh-ro." Hannah quickly said, "Hey Mom, gotta let you go. We will see you tomorrow. Bye."

"What?" Emmeline asked.

Her voice cracked. "Emme, we couldn't afford to keep the monthly payments on your apartment. We put your things in storage. Oh, don't scrunch your face like that. You were gone for months. It may have felt like weeks for you, but it wasn't. We had to decide where to cut."

Emmeline's stomach clenched. She was slammed with all that had transpired. She missed being there to support her mom when she got the diagnosis. She held guilt placing the apartment in the same thought thread as her mom, but it had been a sign of her independence when she scored that apartment her last year of college. Emmeline knew it shouldn't be a big deal, but in the Denver housing market, losing an apartment was huge. She had rented it for a steal.

Hannah touched her arm, "We aren't putting you out on the street. Mom would love you to stay with her."

Pulling out her phone, Emmeline said, "You kept my phone service."

"That was less than a hundred a month. You know rent is crazy expensive. Mom wanted you to have a way to call us."

Emmeline begrudgingly admitted, it made sense. Her brain launched back to Edmund. Where was he? Would directions be enough? She hoped she'd prepared him for what he would see and what he needed to do.

Right now, her mom was foremost on her mind. "Maybe we should go to the hospital now."

Hannah gave a quick head shake. "Like you said, let's leave in the morning. Mom needs her rest."

"I do feel drained. Let's order in," Emmeline said.

"Perfect. I want to hear everything about the hot guy. Then you can tell me how time-travel works."

●●●

Emmeline let go the guilt for not speeding back to Denver. She wanted a beer more than a journey right now. They ordered take out from Juicy's. Emmeline always liked the place but now felt a warm connection knowing it's in the same building as Red's Café was in 1938.

They threw some plates on the table and tossed back a beer. Then they settled in with their delivery and a bottle of wine. Hannah asked questions, and memories flooded Emmeline's brain as she talked. She told of being hypnotized and discovering what triggered the travel.

Hannah sat and listened for a few minutes. Finally, she threw up her arms. "Come on, you know that's all intriguing, but what I really want to know about is Nicholas. Did you guys do it? What is a guy like from 1898?"

Emmeline's skin warmed, hearing his name.

In a lifted voice, Emmeline said, "We got very close—more than friends."

Although ecstatic to be with Hannah, those weeks with Nicholas deserved some privacy. She reminded herself Hannah was not her confidant. She chose her words. "He didn't want me to leave, but I knew I couldn't stay. My romantic bubble burst the moment I heard about Mom. Well, it burst for a while. Crap, I'd love to commute back and forth."

Hannah bobbed her fork at Emmeline, "Good sex is hard to leave behind."

"I didn't say we had sex." Emmeline wasn't ready to divulge that. "But I felt a connection I've never had."

"But Emme, what kind of work is there for a woman in the 1930s? You don't like nursing or teaching. I doubt there was much in business for women. It'd be ridiculous to consider returning."

Emmeline spoke with more commitment than she felt. "I am not returning. It was like those summer flings or those reenactments where you ride a covered wagon on the Oregon Trail or immerse yourself in a novel's theme park. It is over and done, but I must say am basking in the afterglow."

Emmeline changed the subject. "If you remember, the whole reason for my coming to Glenwood originally was for us to go through Dad's coins and decide what to do with them."

Hannah furrowed her brow. "Oh, that's right!"

Emmeline knew Hannah had been preoccupied with her disappearance and never understood the interest in coin collection.

Hannah perked up. "Maybe we hold on to the two most valuable and sell the others. Or we sell the two most valuable. Whichever might bring in the most cash. If it's a lot, I could put the money into updating my store."

Emmeline watched out the window as someone passed by. Irritation settled in. "Let's put it on hold until we see mom and life settles again."

She shouldn't have brought up the coins. Hannah wasn't going to suddenly share Emmeline's sentiment in their dad's old collection. The wine was influencing her words. "I need to grab a glass of water." In the kitchen, she let the water run cold as she peered out the window.

She yelled to the other room, "Hannah, do you want some water?"

Out the window, she stared at the house down the street. She pictured Nicholas in their room, wondering if he was watching the street below from their window. Was he thinking of her right now? Emmeline turned to carry two glasses of water and reminded herself she had moved on.

Chapter 26

The Hospital

They drove a good portion of the way to Denver in silence. The initial exhilaration was seeping away, replaced by the old story of being sisters but not exactly friends. Emmeline watched the road signs pass by wondering if that could change. Could they ever be partners in crime?

They pulled up to St. Anthony's Hospital. Emmeline leaned her head back on the head rest. With her eyes closed she took three deep breaths, preparing for what Hannah had said was a change in her mom's appearance. Agnes had dropped weight and chemo was taking its toll on her skin and hair. Emmeline hoped her mom would be asleep. She wanted time to adjust to the physical changes. Emmeline wandered slowly up the sidewalk, planning for her first words to sound casual. They took the elevator up. When the door opened, her mom was sitting on a bench opposite the elevator, her IV rack beside her. Planning had been worthless. Emmeline's breathing cut, and she turned her head, blinking back tears.

Immediately her mom shifted to strong Mom mode. She smiled and pointed to her head scarf. "While you were gone, I shaved my head to join Hari Krishna and I found a fantastic weight loss program!"

Emmeline engulfed her in a bear hug, then flinched. She may have been too rough. Tears streamed down Emmeline's face. Her mom pulled back, wiping the tears with the edges of her thumbs.

Her mom asked, "What, no quip in return?"

Emmeline mustered a playful smile. "How about, you look beautifully like shit."

Agnes placed her hands on Emmeline's shoulders, "There we go. Isn't that better? I am already tired of everyone crying and feeling sorry for me or themselves."

Emmeline responded, "I think I need a few good cries. Then maybe...then maybe I can be stronger."

They walked slowly down the long hallway back to the room. Her mother's breathing became labored. Hannah had brought Emmeline up to speed about the pancreatic cancer being stage four with small spots metastasized to both the brain and lungs.

Standing straighter, Emmeline growled, "Fucking pancreatic cancer, fuck all cancer." "Exactly." Her mother agreed.

Her mom shared her worst fears of Emmeline being abducted and then the disbelief that time travel could have happened.

After Hannah left to run errands, they sat side by side on the edge of the bed. Her mom said, "Finding the bracelet was proof enough for me that you were okay. You would be too embarrassed to share that any other time."

Medical staff were in and out. Each time they left the room, Agnes jumped back to questions about her 'trip', as she called it. Emmeline watched her blinks lengthen, as her mom fought to stay awake. "I am not going anywhere, Mom. We have the days ahead to debrief my 'trip'." Her mom was out within seconds, face relaxed with a little smile.

For nearly an hour Emmeline soaked in her mom's peaceful look and rhythmic breathing. She cursed the world for having all the advanced equipment. It was equipment of dreams in 1938. Yet, with all of this, they still couldn't cure her mom. She replayed gentle memories and loathed the childish moments of being an ingrate. Emmeline's attention turned to birds out the window when she heard a soft, "Emme." She turned her head.

Her mom had woken and watched her through sleepy eyes. "Emme, I know you have been sitting chastising yourself for whatever you think you did wrong."

"I was thinking what an ingrate of a kid I was and that time I said you made dad do all the real thinking."

"Most kids are ingrates at some point. It's part of finding your own path."

Emmeline's voice cracked, "I just don't know how I make up for lost time."

"It's not about making up time. It's about expanding what remains."

Hannah had told Emmeline the doctors were expecting six months at the most. The treatments may prolong her life but not by much.

Agnes took Emmeline's hand, "I am hoping you will stay with me when I am released. You don't have to worry. I won't expect you to wipe my butt. I will need someone to be the organizer for any providers who might have that job."

Emmeline was not questioning her priorities. In one day's time, the thought of getting that first job out of college had been back seated. Helping family, her mom, was more important. What she'd been through the past six weeks had spun her priorities like whirligigs in an autumn wind. She stayed with her mom through dinner and Hannah's return. Insisting she was fine alone through the night, her mom suggested the girls leave and enjoy some sister time. She pulled each of their heads down and kissed them on the forehead.

Agnes wagged a finger, "No arguing."

Emmeline scoffed. "We aren't twelve, Mom."

They stopped at Platte Street Tavern for a beer. Music bombarded Emmeline as they opened the door. TVs hung in every corner. Each one showed something different. She'd never noticed how TVs constantly changed brightness and volume. It cluttered her senses. It was all noise. Noise which once stirred energy and excitement, now assaulted her senses.

Chapter 27

Edmund's Journey

Standing with Emmeline only moments before, Edmund was now standing alone. Frozen in place, his every sense activated. He'd rarely heard these noise levels, even in New York City. It was not only the dizzying numbers of cars whizzing, but other ambient sounds. Voices, honks, and random music. The sounds bounced off houses and buildings. After his senses calmed, he noticed it was not winter but late spring or early summer. Where was Emmeline? Did they come through to different times?

His eyes wide, he soaked up his surroundings. It had sounded exciting to travel ahead to a more accepting time, but at this moment, also daunting. He was alone but needed to contact someone who provided false identification, yet he couldn't tell why he needed it. Emmeline did say they don't always ask those types of questions. They only cared if you had the money. She gave him hers, saying she had something called a credit card to get her by. She assured him his wardrobe would be of no matter.

His feet started moving, and he found himself in front of Emmeline's sister's house. The entire street had a different feel. It went beyond the trees being a shocking height. It was still quaint but had a busy energy. What he felt wasn't nature; it was activity.

He knocked at the door, but there was no answer. He had confidence this is where Emmeline would go, so he risked leaving a note. Edmund always carried a small notebook and pencil in his coat breast pocket. He opened the screen door and closed it, making sure it wouldn't fall or blow away. It had enough information to be understood, but not so much to be questioned if Hannah or Emmeline weren't the ones to find it.

●●●

Next, he went to the train station to verify the date and check the schedule. Frequency of trains were very limited compared to the 1930s and the prices were outrageous. The money would be needed if that was a sign of the times. It was a couple of hours before the only train heading to Denver would arrive. He wondered about Nicholas's cabin; wondered if it'd still be there. It was not. Only an updated plaque remained, naming a walking path which headed past more houses. Where the outhouse had stood, there was a cement public restroom.

Edmund could people-watch all day. He didn't read minds, but he did read feelings. Sitting at the train station, even though people were talking or laughing, there was anxiety in the room. Sensing something about the era, he struck up a conversation with a woman seated next to him. There was a calm about her that others lacked.

"I am not from around here. Is there any information that will help when I get to Denver?"

"There are likely to be homeless people around Union Station. Overall, they are quite harmless. Some have mental illnesses while others are just down on their luck. The pandemic fucked with people's stability of housing." Edmund had grown accustomed to swearing from his weeks around Emmeline.

The woman chatted openly, and Edmund felt comfortable asking more questions. "How about a place to stay as a newcomer?"

"I don't know of a best first place. You could Uber out of downtown and it would be cheaper. Checking out Airbnb might help you find a room for a night or two."

She used these terms as if they were common knowledge. Emmeline had told him some key terms. "I don't have a cellular phone for calling." The woman squinted and pulled her mouth sideways into a smirk. To cover his tracks, he added, "I lost it in my travels. I wonder if there's a good old-fashioned taxi?"

The woman stared a moment longer, "Yes, there are taxis. Why don't I give you a friend's address? He has a motorhome next to his house that he rents through Airbnb. It's very cheap. I'll give him a heads up you may be calling—or stopping by, and that we had chatted; you seem safe enough."

She excused herself and walked to a vending machine into which Edmund saw her place the coins and retrieve food. His familiarity these machines was for gum or cold drinks. Knowing he would get hungry but not wanting to spend much money, he took the change from buying his ticket and mimicked her. There were candy bars and bags of various snacks. He didn't recognize Fritos or Sun Chips, but he loved potato chips. He went with the familiar.

Edmund walked over to a box holding newspapers. He stooped to read the big print. One headline said, "Apple holds developer conference." Apples must hold substantial notoriety, he thought. His eye slid to the top. He saw the date June 5, 2023-months past their travel time.

He returned to his seat. "Your generosity is appreciated. I worry I might seem an odd bird to some."

"Your oddity as you call it, seems, somehow, reassuring. My name is Carmen. What is yours, so I can tell my friend?" They both noticed the train rolling in.

Her kindness made him feel welcomed. "I'm Edmund." The passengers herded toward the door. Once they boarded, Carmen's ticket took her to a private car, while his was in the coach section. Nodding a farewell, he thanked her for the help. A calm energy hovered throughout the train car as most passengers gazed at the scenery passing by.

●●●

Graffiti littered the other cars and walls pulling into Denver's train station. Edmund had seen messages on trains. People who rode the rails wrote warnings or messages in chalk on train cars. These looked permanent and was a language he didn't understand but in many artistic colors. The train station in Denver was enormous and grand. Edmund stood and studied people's movements and mannerisms to help him blend in. When he got outside, even the few who weren't gazing at their cellular phones, were still walking swiftly. Surely people hurried in the 30s, but this pace was frenetic. He jumped aside to avoid a man knocking into him. "Excuse me sir," Edmund said. The man glanced up, surprised. He offered a half smile and hurried on. An occasional pedestrian made eye contact.

Flagging a taxi was easier than expected. Somethings had not changed. When the seat belt process needed to be explained, he knew he was failing at his desire to blend in. Arriving at the address in Lakewood, he knocked on the door. A man looking older than Carmen answered.

"Hello. My name is Edmund. Your friend Carmen said I might be able to rent your motor coach for a night."

"Hello back, my name is Todd. Yes, Carmen said you might show up. She was correct in saying I would be able to verify you by your word choice and your old-fashioned name. However, she is also a wonderful judge of first impressions, and she said you were genuine."

Smiling a guarded smile, wondering which words were revealing, Edmund said, "I have limited funds until I find a job. What is your rate for a night?"

Todd cocked his head to the side. "Why don't you stay in the room I also rent. It's cool out and it will save my explaining the process of the propane to you. I can strike a deal."

Edmund realized renting rooms now was not so different from the boarding houses. He settled into his room. He saw very few pedestrians out the window. Cars seemed to be the way to get around.

Not having thought much about food, he was glad he had bought two bags of chips. Opening the bag, he welcomed the familiar smell.

As he was crunching, Todd knocked at the door. "Are you hungry? I made too much spaghetti and am happy to share."

"I am, in fact, quite hungry."

Todd suggested he come to the kitchen, since it was such a messy meal. He didn't ask questions why Edmund was in town. Instead, they talked about art and music. Edmund said, "I have a love for jazz. My favorite is Billy Holiday."

Todd smiled. "I love the old classics too. Ella may be my favorite."

"Fitzgerald? Yes, she probably stood the test of time."

Edmund saw Todd's quizzical look before he said, "Yes. she certainly did."

Whether it was time travel or the hectic energy of this new setting, Edmund was exhausted. Todd declined payment for the meal, saying the conversation was a welcome change from the discussions of the twenty somethings who usually rent his room. They were always pleasant, polite, but preferred discussing best bars, and climbing fourteeners.

The following day, Edmund continued the story of losing his cell phone and having limited funds. "Is there a phonebooth nearby or place I could procure an inexpensive phone?" A look told him he had spoken another self-dating word.

Todd skipped over it. "I haven't seen a phone booth since visiting Scotland." He explained about TracFones and prepaid access. Todd's eyebrow flicked when Edmund said he preferred something he could get while being anonymous.

"There's a pawn shop a few blocks away. I don't know, but it may have a wiped phone. Edmund ignored the word, figuring he'd drawn enough attention to himself.

●●●

Edmund ended up with a burner phone. His first call was to Emmeline. There was no answer, but luckily her voice told him when to talk. He told her he had made it through, but she was not around. He chronicled about going to her sister's and the nice woman he'd met at the station. He'd found a place to rent for the night. Edmund talked on without knowledge that his time was limited. He was suddenly informed the maximum time had been reached. Realizing he should have started with where he was, he called back only to hear the mailbox was full. He had no choice but to proceed to the next step on his own.

Edmund located Emmeline's friend Mick, who had recovered from addiction. He should have anticipated the suspicion. Of course, he asked questions such as when had Edmund seen her, where did he meet her. Luckily, he did not know she'd been missing. Knowing his responses were vague, he led with flattery. Telling him Emmeline shared his journey back from addiction and the strength it took. She had never given up on who he was and his ability to find his way back.

Eventually, he offered a possible location. Mick said, "I don't know if the same people still operate there, but if not, someone has likely taken their place."

He was to approach a white van in the parking lot behind an abandoned restaurant. Of course, they only deal in bitcoin or cash. Mick warned Edmund to be alert, cautious, because of the arena he was stepping into.

"If they ask who referred you, have some plan that doesn't include my name. I never want it on their radar again." Edmund thanked him and left.

●●●

Edmund walked a couple of blocks before he saw the place. The taxi driver chose to drop him a distance from the address. He stood down the street watching for activity around the abandoned restaurant. A white van had pulled in minutes earlier, but there had been no other cars. Crossing the street, he saw it was an old diner and the sign, "*Polly's*" dangled from one screw. A large piece of butcher paper hung in the cracked window. The words "*Permanently closed*" had been written in fat black marker. Weeds crept through the concrete beneath his feet.

Edmund walked to the side of the building and peered around to see the van idling, but no movement. He stood his 5'9 body straight, hoping that a puffed chest would be perceived as confidence. He set his jaw and drew in a deep breath. Somebody could be seen in the driver's seat as he approached. Edmund was being watched.

The window rolled down and a man with a mountain man beard wearing a woolen cap and mirrored sunglasses, stared in his direction.

Forcing a warm smile, Edmund said, "Good day, sir. I need a new identity. I was told you would know how I could obtain one."

The man raised his tattoo-covered hand to his sunglass and slid them down his nose. His scrutinizing gaze moved up and down Edmund's clothes.

"Seriously, what century are you from? Get out of here."

"Sir, I may appear odd to you, but I am fully capable of paying cash." He showed some bills. "I do not think you care how your patrons dress."

The man held his stare. "How do I know you're not a cop?"

"I can assure you, law enforcement would never find me suitable for their profession."

The man scanned the lot and gave his head a shake. "Holy fuck, what is happening to people? Get in, weirdo," he muttered.

Edmund's throat tightened. He stood staring into what he could see of the van.

"Well. You want that identity or not?"

Edmund went to the passenger side and checked out the back as he put a foot on the running board. It was empty except for an old mattress on the floor.

"If you're not a cop, try this weed. It's good shit. It'll set you for the day."

Edmund knew of reefer. He had it a couple times but deemed it dangerous to be relieved of his senses and risk acting with impropriety. Edmund took the joint, taking as small of hit as possible. Even at that, his head lightened. "You're right, sir. It is good...shit."

"Glad you liked it, good sir," spoken with a mocking tone.

176

Edmund didn't know if his choice had been wise; getting into the van not knowing where they were going. Oddly, there was no siren sounding in his gut. The van took off.

Chapter 28

Emmeline's Search

A gnes was released days later. She told Emmeline removing residual fear of her where-abouts was healing. Emmeline returned to her childhood bedroom with a renewed appreciation. Her mom kept up with household chores and asked Emmeline not to dote.

Never having accepted much at face value, Emmeline jumped into research about cancer-causing agents. There was too much to dissect. One article associated diet, another lifestyle, some pesticides, others nothing at all caused cancer, just random or genetics.

Her mom didn't have the years that most environmental activists spend championing an issue. In her heart, she knew any torch she may pick up wouldn't save her mom. She just felt better doing something. Digging in and researching is how Emmeline coped.

She came across a statistic in the *Health Hotline from Natural Grocers*, citing a substantial decrease over the last seventy years in the micronutrients found in fruit and vegetables. The food they ate today carried less nutrients than the food grown in 1953. Her mom was born in 1970. Nature doesn't produce perfect looking food, but today, that was what people expected. Emmeline was one of those wanting a flawless shiny apple with no worry about how it was grown.

She assumed in the thirties, even though people were embracing the packaged items, crops were still grown chemical free and much of the soil was likely thriving. The Dust Bowl era had left its mark. In the late 1930s there was renewed respect for the soil. They learned first-hand it couldn't survive overuse or misuse. The Soil Conservation Act taught farmers how to protect soils with practices like crop rotation. Introducing chemical pesticides and fertilizers arrived after WWII. These pesticides and subsequent seed manufacturing would enhance crop yield. The promise of crop increases again overshadowed what was happening to the soil.

She needed to get out of the cyber world and talk to someone. Agnes was reading in the living room. Her parents had never changed the taupe color of the room and art hung in the same place it had when she grew up. Emmeline sat in a favored recliner chair. Its wild abstract pattern of greens, oranges and yellows stood out on the beige background.

"Mom, I know you grew up on a farm, but I never asked much about it."

"I did. Why are you curious now?"

"I have been researching connections to your illness."

"You can say it, Emme. Cancer. You don't have to be afraid to use the word."

"Okay. Some articles associate pesticides with cancers. Others say our nutrients are decreased in our food. How was it when you were growing up?"

"Well, our farm was considered medium-sized. Smaller farms were being incorporated by the larger farms and yes, in the '60s and '70s it was hard to avoid the pesticide use. Bigger and bigger yields were needed to stay afloat and to achieve more perfectly formed produce. What happened to the soil took a backseat."

"I wonder if more people had protested the changes, whether it might have made a difference?"

"Emme, it's hard to stop anything considered progress. Just like you can't stop my cancer by trudging around the internet."

Agnes moved to sit on the arm of the chair. She took Emmeline's soft hand. "Emme, I know it's your nature to dig into the research when you can't control something. But if you really want to help me, then spend time with me. I cherish having you here with me." Emme ran her thumb over her mom's hand. The skin was not as taut as her own but at fifty-three, it had no lines. Her lips tightened. "I'm glad I got back to hang out with you, Mom. You're right. I will treasure this chance."

Chapter 29

Time Flies

Time flies whether you want it to or not. Typically, even more so when you don't want it to. Emmeline had been back in 2023 for months now. She wasn't sure if the initial sweetness of seeing her mom clouded her ability to see how ill she had been or if now she was declining day by day. Although her mom was independent with self-care, her energy level was tanking. She was tired all the time and needed more assistance getting household tasks done.

She knew Edmund arrived in current day. Hannah had found his note tucked into the front door. It read, "I made it safely. I will call when I can." Edmund didn't understand voicemail systems or know to get right to the point and filled Emmeline's voicemail.

She couldn't return his call since his burner phone didn't show a true number and he didn't leave one. The only other option was to visit her friend, Mick. He had kept to himself a good deal since beating the addiction. He spent time with new friends who had a better understanding of his journey. She had distanced herself when the part of her gave up the last hope recovery would hold.

Edmund had found Mick, and he passed on a contact, but what happened after that was a mystery. Mick estimated it was about two months ago, maybe longer. Edmund was intuitive and likely able to navigate many things more smoothly than most. Still, why didn't he reach out again? He must have realized he didn't leave enough information. Did something bad happen? He lived through the Prohibition wars that raged in the 1920s, so seedy lifestyles weren't completely foreign to him. Yet, she worried seedy had surpassed 1930s level.

Any time she thought of Edmund, there was an immediate link to Nicholas. Her guise of moving on from that 'summer fling' idea began to splinter a few weeks after her return. Initially, she easily pushed it from her mind. Then she'd lie on the bed visualizing their last night. Why hadn't they gone for a photo before she left? Why didn't she use her phone?

With months passing, Emmeline spent little time with her few friends. There was a scurry of contacts when she first returned. They knew she was a driven person, but they never pegged her as one who would be admitted to a hospital for suicide attempts. That was the story her mom had made up. With patient privacy laws, it held investigators at bay. Or at least that's what she thought.

Pulling away from her few friends proved easier than masquerading the lie. Emmeline had gone out a few times at her mother's encouragement. One friend wanted her to dive into the shadow side of whatever led her down the path that culminated in the suicide attempts. Another treated her like fragile glass and tip-toed through what would have previously been lively hot topic debates. "Oh, you're probably right. I should check my facts more."

Out at a pub, she glanced around the room. Too many people were absorbed in their phones—swiping up or fingers flying through texts to someone who wasn't in front of them. It seemed everyone was enmeshed in social apps and binging shows. Some of this was driven by a communal worry of being powerless to stem the tide of climate change. Having been the mono-focused sort, Emmeline burrowed into the food production rabbit hole. Being at the beginning of a movement would make it easier to impact its influence than decades into the quagmire when it's a difficult engine to slow. People her age were dropped into that quagmire.

Emmeline was pulled from her thinking by a tap on her shoulder. She shifted her body to see a dark haired man likely in his forties or fifties holding a business card out to her. She spotted furtive glances among the others at the table.

She took the card as the man said, "Hello, Ms. Hammond, I believe?"

Emmeline looked at the card. It read, Thomas Kelly, Littleton Police. Emmeline's eyebrows lifted along with her stomach as she handed the card back. "Yes, I'm Emmeline Hammond. Can I do something for you?"

"I am glad to finally meet you and to see you well." He looked around the table at the others nodding to them. "I have met your friends before while the investigation into your whereabouts was active." She knew she had done little to maintain these connections, but none had mentioned talking with a detective. Her focus had been on the story her mother and Hannah had used for the alibi. "You had many people worried and many confused. When did you return?"

"I have been back for several months." Surprise resentment filled her, thinking everyone had colluded without telling her. Her gaze slid across them. "I am surprised you all didn't tell Detective Kelly that too." Their return stares fell somewhere between guilt and 'what were we supposed to do?'

"Your friends were only worried, and I asked to be called if...when you...when you got out of the hospital. I am surprised myself that it took until last week to hear from them." He continued. "I assure you Ms. Hammond, you are in no trouble. It's relief we feel. You must understand we can't just take another's word for it when they report you back. I preferred seeing you myself. Your departure was very sudden. How are you doing?"

Her tone was curt. "My mother's dying of cancer, so not great if you really want to know. Don't worry, I am not suicidal. I'm helping to care for her." It chided her to be reminded everyone thought she attempted suicide. She understood the reason for the lie, but she didn't like people thinking her fragile.

"I will leave you to carry on with your evening." Detective Kelly extended the card again. "Even though the case is now closed, please, keep my card in case there is anything about your stay you find worth sharing." His eyes bored into Emmeline.

She questioned his choice of words as she tucked the card into her purse. "Can't imagine what that would be."

● ● ●

The allure of the twenty-first century was diminishing and the lingering impact of her six weeks in 1938, confusing. It was annoying recognizing a sizeable part of it could be Nicholas. Independence was her pride and joy. Pages of doodling his name embarrassed her, feeling like a middle schooler. There was a sense of limbo being in this twenty-first century life without him.

Emmeline's main source of easy pleasure was hanging out with Hannah on weekends. Worry for their mom bonded them in a common focus for the first time in years, if not a lifetime. Emmeline could let her facade melt away. She longed to tell Edmund she now understood the freedom that rises when allowed to be authentic.

●●●

The scene of watching Nicholas walk out of her life played on the lids of her closed eyes. Had he found the ring yet? She had removed it and tucked it in a writing desk cubby after Nicholas left for work knowing it would be safe from other eyes. He wouldn't find it right away, but maybe at the moment he needed it most. There was conflict when her words spilled onto the paper. She had tucked the note with the ring. It could give false hope, but she was leaving something, someone, important. She needed to leave a memory. She didn't know then that her love affair with the current day would wane.

Emmeline texted Hannah and asked if she could knock on what some seventy years earlier, had been Helen's door. Hannah had worked her way into the house early on to leave the angel book. She was friendly with neighbors on her block but must have befriended the people living there.

She told Hannah about the ring and which cubby of the writing desk the note was in. Hannah's return text was a series of question marks with a wide-eyed emoji, followed by, "I had a hunch."

Living with her psyche in two eras exhausted Emmeline. Laying back on the bed, Emmeline began watching the in-her-head-replay of the last night with Nicholas. Dozing, she slipped into a dream in 'their room' at Helen's boarding house. There was Nicholas's pungent scent after he left the butcher shop. Nicholas was standing at the window with a whiskey in his hand. He leaned to kick off his shoes and his blonde curls dropped forward when he bent his head. His hair was trimmed on the sides, with combed back waves she longed to rake her fingers through.

In her dream, Nicholas didn't sense her, didn't hear her whisper his name. He moved on into the bathroom and she wished she could follow. She could not.

A knock at the door bolted Emmeline awake. The scent lingered in her nostrils momentarily and then vanished.

"Come on in, Mom." Her mom shuffled over and laid down beside her, taking Emmeline's hand into hers.

She asked, "Are you missing him?"

Emmeline's head turned to meet her mom's. "For some reason, I do."

Agnes gave Emmeline's hand a squeeze. "As this life for me is closing, I urge you to live yours to the fullest. My life with your dad was wonderful, and I wouldn't replace what we had with anything, but there were paths untaken. The kind of path that, in the quiet moments, you wonder where it would have led; wonder what might have been different for you. You are no doubt at one of those intersections with open-ended choices ahead of you."

Emmeline gave a teary nod as her mom continued, "You need to keep in mind, this era has so much more to offer you as a woman. You are allowed to explore and navigate multiple paths at once. The narrow expectations of the '30s would be hard for you. Please consider where the world was headed in the late '30s."

Emmeline stared at the dingy constellation stickers that had clung through the years to the ceiling. "I will never be glad you have cancer, Mom. I know I spent more time with Dad than you. Lately, I've realized a little blessing in his going first. Maybe he knew he needed to. His dying, along with this fucking cancer, has given me a chance to know you differently than that teen who shunned your style, the person who dismissed your depth or purpose in my life. My fear is there will not be adequate time for me to embrace all I missed."

"Inadequate time is what makes it so perfect now. It is why the gift of your helping me is precious. You will remember these tender times forever and I get to languish in daughterly love."

She was right. This was exactly where Emmeline needed to be and exactly what she needed to be doing. Not to be planning. Not controlling what next week would bring. Their relationship was shifting out of child, parent. It was becoming sisterhood. Two women nurturing and serving each other.

Chapter 30

Edmund

E mmeline endured every telemarketer and spam call, in hopes of it being Edmund. Her persistence paid off one day as her phone played the unknown caller ring, Somebody's Watching Me. She answered tentatively. "Hello?".

"Hello from across the universe or at least the country."

Relief slid through her, "Edmund! Oh my God! I am so relieved to hear your voice! Where are you? How are you? Are you ok?"

"I am in California. I am working at the Berkely Psychic Institute."

With curious shock in her voice, she said, "What the hell? What is the Psychic Institute and how did you get there? I was worried you were enslaved somewhere in the back alleys of Denver."

She told him the trail went cold after discovering he'd met Mick. He told her about the van in the parking lot and surmised his odd attire went in his favor.

"Then what happened after you drove away?"

"We went to a small house in a Denver neighborhood with bed sheets hanging over the windows. Their house had a distinct smell of reefer. They kept asking for my contact, but I couldn't give them one. At one point, two burly men towered over me. I decided to tell the truth. I used your words and told them I was gay. I was coming out for the first time in my life. I needed to escape an intensely Christian family who would never stop trying to convert me and wanted to place me in a conversion center."

"Holy crap, Edmund. What then?"

"You were right, being gay isn't foreign to many walks of life in the twenty-first century. One of them had a gay sister. They bought my need to be hidden and gave me an identity."

"What is your name now?

"Still Edmund but now Edmund Reese. I go by Ed because it blends in better. I received a social security number, too."

"Oh, I didn't even think of that."

"They asked me if I wanted one. Mostly government workers had them in the 30s. I have learned now you need them to get a job."

"I know you're working, but do you need money? Need help of any kind?"

"I am fantastic! I feel more alive and accepted than I have ever been."

Emmeline asked for details about the Berkeley Psychic Institute and exactly how he ended up there and how he could have possibly landed a job.

"For some cash, I held a few readings at a store in Denver. I guess they are called New Age or something. By happenstance, the owner was a woman who had studied here and observed some readings. Her clients told her they were more pertinent than any previous. She gave me the name of a gentleman named Marshall.

It was risky to lie to someone working at a psychic institute, but I guess claiming Edgar Cayce is a distant relative was enough of a truth to hide my falsehood and enough of a truth to be impressive."

Edmund still had his burner phone and people embraced he chose to be off the grid. He didn't want people to delve too deeply into his past or lack of it.

"I must get back to work."

"Wait! I have one more question. You left a note on Hannah's door, but we were there the entire evening. I wonder why we didn't hear you or see it when we left?"

"I was shocked to find out nearly six months had been skipped. It was June 5th. Was it the same for you?"

"Huh. Strange. I arrived June 4th. We left very early the next day to see my mom."

Edmund said, "With everything that could have happened, we must count our blessing we arrived only a day apart."

"You're right. If we missed each other by a day, we could have missed each other by years. We are lucky."

Edmund spoke in a quickening tone. "It is wonderful to hear your voice and feel our connection again. We need to talk again soon. Emmeline, are you ok? I am sensing some underlying confusion."

"Your sense is correct, and I would love to talk soon, Edmund, even this evening. Could I have your number and call you back?"

They decided Edmund would call after work the next day. Emmeline stood staring out the window, afraid to break the energy by moving. Speaking with someone who stood by Nicholas, shook his hand, knew he still exists was a lifeline arcing across time connecting her to Nicholas.

Chapter 31

Food as Medicine

Agnes was sleeping peacefully under her light lavender quilt. In sleep, her face relaxed and her small round face wore the bald scalp comfortably. Not everyone could pull that look off. Emmeline for one, having inherited her dad's sizable head.

Her desire to treasure this time with her mom only grew. There were still long evenings since her mom tired easily. Emmeline scrolled through Instagram. Feeling bored with social media that once endlessly entertained her, she switched on the TV.

There was a docu-series hosted by an MD talking about food as an important player in health vs. clinging steadfastly to Western medicine. The discussion concentrated on buying food locally and knowing your farmer. Eat by the season. Emmeline barely knew what country her food came from, more rarely, what state. Living by those described standards, she wouldn't have her mangos or almost anything juicy in January. She could learn to can fruits or freeze vegetables but that wouldn't happen. Her mom's voice played in her head; 'never-say-never.'

She watched another episode, then another. Instead of bingeing a season of The Mandalorian, she binged these. She accepted she couldn't alter her mom's fate, but she still digested all the information she could.

Chapter 32

Hope Answers Nicholas's Worry

Helen and Nicholas had been sharing more time together in the kitchen, away from the other guests. He enjoyed her humor, her interest in his work. She was the second woman he could say he had experienced comfort around. It had been complicated keeping the story alive that Emmeline was visiting her ill mother back east. He had stuffed stationary in an envelope and addressed it to himself using the typewriter in the office at the butcher. If Helen had noticed that the postage was stamped Glenwood Springs, she didn't let on.

Nicholas had placed a note to Emme in the angel book days after she left. It remained there. Nicholas often replayed his final glimpse of her. He had gone to the train station after all, watching from a distance wishing it had been his hand, not Edmund's, to catch her slip. He no longer counted the number of days he returned there and watched the people coming out, longing for one of them to be her. When the last person had emerged, he turned and slowly returned to the house.

Work had been a welcomed distraction. He brought in an elk he butchered and shared stew pieces and occasional steaks with Helen to serve to guests. The food in the stores caught his attention now. Customers were giddy about the convenience of canned or frozen foods. Chicago was the hub of the meat packing industry when Nicholas was a child. By the time he was in his teens, railroads had made it possible to ship cattle and hogs east, and ice-laden rail cars made it possible to ship foods west and east. Now, in the 1930s, reading about the first refrigerated vehicles, food would soon travel even farther.

●●●

One evening after dinner, Nicholas and Helen sat in the kitchen sipping coffee. She poured a bit more coffee in his cup. With a little smile, she walked to a cabinet. She turned and asked, "Would you like a splash of whiskey?"

His eyebrows rose in surprise. "Why certainly! Thank you."

She shot a glance at Nicholas while adding a healthy pour to his coffee. "It's been over four weeks. You must miss Emmeline greatly." It was subtle, but the glance made him wonder about her level of suspicion.

"Greatly. We had just begun our adventure here."

As he spoke, his gut churned. He couldn't keep Emme out of his thoughts, but he was considering Emmeline may...probably, would not be returning.

"Helen, you have made it easier to deal with her absence. You have become a good friend."

She stood, taking her coffee cup to the sink. He heard it clunk on the porcelain. Her back was to him, "Some days are very hard when you are widowed. I understand your loneliness."

Nicholas was conflicted by his comfort with Helen. The evenings went faster with their conversations. She was lonely, as was he, but Helen's attention was a diversion from his heart's desire.

●●●

Nicholas sat at the writing desk, staring at the squiggly horizontal grains of the oak. The drop-down flap open, he gazed at the slots for stationery and letters. He pulled on the small 2x4 drawer on the right and closed it. Mindlessly, he opened the drawer on the left and his eyes fell upon the small delicate ring with a garnet stone. His stomach dropped. Emmeline left it behind. He hadn't considered she'd do that. As he scooped it up with the nail of his index finger into his thumb, a slit of paper sat underneath it. Holding it gingerly, he read, "Keep it safe for my return." His head tilted toward the ceiling, eyes closed, and a smile spread across his face.

If Emmeline was correct about time passage, he calculated months had passed in her time. Even after weeks, he had stopped regular checks of the angel book as hope faded to memory. He had not sat at the desk since her departure.

Pulling a pen from the horizontal shelf, he flipped the paper over. He wrote, "It'll be right where you left it, as will I." He slumped back in the chair, releasing a sigh, whispering 'huh'. A door had creaked open offering renewed hope. Needing to be at work at six in the morning, Nicholas slid into bed. Every now and then he was sure he whiffed Emmeline's scent as he lay beaming up at the ceiling.

Chapter 33

Truth be Known

Emmeline paced, waiting for Edmund's call, willing the clock to move faster. She cocooned herself with the only two people who knew what the hell really happened to her, and to have another in that group cut into her sense of being an anomaly. She suspected Edmund felt the same. It can be hard to stay masked. She had chosen to cocoon with those requiring no explanations.

Even with the phone on full volume, she didn't let it out of her sight. She wouldn't miss this call. She answered on a partial ring. "Edmund. I thought the phone would never ring."

"As I said yesterday, I am grand. I can't talk long but tell me what you are thinking. My intuition tells me you are having some realizations. Am I right?"

"Don't get me wrong, I know from the bottom of my heart that I made the right choice to return to the twenty-first century. But I expected to slide right back into my life. I expected the weeks with Nicholas to be like a summer fling. It would fade into the fabric of my day to day, becoming a fond memory. I expected to leap into a job with occasional nights at the bar, but none of those things have the allure they once did. The bombardment of noise and activity irritates me. I hung out in a vintage store the other day to help me remember those six weeks. Maybe I was drawn to vintage fashion for other reasons than just clothing."

Edmund broke in since there had been no pauses. "You mean like maybe you already knew Nicholas or knew something about the 1930s?"

"Is that crazy?"

"Not crazy at all. Many religions believe in reincarnation. There are accounts of people's uncanny knowledge of an era without having read about it or experienced it."

"But I likely learned about the 30s from history and Pinterest fashion pins."

"That is true, Emmeline, but it's not the historical facts I am referring to. You have read about many eras, yet you feel drawn to a very specific time. It isn't the intellect coming through, it's the emotion as if you were reminded of something you forgot. You may not have known Nicholas before, but you may very well have lived during the time."

"I've never thought much about any of that. Thinking I knew that era is kind of sweet. Not sure why, but I feel comforted by the idea." Emmeline paused. "Now I have a question for you. If the psychics are psychic, why don't they suspect something about your true story?"

"I sense some question my beginnings, my travels, but may not know how to put those pieces together. Just as I had never considered time travel, my colleagues don't look at that as an option. Anyway, these people are not deterred or surprised when someone hides or disguises a part of their past. Many have stories they hide and try to heal from privately."

"That might be why friends accepted the story of me being in a psych hospital. Mental health and addiction issues can be kept hidden for a long time before being discovered."

Emmeline drew out her words with a whine. "Oh, I know you can't talk long but I wish we could. I feel so seen. You recognize things about me I don't." She was crossing linear time in talking with him. The cosmos was meeting in Kairos time. It was beautiful.

"I will call again soon. I too enjoy being understood without explanation. In the meantime, another way to reach me is through the switchboard. Well, phone tree is the term now. Let me give you that number."

Chapter 34

The end...of a generation.

E mmeline spotted her copy of _Timeline_ on her bookshelf. Her body molded into her too-soft mattress, and her head nestled into the pillows. She read a few pages but found herself watching shadows on the wall, worrying about how much longer her mother would live.

Agnes got up most days and put on a smile, or at least a game face. She had been tiring easily, but Emmeline noticed tired began lasting all day, then days. The latest scan showed further metastasis to the brain, and she experienced rolling headaches. There was a period of drug trials with no impact. Medications increased, which helped the headaches and the pain in her abdomen but caused nausea. Agnes knew her body was deteriorating. Some doctors would look at her gaunt face but tell her to remain optimistic.

Emmeline was sitting with her on a visit when the oncologist looked her in the eye. "Agnes, none of the trials have worked for you. Our treatments kept the tumor from growing, but it did not stop the metastasis to other areas. Your body will continue to weaken, but you have some time. I just don't know what time to place on that."

Her mom swallowed hard. She took Emmeline's hand and squeezed. Agnes's eyes squarely met the doctor's, "I have always known my body. I appreciate one of you being straight forward. There's terror in your words but also some weird relief. I prefer knowing the truth, and I don't have to consider myself a defeatist by accepting what my body has already been telling me." Emmeline sat in awe of her mom's well of strength. She had learned repeatedly her mom was so much more than she credited her for. She had let go of guilt from those years, but she vowed her mom would feel the breadth of her admiration before she died.

●●●

Agnes called Emmeline into the dining room, where papers were strewn across the table. Her mom explained what each was. She shared all the passwords—all written on a sheet of paper. Hannah and Emmeline now had access to bank accounts and subscription plans. Her mom's lawyer was the rare breed willing to travel to the client's house. They reviewed the most current will.

One day when both Hannah and Emmeline were at the house, their mom offered a short lecture, "I know you girls haven't been the closest of sisters or the best of friends, but once I am gone, I want you to stay in touch the way you have been these past months. It has injected joy into this shitty time. I'm taking care of all finances to ensure there will be nothing to argue about. The house will be left to you both. It was paid off at your father's death. It is perfectly fine that you will eventually sell it."

"Mom, I never gave you credit for being financially savvy. I thought it was all Dad."

"Emme, you are not far off, but certainly in the past couple of years, I have had to learn the financial ropes."

They walked through the house taping names on the bottoms of items they'd each want. Emmeline wanted the original generation Rubik's Cube. After Hannah taped her name on the Cabbage Patch doll she exclaimed, "Emme, surprise! We haven't wanted the same thing! Finally, our difference in tastes has come in handy."

The chrome framed caned chair and bread box that had been in the house Emmeline's entire life, drew honest remarks. "Mom, I just don't see myself using these." Agnes knew not all her treasures would be theirs, but asked they hold on to some for a time.

● ● ●

Gradually, Agnes began forgetting the day and which meds were needed at which time. She remained in bed most of the day. Hospice was called in. The doctors said the last days are exhausting for the caregivers and Hospice workers help the dying as well as those remaining behind.

A hospital bed had been placed in the living room as stairs were difficult to manage. Emmeline appreciated sprawling in a red love seat and watching reruns of MASH and Seinfeld with her mom.

One day, she was sitting in the chair with her feet up on her mom's bed. Agnes turned her head to Emmeline and asked, "Have you given much thought to what happens when we die?"

"I gave it some thought when Dad died but even though I am not an atheist, I never lingered on what happens to someone. Or at least I hadn't until recently."

Emmeline was too pragmatic to give it a good deal of thought; there were too many other things to consider at her age. Agnes, on the other hand, had given it much reflection over the years and certainly more recently. "I don't think it's a one-shot and done. We get more chances to be better human beings."

Emmeline told her mom that Nicholas had died in the year 1925. Yet he traveled from 1898 and was somehow alive in 1938. "Nicholas died in one year, but somehow skipped over that death to land in a year he never lived. Was the soul retrieved from wherever it goes? Did he pass himself going out of the human realm when emerging from the train station?"

Agnes giving brief nods suggested, "Maybe time is circular, not linear. Episodes can overlap, intersect like a Venn diagram without serious impact, and then they rotate away. Hmm. I like that visual. Who knows, maybe we will see each other again."

Emmeline thought back to that conversation as days passed. It turned out to be their last serious conversation. Agnes became more somnolent. She became hard to wake even for her pain meds. During her wakeful minutes they would be sure to give her whatever she could swallow. Emmeline stayed close, leaving the house when only shooed away by caregivers. For those hours she wandered the vintage section of Rewind touching belted dresses and pretending she liked hats.

A nurturing trait blossomed Emmeline had never felt. She wasn't sure if she had dismissed the trait or if she had been meant to experience this labor of love to release the dormant trait. As she woke to the new tenderness, she pictured the Grinch's heart growing three sizes that day. While her mom floated in and out of consciousness, she knew this nurturing was working reciprocally.

Emmeline watched Agnes as she slept and softly adjusted a pillow or sheet the moment her mom shifted or offered the tiniest grimace. She learned movements that made her mom's face and body relax, then reported them to Hospice workers to implement. Emmeline enjoyed streaming her mom's favorite soft jazz. In the echoes of the still house, she heard her mom's words of their meeting again somewhere in time. It eased the grieving and gave her hope.

Chapter 35

The Clearing

Three months passed after Agnes's death before Hannah and Emmeline were ready to clean out their mom's house and put it on the market. Even if Emmeline planned to stay in this era, it wasn't where she wanted to remain. It took considerable energy to say goodbye to so many items she never cared about but knew they had meaning to her parents.

It was a reflective time. Emmeline said, "This is the passing of the baton. It's too much adulting."

"Yeah, it's bizarre. We are the oldest generation. The last unless one of us has kids."

The attic was at the end of the upstairs hallway. They entered the small door with arms swinging to bring down cobwebs. The attic was a place of both fascination and petrifying imagination. The long room had a slanted ceiling with one small window, which kept it dark at the opposite end, even when the dangling pull-string bulb was lit. It was the last room to clear. Deciding what to keep or throw out was tiring. They resisted mindless tossing but, wanted to be finished.

As they sat on a long row of boxes, Hannah rhetorically stated, "Doesn't it seem odd that we have lost both parents? They were young, we are young. It's not the norm."

Emmeline agreed. Losing both parents by twenty-three had left her feeling adrift. A couple of aunts and uncles remain, but they weren't close growing up since they and their kids were older.

They worked methodically from one end to the other, placing more into the toss pile than the donate pile, keeping a couple pieces of clothing worn by each parent.

"Oh, Emme look, the angel costume we both wore for Halloween," Hannah said in a reminiscent sugary voice.

Emmeline laughed. "Oh, and Hannah, here's your fourth-grade report card. I'm so shocked it has a note saying you talked too much in class."

"Well, I prefer that over the most studious award," Hannah jabbed back.

Judging by the number of ribbons and small trophies, it was apparent they were part of the 'everyone's a winner' generation.

Part way through, they found a box of old photo albums. They chuckled at the tintype photos—the kind where it was rude to act as if one was having any fun. They didn't recall ever seeing those before, and some had names underneath. As they flipped through the photo album, Emmeline stopped at one that said Agnes. She was, beyond a doubt, the woman living in Hannah's house when she and Nicholas were looking for the boarding house.

"Hannah, meet our great-great-grandmother. In 1938 she lives in your house. Plus, she had two children." Adding a snarky grin, Emmeline said, "By the way, the yard looks a whole lot better when she's tending it."

Hannah squinted her eyes, stuck her tongue out and then said, "Do you think anything changed by your looking at her? Did we ever meet any great aunts or uncles as their old selves? One of the kids would have been our great-grandmother or great-grandfather, right? At least I think so."

Emmeline shrugged. "I never went back to her house. I was curious about her, but I didn't want to mess with time travel rules." She switched to a serious tone. "Hannah, I know I haven't talked about it much but if I can, I am going back to 1938. I have no idea if what worked before will work again. I don't know if Nicholas will be there. I have to try."

"You've been researching in true Emme mode the history of food production. Does that have anything to do with it, or is it to get back in Nicholas's arms?"

Emmeline pulled in her lips to fight her smile. "It is Nicholas, pretty much all Nicholas."

"What if he has moved on?"

Emmeline stared at her finger where she hoped to see her garnet ring again. "I don't think Nicholas will have moved on yet. He said he loved me."

"But what if he has?"

"Believe me, I have run through every scenario over and over. In planning for the worst, the way I do, and it would be the worst if his feelings have changed; I know I have a friend in Helen and in another woman who was boarding there at the time. If he's gone, I tell myself I will get busy trying to influence the direction food production takes. There is no way to meaningfully impact it from here."

She turned her gaze to Hannah. "I bet we could figure out a way for you to travel with me. I wish you would."

Hannah squirmed on the box and shook her head. "I love that all of this has brought us closer to each other. I can't stand the thought of losing the friendship we waited a decade to develop. I am more suited for this century. You were always the directed one. I doubt Nicholas has forgotten you either. I just hate to see you go."

Hannah's eyes were focused on photos she wasn't really seeing. "At least we know we could communicate occasionally. It can be like when people left the east coast for the Oregon trail before trains. They said goodbye forever, only communicating with letters. If this world ever goes too much to shit, maybe I will consider it. Besides, unless one of us remains, what would we be doing to the timeline of our family? There must be some impact."

Hannah leaned her arms on her legs and groaned, "Okay, I'm embarrassed, basically feeling horrible now. I never let you know I got into the room with the desk. I knew what it might lead to if I told you. But it's not stopping you anyway."

Emmeline jerked her head up from a box with some old '80s clothes. She stared at Hannah and said, "I've been afraid to ask again. I held out no news was good news." She leaned her shoulder against Hannah's, as if to brace herself, "So.....?"

"I left his note behind in the cubby, but it said, "It'll be right here where you left it, as will I."

Emmeline closed her eyes as her heart thumped in her chest, pushing away annoyance with Hannah, letting in relief and joy. Nicholas had found the ring. He was waiting.

Chapter 36

Try, Try Again

As Emmeline stood rolling the Liberty Nickel around in her hand, she and Hannah hooked arms at the road, soaking in their parents' house one last time before putting it on the market. Her nickel had become a tangible memory of a time as much as her ticket back to Nicholas.

She reached Edmund at school through the phone tree. She had told him about her mom but wanted him to know about selling the house and seeing her great-great-grandmother in a photo. She told him Hannah had found a note from Nicholas. He was waiting for her.

"Did you seriously have any doubt? The scathing expression I saw that day at the cabin when I asked to travel with you sealed his feelings for you in my mind. I thought he might trounce me."

"Ha! That was a tense moment, wasn't it?" Emmeline giggled.

"Besides, it's only been a matter of months for him. When you return, do you have a plan for changing the trajectory of food production?

Seething, she told him of connections she'd found between pesticide use and cancers.

"You need to keep in mind somethings must swing the full arc of the pendulum to wake people up and cause a sustainable shift."

"You might be right. Maybe if opposition voices had been louder at the start, the arc could have been shallower. I'm fortunate to have leaped across fifty years and have hindsight." After a pause, she continued. "I have names of several women who had foresight in the 1930s and 40s. I'm going to connect with them somehow. More joined voices in the conversation early on may make the opposition more powerful."

The conversation shifted to reviewing the travel steps. Emmeline needed to have the coin on her person. She needed to walk to the place out of town where she and Edmund parted ways.

"This seems too simple. But it worked twice before."

Edmund asked, "Does your sister want to go? I would get my coin to you. You said there aren't any other close family members."

"She doesn't want to go. We have become so close, but she has a solid tribe here. They are her family too. Edmund, do you feel like you can be your authentic self here? You could return with me if you have any doubts."

"There is prejudice and sometimes the hate feels ever growing. But I have found what you call my 'tribe'. I no longer hide what my soul screams to share. I will cope better here with whatever lies ahead. I can't return to a life of oppression. You may be able to stem the tide on the food production pathway but the cultural disdain and fear of gay people in the 1930s may have had to take the arduous path it did."

"Then will you keep in touch with Hannah? She has a broad friend base, but I'd feel better if someone older...not that you're old but more mature, kept periodic tabs."

"Of course. She can call me anytime. I still prefer it to the internet. Remember, you two have a gift for getting messages through. Hopefully you can still do that. Tell her to call me if she hears from you."

"That'd be wonderful if we can. Edmund, you know I'll miss you too. We don't talk all the time, but you lift me when we do."

There was silence on the phone. "Is there something else, Emme?"

"I am doing this solo. It's scarier than when we came back together. I was hopeful and you were so excited for the adventure. If something goes wrong this time, I have no one."

●●●

Tears welled in both Hannah and Emmeline's eyes as they stood near the spot that should return Emmeline to what was now 1939. They held a loving hug. Emmeline stroked Hannah's hair. Both whispering words of love that still had a foreign but sweet ring.

Feeling the nickel pressing into her skin, Emmeline closed her eyes after reaching the spot which should end with her seeing old cars and stores with window displays. She opened her eyes and pivoted. Her heart sank when she saw a Prius drive by. It hadn't worked. Hannah saw her ashen face. Hannah met up with her.

"Maybe it was because I stayed, to watch you go."

Her head bowed, Emmeline responded, "There were people around each time, although they weren't observing us or anyone we knew. Maybe I should try it without you here."

Hannah squeezed her hand uttering, "Ok, I'll go." With another quick hug, "Safe travels Emme."

Emmeline returned to the beginning point. She grasped the nickel and pictured Nicholas pressing her to his chest, squeezing out even the air between them. Still nothing. Bewildered, she trudged following the tracks. 2023 remained all around. She had the nickel. That was all they needed before. Crestfallen, she cursed each modern car that passed and every jet overhead.

Emmeline walked up the sidewalk to the stoop. Her shoulders were slumped, eyes pointed down to her feet. She glimpsed Hannah watching from the living room window and she opened the door before Emmeline touched the doorknob.

Hannah greeted her with a fake smile. "Long time no see."

"I know you are trying to lighten the mood. But fuck, now what? Has the portal, or whatever it was, closed? Was there a time limit on travel? I am stuck in my own time."

Emmeline stared blankly as she took a slug from the beer Hannah placed in her hand. They'd sat silently for fifteen minutes when Hannah stood. "I hate to leave you like this, but I need to get to my shop. Are you ok alone?"

"I'll be fine. Drunk maybe, but fine." As Hannah headed to the door, Emmeline asked, "Hannah, who lives in the old boarding house now? How were you able to get in there and up to the room with the desk?"

"It's the daughter of the original owner. Well, technically, it's the owner's granddaughter who lives there caring for her mother who has dementia. What was her name?"

Emmeline responded with, "Helen Miles. Her daughter's name was Ruth. Is that who has dementia?"

Hannah nodded. "I can introduce you to her soon." Opening the door, "I really need to go." Stopping and turning toward Emmeline, "I am probably stating the obvious, but you can't start off by saying you knew her mother."

Emmeline scoffed. "I am desperate, but you know logic has always taken the front seat with me. But I do want to get my hands on that desk."

●●●

Edmund answered the phone on the second ring. Emmeline wondered if he could feel sadness through the airwaves as he spoke his hello.

Sitting at the dining table, Emmeline spoke flatly. "It didn't work. If you're a psychic, can't you figure out why?"

He chuckled at her brashness, "Well hello to you too, Emme, and Psychic 101 teaches you it doesn't work that way."

"Ugh. I'm sorry. My hopelessness is tainting my ability for tact."

"Presuming you had the same nickel, and you followed the same path, there must be something influencing the moment we are yet to discover."

"This feels like a perfect crystal ball time."

"Emme, remember you discovered the nickel connection yourself. Not me."

"I don't know what to do next. I could try every day or different times of day and hope whatever commonality those days shared is present again."

"If we remain open to possibilities, the answer may find its way to one of us. I know that doesn't sound logical to you, but this might be the time to step away from logic and learn to clear your mind. Sometimes being vulnerable is beneficial."

"Abandoning logic and being vulnerable are not my strengths."

"Bringing nothingness into your mind and making room for the unknown isn't stepping into a void, Emme."

"Okay, tell me more."

"We have a physical item, and we have a general place. There may be something else about the timing or another aspect. We have thought of it as a dyad, but maybe it's a triad or even more. I will meditate to see if I can recall any other element we may not have noticed."

Emmeline sighed. "Edmund, the little hope window is opening. I can't fathom clearing my mind for answers from the universe, but you know what they say about desperate times."

"I don't need to be psychic to know going back every day, doing the same thing over and over, will only plunge you farther into despair. Certainly, try another time or two but recognize when the value is not worth the disappointment."

Emmeline agreed with Edmund, then apologized again for her surly start. Edmund asked her to try clearing her mind before dismissing the idea. They hung up and she headed to the fridge for a beer. Soon after, Hannah walked in to find Emmeline sitting on the back porch, a beer resting on her leg, eyes closed.

Hannah looked around for empties. She saw one other. "Did you pass out from one too many?"

Emmeline's eyes fluttered open. "You sure can be a buzz kill. I am taking Edmund's advice and clearing my mind. He says it may allow the universe to reveal another element that triggered the travel."

"Whoa! You would have said listening to messages from the universe was too 'woo' a year ago."

"Many things have turned upside down. God, I don't think the same about anything! Could you introduce me to Helen's daughter and granddaughter sooner than later? I need to sit in the room and lay my hands on the desk. I could leave a note for Nicholas. Even though I know less time has passed for him, I still worry he might give up hope. I just want a connection."

"We can figure out a reasonable excuse to tour the house."

●●●

Emmeline groaned. For hours she flipped from stomach to back to side in bed. She knew it was hours because she checked the clock with every flip. Her brain was looping replays of her travel episodes, hunting for that unknown factor.

She moved downstairs to the overstuffed chair, gazing out the front bay window. Her breathing slowed with the quiet, and the stillness of the street relaxed her body. She noticed a slow movement on the sidewalk a couple of doors down. Alarm rose but as she stood to get a better angle from the window, she realized it was an elderly woman. As the woman moved under a streetlamp, she could see a broom in hand and an apron tied at her waist. The lady was sweeping the sidewalk!

"What the hell?" She connected this must be Helen's daughter, the woman with dementia. She gasped knowing she may be looking at little Ruth as an old lady. Quietly opening the front door, she stepped onto the porch with wonderment at seeing Ruth. Emmeline shivered with the chill of the night mountain air, but she was glad the woman wore a light sweater. The elderly lady's head jerked up from her sweeping when Emmeline quietly cleared her throat. Her eyes widened, followed by a smile.

"Hello dearie, you gave my old heart a start."

Emmeline casually walked towards the woman. Would she recognize her as Emmeline? "I am Emmeline." She pointed back to Hannah's house. I am staying with my sister for now. It's kind of cold to be out doing housework. Can I help you back home?"

"I do feel a chill. This is clean as a whistle, so I will move on to doing dishes."

At that moment, the door to Helen's boarding house opened and a woman shouted in a panicked whisper. "Mom! It's cold out here." Hurrying to her mother, she looked at Emmeline, who quickly explained again who she was and that she'd been awake in the middle of the night and noticed her out sweeping.

"My mom has sundowners and cleaning is what she likes to do. Unfortunately, it is often at most inopportune times. I must have forgotten to turn on the door alarm that triggers when opening. Thank you so much for helping. I too have many wakeful nights listening for the patter of her feet. You say your name is Emmeline?

I met Hannah some time back. My name is Susan." Based on the lines and gray hair, Emmeline judged her to be somewhere in her seventies.

The elderly woman said, "Emmeline, that's an unusual name. I knew an Emmeline as a child. Nice lady. She had your hair color." As Susan took her mother's hand, she smiled and said, "Do come for tea sometime soon."

Emmeline reached for the elderly woman's hand and searched her face for a resemblance. She said, "I didn't catch your name."

"My name is Ruth."

"So nice to meet you, Ruth." She turned to Susan. "I would love to come for tea."

Emmeline watched as Ruth was guided back to her house. She warmed at glimpsing both her worlds in this one person. She would be sure to tell Edmund his 'universe acting' stuff had merit after all.

Chapter 37

Time for Tea

Hannah arranged for them to visit on Wednesday. To keep Emme from dashing over at eight in the morning, she threatened to leash Emme to the chair. Hannah told Susan her own home had been updated more than once, but her sister admired vintage and was eager to see the inside.

They were welcomed in. A musty smell met them as if many treasures needed a dusting. As her eyes glided slowly about the dining area, a sense of home washed over Emmeline. She recognized the oak dining table. It was now round with all the leaves removed. They weren't needed without the guests.

She rubbed her fingers back and forth across a few square inches on the table before she sat down. "I love this table. It must be at least eighty years old. I have seen similar at antique markets in Denver."

Susan said, "It's the only table I remember, so that's at least sixty years. What do you remember, Mom?"

Ruth perked. "Oh yes, so many good stories were told at this table."

Emmeline said, "Yes, I remember." Seeing Susan and Hannah's expressions, Emmeline straightened her back and rubbed a hand on the table. "Dinner tables are the center of so many life stories."

She sipped her tea and turned her head to the china cabinet. "Is the glassware new? I don't remember, I mean, glasses from your childhood can't possibly be intact."

Hannah's eyes flared a look of 'You better be careful'. Emmeline pushed back in the chair and pried her eyes away trying to act casual by glancing about the room.

"Mom why don't you give our new friends a tour. It'll give me a moment to start some laundry."

The kitchen had been completely updated with stainless steel appliances and small glass tiles on the backsplash. Conversations with Helen about the kids or the weather filled Emmeline's head. Approaching the stairs, Ruth gripped the railing and slowly climbed each step with a slight lurch and pull. Emmeline paused on a step, swallowing her urge to blow past Ruth. She wanted to get inside their room. Her body heated all over when they approached the old guest rooms.

The doors were closed to keep heating costs down. Hers and Nicholas's room was in the middle of the three. Emmeline's belly fluttered when Ruth placed her hand on the doorknob. She grasped the door frame to keep her knees from buckling. Emmeline crossed her arms, hiding her shaking hands. She ran fingers across the dresser when her body settled. The dresser dust came off on her hand and she had a childish urge to write Nicholas's name in the dust.

Ruth was chattering away about pieces of furniture. Emmeline passed by her, going to the window. She breathed in memories.

With a slow turn, she spotted the writing desk. She walked over and stood behind the wooden rolling swivel chair.

She pointed to the desk, "It sounds silly, but I love envisioning what must have been written long ago. Do you mind if I sit?" She knew that wasn't it at all. There was a time when the past would have been the past. Her admiration of vintage clothing was as much about it being economical and making sense, as it was romantic.

Hannah came to the rescue. She suggested she and Ruth go back to their tea. "Emme becomes entranced with these old items, it could be a while." Ruth happily followed.

Emmeline sat in the chair. Memories coursed through her veins. Her neck tickled remembering Nicholas kissing her there as she read. He didn't sit at the desk often, but he swiveled when he did. After pulling down the writers table, she immediately reached to the cubby that should hold the ring. Her fingers rested on the knob. She closed her eyes as it slid out. A deep breath in gave enough courage to handle whatever she may find. Her eyes dropped to its contents.

Her hand flew to her mouth as she sucked in air. The note and the ring were there. How was this possible? Had no one looked through here after all this time? Lifting the ring, she placed it on her finger and then read the note she had written twelve months or eighty-four years ago. Turning it over her heart soared seeing Nicholas's handwriting, and reading his words that he would wait for her. Emmeline touched the note to her lips and set it down. She laid her head on the desk, resting on her crossed arms longing for the realness of him.

Her head swirled every time she considered the sequence of this time travel experience. It was sweet to see the ring but why was it there? Was the ring there because she never made it back, or because not enough time has passed? Eventually, lifting her head, she realized she couldn't stay there all day.

Emmeline pulled a piece of paper from her pocket, reviewing the words she had written before coming over. She wanted to write pages but held it to the essentials.

She re-read her words. Folding it, she squeezed it into the box, replaced the ring, and returned them to the cubby. Her finger lingered one more moment before a sound downstairs jolted her back to reality. It was time to leave.

Rising from the chair, she cast a last look around the room and walked to the door, closing it behind her. She leaned back against the door and whispered. "Someday soon Nicholas, someday soon." She walked to the stairway. Straightening her spine, shaking her head to beckon the return of her merely interested persona, she merrily sprung down the steps. Calling up her most frivolous voice, "Antiques are fascinating to me. That writing desk is spectacular!"

●●●

Back on Hannah's porch, Emmeline stopped, and her hands went to her hair, pushing it back in frustration. The merely interested persona fell away. Hannah pulled her in for a full embrace whispering in her ear, "I am so sorry, Emme. I know that was incredibly hard for you." Pulling back, her hands on

Emmeline's arms, Hannah cocked her head and gave a slight smile. "That return to the dining room from upstairs might have been an Oscar worthy performance though."

Chapter 38

Nicholas-Back and Forth

Nicholas shut the door to their room. It'd been six weeks since Emme left. Each week was dragging on longer than the one before. He had hoped this would get easier, not harder. He worried others could hear the truth as the story of Emme's mother grew stale. No one thought a daughter's duty was a stretch. What was wearing out was his lack of control over the outcome. Emmeline implied she was returning, but the holding pattern wore down his hope. His enjoyment of dinner conversations with Helen led to increased guilt. He wasn't attracted to Helen, but she was a kind and generous woman. It filled a void deeper than he'd ever felt. Nicholas knew it wasn't fair to a widow and was thankful a new guest had recently come to stay.

Nicholas sat at the writing desk with a vacant stare, one leg stretched out long underneath. His gaze slid to the cubby holding the ring. He'd resisted checking it for the past two weeks. It'd become too disheartening. Despite the dread, his hand pulled the knob on the box. A piece of paper wedged into the space sprung up. Thinner paper than he'd seen, he nearly ripped it hurrying to unfold it.

It read, "Dear Nicholas. I hope you haven't given up on me. Mom died. I tried to return, but something is missing. The place and nickel didn't work. Edmund and I are trying to figure out what else is impacting travel. It is my solitary focus."

A slow smile spread across his face and a moment of giddiness followed at seeing her handwriting. A scowl soon replaced the smile. He muttered under his breath. "Blast! One more thing keeping us apart and I have no idea what it is."

●●●

Nicholas established a routine of hunting every couple of weeks to bring wild game into the butcher shop. Customers looked forward to options beyond the pork and beef they commonly found. Even when he wasn't successful, the solitude made it his favorite day.

Nicholas sat hidden, scanning the trees and watching for bending of branches, indicating a creature may be on the move. Knowing animals may come for a drink, he had positioned himself on a hill overlooking a branch of the Roaring Fork River. All had been still when he jumped at hearing a violent rustling among the treetops. He cupped his hand over his eyes to shield the sun and saw a mass exodus of birds soaring into the sky. Nothing had moved to startle them. He noticed a sway among the branches, even though the air remained still. The sway likely caused the flight, but he wondered out loud, "What in tarnation caused the swaying when there was no wind?" His eyes scanned the river. There were ripples, but no wind to cause the movement. The ripples covered a larger area than a fish jumping for a mayfly would cause. This was not the day he would bring venison to customers. Rubbing his jaw, he put his gun strap over his shoulder and headed back to town.

A few days later, Nicholas was flipping through the Denver Post while eating lunch at the diner near work. His eyes fixed on a headline citing an earthquake in Chile that had killed 30,000 people.

Nicholas turned to the man sitting a table over. "Have you lived here long?"

"Born and raised here."

"I'm wondering— do you know the population of Glenwood Springs?"

"About 3,000, I think."

"I read about an earthquake in Chile killing 30,000 people! That'd be much of Denver. Gee, hard to imagine the power."

● ● ●

It was a slow time of day for the butcher shop. Pete and Nicholas's friendship had blossomed during these slow times. Pete's wife had left him some months back for what she described as a 'more exciting man'. Nicholas shared his own loneliness without feeling like a fraud.

"Hey Pete, I had an odd experience last time out hunting."

"How so?"

"I was watching for wildlife and saw a massive number of birds burst from the treetops. The branches were swaying but the air was still. Then I saw some ripples on the river too large to be from a jumping fish. I would have noticed if someone canoed by."

"Huh. You would have seen a bear or cougar dash across or climb a tree."

"Yeah, I'm sure it wasn't anything like that."

Pete raised his eyebrows. "I can't help you but Marjorie at the library is a smart lady. She probably reads books all day. Maybe she could help you narrow something down."

●●●

After work, Nicholas visited the library. "I am wondering about something that happened while I was out hunting the other day." He told Marjorie about the birds taking flight, the swaying of the branches and the ripples on the water.

"Go to the card file and look up earthquakes. It wouldn't be the first around here."

"How in the world does one track earthquakes?"

"They have been documented since the Chinese Dynasty in B.C. times."

"Hmmm. I didn't feel any movement of the ground. I heard of earthquakes in Colorado, but no one knew much in my time."

Nicholas was surprised he'd made such a slip-up after all these months. Marjorie tilted her head, and he covered by adding, "As a kid, I don't recall hearing about tracking or measuring earthquakes, you know, in school."

Nicholas quickly thanked her and walked to the card file. He read that some people believe animals can sense an earthquake and display unusual behavior before it occurs. Water movement is also a natural result of underground movement. He left convinced he had witnessed effects of an earthquake.

●●●

Nicholas's eyes bolted open in the middle of the night as this event kept seeping back into his mind. Something about it may be the third trigger. Maybe it was the key event causing his and Emmeline's time travel. When they arrived in 1938, they had each been too shocked and too overwhelmed to notice subtle details. When she left, his eyes had been on her only, nothing else. He only recalled his own quake in watching her disappear.

Throwing back the covers and putting his feet on the floor, he dashed to the desk, pulling the drawer from the cubby. He pulled out Emmeline's note, set it aside, and wrote another to her. "Check earthquakes in the area. It may be the key." He pushed back in the chair, and stared at the dark ceiling as he rested his head on the chair's back. Hope filtered in but was outweighed by frustration with not being able to do more from his end. For the first time, he felt a tinge of regret at staying behind. If Emme got the message, he knew there were vast ways to search for information in her era.

Chapter 39

Shaky Ground

E mmeline bit her lip considering her guilt. She liked both Ruth and Susan. Ruth was a link through time. She marveled at witnessing Ruth at both ends of her life. Emmeline's guilt stemmed from nurturing the friendship for ulterior purposes. She needed access to the writing desk.

Susan jumped at her offer to provide respite by spending time with Ruth. She insisted on a small stipend in exchange, even though Emmeline's guilt had tried to reject the idea. She didn't need the money considering her parents' will and the sale of the house in Denver. She wasn't set for life, but she hoped to be traveling soon.

"Ruth, I remember...I mean, Susan mentioned you had a brother. What happened to him?"

"Richard died in the Korean War. He was too young to be part of the Great War, so he enlisted at the first opportunity. Richard was too young to die. Mother had already buried our father and even though she remarried, burying a son was too much. She never fully recovered."

"I am so sorry. He was, must have been a delightful soul, knowing you, I mean." Emmeline was becoming too comfortable with Ruth. This room felt like home and she was slipping in too many knowing words. Ruth may have dementia, but one never knows what words get held and what fades in moments. She needed to be careful. Her heart ached envisioning Helen's devastation from burying a husband and a son.

"What about you, Ruth? You obviously married because there's Susan. Did you stay in Glenwood?"

"I did. I earned a nursing degree and eventually became one of the first nurse practitioners in Colorado."

●●●

Ruth never questioned Emmeline's interest in spending time upstairs at the desk. Ruth was glad to be with her and watched out the window of the sitting area. Emmeline wondered what happened to the angel book, but it was another one of those conundrums about what occurred first.

On a day when Ruth was dozing in the sun, Emmeline slowly, silently pulled the drawer from its cubby, watching Ruth from her peripheral vision. Her breath caught as her stomach flipped. Her note was gone and there was another. She glanced at Ruth, who was still napping, before carefully unfolding the paper to avoid any sound. "What the hell!" she mouthed. She re-read the short note. Earthquakes? The key?

Raising her head, she saw Ruth watching her. "Why are your eyes so wide? Did you get some bad news?"

Quickly reaching for her cell, she looked at it as if that was the source of the news. "Surprising news, not bad, I don't think. Just enough to make me postpone a trip I was hoping to soon take."

Emmeline slipped the note in her pocket. She needed to process these words. She usually hung around and chatted with Susan on her return. Today was not a day for small talk.

●●●

Walking the two houses down and flinging open the door, Emmeline hit Edmund's work under contacts. At this moment, the phone tree directions were particularly irritating.

"Oh good. I got you."

"Of course. You are about the only person calling this number. You're excited."

"Something like that; not sure that's what it is. I got a note from Nicho...."

"Well, that's stupendous news, isn't it? How is he?"

"Not sure we can communicate with newsy notes. This isn't the Lake House. Another movie for you to watch. It only said, 'earthquakes may be the third element for our travel'.

"That's interesting. I am getting quite familiar with them out here in California. Wonder why he thinks that?"

"It didn't say, but if I can infer from the wording, something must have happened. I don't know a damn thing about earthquakes, and I don't know anyone who would know much more about them than I do. Why can't this be simple? It sure as hell was simple the first time."

"The only choice is to research the frequency of earthquakes in Colorado or find someone who knows. I can ask some questions around here. Being new to the area, I can justify the curiosity."

"Thank you, Edmund. Ed, I should get used to calling you Ed. Thank you for being my crisis mode go-to person. You're wonderful. So, anything new on your end?"

"Uhm, yes. I am seeing a guy. He's wonderful, oooh, and very fit for our age. He's got me exercising, which wasn't much of a thing back in the day."

"That makes my heart sing! I hope your good fortune leads to mine."

Edmund asked, "When not trying to time travel, how are you spending your time?"

"I have been hanging out with two women who live in the old boarding house. Oddly or not, the elderly woman is Helen's daughter. I am lucky the passage of years or her dementia have led her to not recognize me. Sometimes I catch her studying me, but she doesn't say anything or ask questions."

"When you do travel back, if you can, let me know how this plays out. You saw your great-great grandmother, but she didn't know you. Now you have spent time with someone you knew eighty years ago. Wouldn't it be nice to know someone else that has time traveled who might tell us about the impact we caused or are causing?"

●●●

Emmeline still scoured the internet. Now, with no absolutes about cancer, she dug deeper into when and how the shift started toward mass food production. She maintained copious notes on her phone with dates and names of influence. Emmeline knew she'd be wise to leave her phone behind, but it would go with her. The battery would last a long time if turned off in between writings.

Staring at her laptop, she saw her reflection in the screen. Emmeline heard herself exhale as she muttered, "It really was a perfect storm."

New farm machinery was easing the time spent in fields. Fewer people in a family were needed to tend more acreage. The young moved to cities. They grew accustomed to the conveniences. Then it all made way for bigger farms and livestock companies, eventually increasing crop yields, and decreasing the pressure on farmers to work more land, all while lowering consumer food prices.

Even the packaging that started as glass and tin before morphing into plastic were wonderful advancements. Packaging had a trajectory all its own. Plastic was invented in the late 1800s to replace ivory and turtle shells being used for pool hall cue balls. But then plastics slid the slippery slope of single-use plastics in the late 1940s. Even that path had a great beginning, ready to serve rations to soldiers.

She grimaced at her reflection, "Oh, enter the solo cup revolution. How many games of beer pong have those served up?"

She was in a house of mirrors. Everywhere, she found another spin on product design or use and that entwined with companies seeking a profit. They sniffed out their target audience for marketing. But the risks to the health and environment weren't known. Even DDT was originally a low-risk venture. In 2023, most freezers held at least a few prepackaged, processed meals. Emmeline grappled with her own contradictions. She loved her easy meals and delivery at her fingertips. Her thinking was evolving and recognizing what those represented about the current day world. The calculated marketing annoyed her.

A perfect storm had truly been served up on a platter. Emmeline was grasping what, in her opinion, had become a shit show.

●●●

Emmeline remained hopeful she could get back to 1938. She kept Nicholas in the forefront of her mind. She knew her longing to be with him went far beyond knowing he would support her efforts. To other men, she would be an upset woman who needed to mind her own business, stick to housework, and raise babies whiling away the decade waiting for the pesticide revolution. If not for Nicholas, she'd question if it was all worth it. She couldn't change anything about her mother. As she looped through scenarios, doubts bubbled if events could be changed once they happened on some timeline. Had this been destiny for the world, particularly America, to get to this point?

Doubt haunted her nighttime. 1938 was a time when women were barely seen and rarely viewed as influencers beyond the home. Questions percolated. How would she explain what she knew? How would she meet the players she needed to meet? Pesticides were still heralded as a positive. She'd be lonely in her disdain.

She'd wake with her mind playing out scenarios she didn't entertain in the daylight. Could she and Nicholas pick up where they left off? What if she got back there and the chemistry was gone? What then? She'd be left living in an era where women have few choices and with a man she barely knew. Her body warmed as she questioned. She had no doubt he'd still be good looking. He'd still be hot, very hot.

Suddenly, a conversation with her mom lying beside her on the bed played like a movie. Tears prickled her eyes. Her mind still saw her frail head-scarfed body, but it was beautiful to feel her presence and be comforted by her words.

"Emme, Nicholas is something some would call your destiny."

Old Emme would pretend she was going back to change a trajectory. Her brain was speaking less and less. Nicholas's waiting spoke to her heart. Her mom had said love wasn't found in the brain.

Chapter 40

Science Intervenes

E mmeline answered her phone as soon as she heard it. Edmund joked, "I feel so important to warrant the first ring."

"Hiieee, I am ever hopeful it's you. Not like I get many calls from people anymore. Your voice calms me."

"Do you need calming?"

"I was doing some major catastrophizing last night. I always found it too annoying to have it part of my psyche. But there I was, three in the morning ruminating on the logic of this decision to return to 1938 and Nicholas."

"Emmeline, I don't know about your mission to change the world's trajectory, but I am quite sure what you and Nicholas were feeling, even for those weeks, was genuine." Following a brief silence, he continued. "I have news that might get you back on track."

"You do!? Tell me!"

"I asked a friend, who turns out has a friend working at a place called the U.S Geo Hazards Science Center."

"That's a mouthful," Emmeline responded.

"Yes, but the nice part is it is near you. You probably know Golden, Colorado."

"I love Golden. What'd they say about quakes?"

"There is some kind of earthquake called Slow-Slip. Generally, they aren't felt by humans, yet the seismic activity can be measured. They aren't sure what causes them, and they can't predict them."

Doubts swept away like a tidal wave. Hope burst in her chest. The doubts weren't real. It was the fear of the task and the unknown. She knew it was her psyche's attempt to let her down gently if going back never came to fruition.

"Have I told you before, Edmund, you have saved me more than once now?"

"When it came to saving, you saved both my psyche and my life; my coming to 2023 with you breathed real life into me."

"What's the place called again?" Pacing the room, she looked to the heavens she usually ignored. "A piece of hope, finally."

Edmund told her the name. "I've got to go. I knew you would need this."

Emmeline googled the Hazard Center. She picked a female geologist from the massive list. She had to fabricate yet another story for why she was seeking information. Obviously, it couldn't be so she could time travel. She pictured the internet door slamming in her face after they flagged her as crazy.

She ended up writing Tatiana Meylp. Emmeline portrayed herself as a freelance author but had hit a dead-end while writing an article about predicting earthquakes using sensors in the ground transmitting to GPS satellites. Emmeline asked for an interview on the subject.

To her delight, she heard from Tatiana in a matter of days. She was happy to share the facts she knew but warned predictability was way down the road. All Emmeline wanted was some tidbit to run with.

●●●

The appointment with Tatiana was for the next week. In the meantime, she kept researching food production and hanging out with Ruth who was studying her with ever more curiosity. Once, when Emmeline looked up and saw Ruth's head cocked to the left and eyes squinting in puzzlement, she decided to ask.

"Ruth, it seems you spend more time gazing at me as if you are wondering something."

Emitting a cracked voice giggle, Ruth responded, "Oh my lands. I am sorry to be caught, but yes, I have been trying for some time to figure out who you remind me of. This old brain won't give me the answers. So, I stare to see if it will surface."

Emmeline felt a bit too seen. "When it comes to you, I hope it's a person you enjoyed. I hate to see our friendship discolored by the face of a memory."

"I am quite comfortable with you, so I am sure it is someone I liked."

●●●

Shaking Tatiana's hand, Emmeline sat down in the sparsely decorated office. As she scanned the room, she saw a mound of rocks. Beautiful greens, oranges, and long tubular rocks that Tatiana told her, were core samples. Sitting with her tablet and pen, Emmeline had twenty minutes to get some answers for two basic questions.

"I'm curious about earthquake activity in Colorado. However, because my family has a house in Glenwood Springs, more specifically about that area. I believe it'd add a personal twist to my article."

Emmeline checked Tatiana's email she brought along. "You said science can't predict earthquakes yet. Is there progress being made? My other question is what can you tell me about slow-slip events?"

Emmeline learned there was very little earthquake activity in the Glenwood Springs area compared to active places, such as Los Angeles.

Tatiana continued, "There is a young volcano nearby, so one can never be sure when a volcano may decide to become active. Slow-slips are not sensed by humans since the energy released from them is spread across enough time that it's too small to be sensed. Sensing a mild quake can depend on the type of ground a person is standing on. What you feel may vary if you are in a building, on soft ground, or a rock outcropping. If it's shallow ground, it's more likely to be felt than if it occurs deep in the earth."

Looking at her computer for a moment, then glancing up, Tatiana verified, "There's no current data showing slow-slips in the Glenwood area."

Emmeline's stomach tightened, feeling her optimism slipping away.

"Let's go back to the predictability aspect. What progress is being made with that?"

"There's no consistent and reliable way to predict earthquakes. We can only estimate the probability of them occurring in a certain area across spans of time, maybe a thousand years."

"I'm feeling a bit deflated for what I was hoping to achieve with an article. People enjoy a bit of science fiction. I know I sound stuck on it, but is there any research going on that hopes to improve the capacity for predicting?"

"There is one person, a woman who's considered an outlier in our field. I would caution you against stating anything as fact. She's considered a bit of a 'mad scientist' in our arena. However, she managed to secure private funding from think tanks to move her work ahead. Do you want her name?"

"Oh please!" Tatiana wrote the phone and email on one of her business cards and handed it to Emmeline.

Emmeline couldn't help but feel the time-travel carrot was moving further out in front of her. She glanced at the information on the business card. "Thank you so much for your time. I understand the facts as they are now. If she's willing to talk with me, Ms. Crawford may provide my readers something to pique their imaginations. I truly appreciate your time."

Tatiana said, "I must ask, there are so many geologists on our website. How did you choose my name?"

"It was related to something I heard on the news recently; not many woman scientists are utilized as experts in their field. That needs to change."

"True. More women are going into science, but in some ways, it's still a 'man's world'. Thanks for being aware. Too many don't think about it." Emmeline nodded and thanked her again for making the time.

●●●

Sitting in her car, Emmeline considered emailing once she got back to Glenwood Springs. But never one for procrastination, she picked up her phone and punched in the numbers Tatiana had written down. As it rang, she realized she had no idea where Dr. Crawford lived. She could be calling in the middle of the night.

She was mentally preparing a voicemail when a rough female voice answered with, "Make it quick. I am a busy person, ya know!" With a sudden sip of air, Emmeline scrambled to hang up when the voice went on, "Ha! I have always wanted to say that. What can I do ya for?"

It took a moment to compose herself, but Emmeline finally said, "Hi, my name is Emmeline. I got your name from a geologist in Golden, Colorado, who indicated you are involved with innovative research for predicting earthquakes."

The woman spoke slowly. "Call me skeptical but did she really say that?"

"Well, not in those exact words, but that's how I interpreted them."

"I suspect she really said something about my being a Mad Hatter. No matter, Emmeline, what can I help you with?"

"I am a freelance writer researching the latest technology for predicting earthquakes."

"I currently research that, but don't have any comments for an article at this point."

Emmeline quickly calculated the next move. Should she be desperate, an author looking for a break? She opted for both.

"Dr. Crawford, I am competing with men for having my article selected. I am pulling the woman-to-woman card and asking for any crumbs you can throw my way. I know it may not yet be fact, but it would excite my readers' minds to present a new possibility." Emmeline made herself stop talking and wait out the silence. It was never-ending.

Eventually she heard, "Please, call me Abby. I am a better judge of a person's truth when I am face-to-face with them. Let's set up a Zoom meeting."

Knowing she was lying, Emmeline swallowed hard. Even though Abby may judge better face-to-face, Emmeline hoped she still wasn't that great. They exchanged emails and Abby said she'd check her schedule and send a link for some time next week. Emmeline said she looked forward to it. She moved her carrot to the next week on the calendar.

●●●

Finally settling for the bay window backdrop, Emmeline propped her laptop on one of the large windowsills. Sitting in the overstuffed chair, she shifted from one hip to the other, nervously waiting for Dr. Crawford to open the meeting. She'd worn a white shirt with a thin cardigan sweater, trying to pass for however a freelance author might look like.

Dr. Crawford appeared on screen. She seemed to be a woman in her sixties with salt and pepper hair that was cut short in that spiky early 2000s hairstyle, except hers was randomly spiked, with most occurring on one side of her head. It was obviously a few days old, and she, apparently a side sleeper.

"Good morning, Emmeline. What article is it you are working on and for whom?"

Expecting a few moments of social chit-chat to gain her stride, Emmeline threw her playbook out the window. She was glad she had googled some fringe online journals.

"I am hoping to have my article selected from a call for papers on earthquakes. I live in Colorado where earthquakes are infrequent. Where are you located?"

"I am in San Bernadino, California, positioned along the San Andreas Fault. Who are you submitting to again?"

"Oh, it's a small online journal, Emerging Technology. They put out an E-paper that is typically focused on environmental issues but like to tip toe into the unknown."

Dr. Crawford retorted, "Sounds like a bit of Science Today with a sprinkle of tabloid?"

"It's not into space alien territory, but yes, a dab of science fiction."

"Why are you interested in the prediction of quakes?" Abby asked.

"I could say it's purely from benevolence for the people, but it's frankly more to do with adding a dimension other writers may not be considering."

Abby jumped into her research explaining she was edging closer to accurately predicting earthquakes ten to fifteen minutes ahead.

"Is fifteen minutes really very helpful?"

"It's only a start, but yes, it could help a good many prepare."

Emmeline inquired if that fifteen-minute notice included slow-slip type of quakes. Abby turned her computer to room view as she walked over to a machine that she explained receives seismic activity information from a satellite that picks up movement five thousand feet below ground where sensors had been placed.

"At this point, I get information only seconds ahead of the activity. Technically, I am predicting, but it won't yet have a safety benefit.

Emmeline was chewing the inside of her lip while clicking her pen. Abby asked curtly. "I am sensing a shift in your demeanor. Is this not what you were expecting?"

Emmeline jolted her head a bit, recognizing her mind was questioning how this was going to help. She sat straighter, struggling to regain her composure. "I was hoping this was farther along and wider spread, such as to Colorado."

Abby watched her for a moment, sizing up what might really be at work. "Other than my benefactors, there's little belief this research will go anywhere. Most scientists working at seismic activity centers consider me loony. Emmeline, it's time for truth. You seem too naïve to be a spy for trade secrets. Yet why would predicting earthquakes in a place that has only occasional events interest you?"

Emmeline's lids lowered and she looked away from the screen, weighing her next words. Any façade of the ambitious journalist melted away. "Maybe because we don't know each other. Maybe because you used the word loony and what has happened to me aptly could be described as loony." She stopped again, averting her eyes.

"Go on," Abby said. "I am a believer of much, surprised by very little."

Emmeline's shoulders raised as she used every muscle for an inhale to prepare for her words. "Don't say I didn't warn you. In Glenwood Springs, Colorado, a bit over a year ago, I stepped off a train and walked into the year 1938."

Following a scoffing chuckle and scanning Emmeline's face, Abby said, "Okaaaay. I am in the business of predicting, but that is one I did not expect."

"I am glad I could offer a surprise in your day, but I am feeling like I go down one rabbit hole only to emerge from another and right into some other."

Abby took over. "I have been watched, mocked, and chastised by the science community for forging a path beyond what the community accepts as procedure. I cannot take such a fantastic story at face value and risk your being someone other than you say."

"I realize you don't know me. Seeking fringe help or feeling the urge to reach the level of pleading my case to a stranger is far from my realm of typical controlled behavior."

"Just to confirm, you want me to believe you have time traveled?"

"Yes. I couldn't make this up. If I were spying on your work, I would make it more plausible."

"Playing devil's advocate—you are here, in 2023...so you got back...without my help."

"True. We thought we knew the conditions which triggered it. I recently tried twice to return to 1938, but..."

"We. It's not just you? You have a merry band of travelers?"

Averting her eyes from the screen, Emmeline was once again weighing how much information she would share. She could share about Nicholas but exposing Edmund could put him at risk. "A man traveled forward from 1898 to 1938 at the same time I went back."

Abby gave a loud cackle. "This gets wilder and wilder. The community thinks I am loony!"

Knowing how absurd it sounded, and with fear of near defeat, Emmeline pressed her lips together then quietly spoke. "Wild, but true."

"Just for grins, keep going."

Emmeline's irritation grew, borne from dying hope and not enjoying seeming crazy, "I am not here to entertain you. I know I sound delusional, but it could also be dangerous to tell someone unknown to me about this. Can you be of any help?"

"So why seek me out? Something about my work must relate to something you need."

"The man who traveled from 1898 is still in the year 1938. He experienced something he believed was earthquake activity. It's grasping at straws, but that is the rabbit hole I am currently traveling down."

Abby's lips smirked sideways as she toggled her head. "Okay, so you two communicate...across time."

After saying each piece out loud Emmeline knew how preposterous this sounded. She hadn't explained it to anyone in over a year.

She thrust her torso back into the chair. "I know, I know. It even sounds ludicrous to me when I say it out loud."

This was going nowhere, and she was embarrassed. Emmeline clicked Leave Meeting and slammed the screen on her laptop. She spat out, "Fuuuck!" as she grabbed a pillow and hurled it across the room.

She sat pouting as she felt stabbing emotions she rarely allowed, desperation and rage. She despised having absolutely no control. Having to rely on others to intervene. As she finished the conversation going on in her head, she whispered, "Shit." She needed a deux ex machina.

● ● ●

Emmeline hashed the conversation and emotions through with Hannah and a bottle of wine. Or was it with a bottle of wine and Hannah? Either way, they sat thigh to thigh with their backs against the headboard in Hannah's room.

"Ya know Emme, it's sweet to see you let go of being the lone wolf. I know you thought Dad was one, but Mom had certainly melted some of that energy along the way. He likely knew it brought you comfort when he played that part. We all have different faces we show for certain people. It's not who he was with Mom. Emme, it makes others feel good to help. It can be liberating to let another take the lead with ideas, to toss your hands up in exasperation and just scream HELP!"

Curling her legs up on the bed and hugging her knees to her chest, Emmeline said, "I am being forced to rely on others. Not loving it, but it's not as horrible as I would have expected."

Emmeline made air quotes with her fingers. "I wonder if this is that shadow work you read and hear about these days." Smirking, she added, "Maybe that's what draws me back decades to an era when people didn't spend all their time talking about upbringing issues but instead swept things under the rug."

"Dear sister, at some point, you will be more peaceful, freer for having done it," Hannah assured her.

"What could be the next steps? I can't just wait for someone to rescue me and take me back to 1938."

"How sure do you feel it was seismic related? What about all the geothermal activity going on all the time? You should investigate with a more open mind. I know this is likely too woo for you but be open to messages and possibilities."

"If I can time travel, apparently much is possible that I have been dismissing as bullshit."

●●●

Later, laying on her bed in Hannah's spare bedroom, she got ahold of Edmund. Emmeline reiterated the conversation with Hannah and the ones with the two geologists. "I can't believe I hung up on Dr. Crawford. It was embarrassment and frustration taking over."

"Oooh, that's a difficult one to come back from. You know, you may have been persuading her."

"I know. It was stupid of me. In hindsight, it was my vulnerability that really did the reacting there."

"Hannah could be onto something, too. The Geothermal may be a route worth pursuing."

"No stone unturned. Feel free to ask anyone you know about geothermal activity, and I will go back to my internet searches." She paused. "Actually, I need to keep finding real people versus hiding on the internet."

"Ah, listen to you. Nicholas punctured that shield of independence and now it's fracturing from all sides. That's a good thing Emmeline."

"I feel naked, though. My barriers served a purpose."

"Needing others covers you in support. You view it as vulnerability but it's really letting in others' strength."

Chapter 41

Rejoice

Emmeline opened her email. Her inbox was sparse now and she liked it that way. It was the upside of her new indifference to the mindless offers and unsubscribing as soon as something showed up in her inbox. Her head jerked closer to the computer when she saw a Zoom invite from Dr. Crawford, from Abby. Weeks of dead ends had passed since that hang-up. She'd written off that thread. The meeting request was for the next day. Her heart pounded. Maybe something in their discussion worm holed its way into Dr. Crawford's brain. She prepared as if she was getting ready for a big interview.

She sat fidgeting, anxiously tapping both feet under the table. She signed on five minutes early and was willing the words 'Your meeting will start in...' to shift over to 'the host will let you in'. Dr. Crawford appeared on the screen.

Jumping in, Emmeline gushed apologetically. "Dr. Crawford. I am so sorry I hung up on our call a few weeks ago. You surely had every reason to be wary of my story. I can't imagine what made you want to hear me out or give me a second chance."

Dr. Crawford was sliding the screen to her left, as she said, "Remember, call me Abby."

Emmeline vaulted out of her chair, squealing, "EDMUND!"

His head tilted back to release a full belly laugh. "It is the bees' knees to see your face too!"

"What is going on? What are you doing at Dr. Craw...Abby's, or is she with you?"

"I am indeed at her laboratory."

As she was blurting why and how questions, Abby shifted the screen to include part of herself. Emmeline's lips trembled as tears formed and slipped from the corner of her eyes. She wiped them with a giggle. "Edmund, I mean Ed, seeing your face is incredible. I'm so happy! I didn't consider you might put your face on a screen or embrace this technology."

"Once Abby could show me how secure she keeps her connections, I agreed. I might've agreed either way at the chance to see your face."

"I still don't understand what's going on. Why are you there?"

Edmund glanced at Abby and back to the screen. "I thought if another person had the same story as you and if I could offer some proof of authenticity for my era, it might turn your rude behavior around." Edmund gave her a wink. "Plus, I explained how out of character the outburst was."

"But Edmund, you took a great risk exposing yourself to someone else." Placing her hand over her heart, "You did that for me?"

"For you, for love, and the future of the world, remember? It gets heavy living a lie. Starts to fester in you and it was soothing to release it to someone. I have started telling people I am reincarnated from the '30s. They just think it's quirky and either embrace it or move on. But with that shift in thinking I feel free to be more, me. I lived too many years hiding who I really was. Had to give some credibility to some of my old-fashioned ways."

Regaining her composure, Emmeline joked, "Look at you! You are looking all twenty-first century-ish. What's up with the size of that shirt collar?"

Edmund tugged on his shirt and chortled. "Best dressed man. I live in Cali, you know."

She acknowledged Edmund with a smile and nod then returned to a more serious face, looking to Abby, "Even if you believe me, you can't help me if you can only predict seismic activity into the seconds—short of my camping out in the spot we think is the trigger. That would carry its own weirdness."

Lips moving into a wry smile, Abby said, "I was hardly going to share my guarded secrets, my proprietary information with a freelance writer on the other end of a Zoom call. There is much more happening in these walls and with shadowed satellites than the science community knows. They all know I have achieved the few second advanced notice but judge it to hold little value."

Emmeline perked up. "What can you do?"

"My former colleague was right in telling you there isn't much activity occurring in the Glenwood Springs area. There was a documented quake in a town about 20 miles away several years ago."

Emmeline agreed, "I did find that in my searches. Beyond that, not much since the 1800s in Colorado."

"Just for clarification, there was another small quake beyond Glenwood Springs that same year, as well as one south in a town called Alamosa. So not a complete anomaly. If there are slow-slips, they have been undetected."

Emmeline leaned into the screen and raised anticipatory eyebrows, "Yet I am hopeful you have something more for me."

"Even though I do believe your story, it's not wise for me to share my science with you or anyone else at this point. There are regular attempted hacks into my systems. Groundbreaking research can be a cutthroat arena. I guard it closely. I am sure you are a bright woman, but you would likely need to google all the scientific terms anyway.

Abby continued. "When I give the signal, you should go to the coordinates immediately. I can't predict how long the window will be open but likely only fifteen minutes or so. You should have your coin in your possession."

"Of course, I have guarded the coin closely, but I live in fear of losing it daily. Why is it so instrumental?"

"Edmund showed me two nickels. One contains older carbon-dated copper and has more nickel content than most. It may have been an anomaly in the minting process. The earth's core is comprised of nickel. Our earth's magnetic field exists due to the earth's core metallic content. I am not sure of the interaction, but somehow it must serve as a trigger."

Emmeline asked, "Do you have any time frame of when this might happen? It's not like I can lounge around the house dressed in my 1938 finest with my suitcase readied by the door."

Edmund chuckled, "A good excuse to go find some more vintage items."

"I guess I should just be grateful for your help and for the sliver of hope. If I miss one window, when might there be another?"

"I can't tell you that. It's not that I won't, it's that I don't know. I can't predict the prediction time frame."

"Ugh. I can only hope you aren't in the bathroom or sleeping when the signal comes in. Fingers crossed the quake knows to happen during the workday."

"Good news for you, every day is a workday in this lab. It is true, I do sleep, and I even eat, but am rarely out of range of notification. This is as good as it gets, Emmeline."

Not wanting to sound ungrateful, Emmeline lifted and shook her head. "Oh, please don't interpret my whining as anything more than fatigue and desperate worry that I will miss my chance. I am extremely grateful for your willingness to help me."

Emmeline knew their talk was nearly over and she gazed upon Edmund with a soft smile. "Edmund, I hate to lose this close connection by hanging up. I know this isn't your usual mode for conversation."

"Since you are now glued to Glenwood Springs, maybe I will need to make my way out to see you off."

"You won't fly." She smirked. "You know trains can be dangerous for arriving where you think you are going."

"It would constitute a nightmare to wake up in 1938 again."

Abby shifted the screen showing only her face. She said, "I need to wrap up here. I will be in touch when I think the window is open. I caution you not to get your hopes too high."

"Bye, Ed. I'm sorry, I like the sound of Edmund better. Abby, I can't thank you enough." Abby gave a slight nod. Emmeline gave a wave. Edmund blew her a kiss. She quietly watched the screen until the message, 'Host has ended the meeting', left her sitting alone.

Her gaze drifted around the room but not seeing a thing. Emmeline pondered her next steps. She would pack the bag immediately and leave it by the front door. She'd buy a few added vintage pieces and trade them out each day. At the shop, a sweet burnt orange tapestry purse caught her eye. She loved the angel embroidered on one side. Emmeline knew it'd be perfect for the 1930s. She had to buy it. She'd write a goodbye letter to leave for Hannah. It dawned on Emmeline she could no longer provide respite for Ruth. It had become routine and a relief to Susan. Something they all looked forward to, but she wasn't leaving Ruth. Soon, she would be with the much younger Ruth.

Chapter 42

The Wait is Over?

Emmeline had always been too connected to her phone before her time travel. She used to consider it a necessity. Living in a different century had broken the habit, but now, it was an obsession. She didn't even silence it at night.

Each day Emmeline saw Hannah's look of sympathy mixed with a degree of relief. "I want you to return to Nicholas. But I do struggle supporting it. I treasure that when I see the social media posts, 'My sister is my best friend', I whisper yeah, mine too." She said she'd always read those, void of any emotion other than curiosity and jealousy.

Emmeline told Susan she'd picked up work as a freelance writer but was on call to travel for spontaneous interviews. She hoped she could continue spending time with Ruth while Susan was home. It would still allow her time to be out gardening or be on a different level. Even though disappointed, Susan welcomed Emmeline's offer. She could apply concentration on needed house projects. Weeks passed with this new routine.

Emmeline had put the coin in a large locket necklace around her neck. Her phone was always with her, and she had hidden some 1930s bills within the phone's case. With this plan, the worst that could happen was she'd travel without her bag. It allowed her to establish a larger radius she could maintain while still being within a hurried fifteen minute window. At least she could grocery shop.

●●●

Hannah and Emmeline walked to grab a beer and a bite from Casey's Brewing.

Emmeline said, "Hannah, you never seem annoyed, even though I always have that one foot out the door."

"Looks can be deceiving." Hannah looked at Emmeline. "I know this move is following your heart. It's hard to resent that. But it will be like no other goodbye we have had. I think it may feel like Mom dying. A friend who is no longer in the same realm."

"Hannah, I have an idea! What if we set some rituals, we can each do in our eras. You know I love popcorn for dinner. We can start making it in a pan on the stove even now."

Hannah said, "Ooh, we could both plow through some pre-1938 novels." Googling some she said, "Let's start with...oh my God it won't have to be arduous! Listen to these! *Gone With the Wind, A Brave New World*...that's appropriate. Oh, here's a new-to-me one, The *Metamorphosis*. A man wakes to discover he's become a giant insect! That sounds like something they'd make a movie of today."

Excitedly, Emmeline said, "Time travel, google time travel movies!" Hannah did and said, "If we are aiming at pre-1940, we'll have to settle for *A Connecticut Yankee in King Arthur's Court.*"

"That's okay. I'll write one about a sister that time travels and falls in love. I'll dedicate it to my sister Hannah."

"Emme. These do make it a little easier to let you go. We will be threaded across time."

●●●

Ruth and Emmeline were drinking tea in the dining room. Emmeline's phone played the alert text assigned only to Dr. Crawford, I Run for Life, by Melissa Etheridge.

It read only, "I believe this is it. I will send the GPS coordinates."

Emmeline screeched and didn't take the time to explain the outburst.

"I gotta go, Ruth!" She dashed to the front yard where Susan was and with the same few words, "Susan, I'm so sorry, but I've got to go." She turned around, seeing Ruth had followed her. Her eyes were sad and her lips tight with a slight quiver.

Emmeline embraced Ruth. "I'm not sure when I can get back, but I do believe I will see you soon."

Emmeline bolted from the yard, ran two doors down, swung open the front door, and reached inside to grab her case. Ripping open the latches, she removed the letter for Hannah. She brought it to her lips for a gentle kiss before dropping it to the floor where her bag had been these past weeks. She calculated only five minutes would have passed. That left ten. Emmeline passed Ruth's house again as she hurried down the sidewalk with her case and tapestry purse. She didn't register Ruth and Susan still in the front yard. Ruth's eyes flew open as she straightened her spine.

"Why are you looking so shocked, Mom?"

"I have seen that purse before, but it was as a little girl."

"You know Emme likes vintage gear."

"I can't believe she found one with an angel on it. It was one of my first embroidery pieces."

Susan smiled that smile one gives when it's not worth correcting something a person with dementia believes.

Chapter 43

It's Happening

Arriving at the coordinates, Emmeline knew the exact place for the first time. It might not be the same place as the last slow-slip quake, but it was close. Was the range ten feet? Sixty feet? She arrived down the block and the tracks were in view. There may be no other chances. She stood on the target and leaned against a tree. Should her eyes be open? Closed? Did it matter?

Her hand flew to shield her eyes. It had been a rare, cloudy day for Colorado when she left the house. It was glaringly bright. She raised her head to witness a Colorado blue bird sky. Not a single cloud. Hope bubbled in Emmeline's chest. Seeing the train station in the distance, she still wasn't sure. Her eyes did a slow arc, first looking east, then west. Her heart leaped seeing 7th Street unpaved. Heading toward the station, she saw others dressed as herself. A smile spread across her face and her stomach flipped in excitement. She resisted an urge to jump and click her heels together. Her mind raced, taking in everything old but now familiar. She briefly debated whether to go to the butcher or the boarding house. She was excited to throw her arms around Nicholas. It was mid-day. She'd peek in the butchers.

She cupped her hands to peer in the window. She didn't see Nicholas, but Pete glanced up from his carving. Pulling back abruptly, she started to walk away as Pete popped his head out the door. "I am surprised to see you here," he said with eyebrows raised.

Not wanting to say the wrong thing, she asked, "Oh! Why is that?"

"Nicholas left a few days ago, saying he was going to surprise you at your mother's."

Her throat tightened and she worked to find air for the words. "I must have, I didn't, maybe we crossed...I wanted to surprise him." Her mind jumped to a worst-case scenario of his leaving her. "Did he say how long he'd be gone?"

"No, but he specifically asked that I hold his job for as long as I could. He's a darned good worker and a good friend. It's here for him upon return. He will be equally shocked to find you gone." A customer approached the door and Pete excused himself to go back inside.

Emmeline stood frozen, whirling in possibilities. Something was wrong since obviously caring for her 1938 mother had been a ruse. She quickly dismissed her fear of his moving away. She refused to doubt his feelings, but then what? What would cause him to leave, fabricating a story? Emmeline shifted over a block from the main businesses. She needed to sort out her worries. She sat on a bench to think before going to Helen's. Nicholas would have told her the same story. It was important to solidify her own version before facing someone else.

On her way, she noticed how small many of the trees were compared to 2023. The house on the corner of Cooper still had a stunning wraparound porch. By the 2020s, it was gone. She couldn't come up with a reason Nicholas would suddenly leave. Maybe Helen could fill in a blank or two. At least she'd seen Pete first. He knew her less and couldn't read her mannerisms or expressions. More scrutiny was possible from Helen.

Emmeline stood silently as she stared at Hannah's house. She had left both a sister and a friend behind. Her heart ached in a way it never had. As she stepped up to Helen's door, she knocked but retracted her hand. She reminded herself this is what she wanted. It is where her love and mission had led. She knocked firmly. A young Ruth opened the door. Emmeline squealed. "Ruth, you've grown!"

"Emmeline! You're back!"

Hearing the shouted words, Helen came rushing from the kitchen, rapidly drying her hands with a cloth towel. Confusion and thrill overtook her face. "Emme?"

She rushed to Helen and wrapped her in a hug. Pulling back to arm's length, Emmeline said, "I saw the butcher. I missed him, didn't I?"

"You did, but I am confused. He said he was going to surprise you. He couldn't wait anymore."

"How long ago did he leave? Seems we crossed trains."

With a quizzical look, Helen responded, "Three days ago. I am surprised he didn't get there before you left."

Emmeline said the only thing that occurred to her. "I wonder if there were train issues, a reroute or something."

Helen flicked an eyebrow and tilted her chin down. "I'm surprised with as many letters as you have written that he didn't anticipate your return."

"I wanted to surprise him, but it was a spontaneous decision. My sister stepped in to take over."

"How is your mom?

"She's recovering, but she will never be the same." Emmeline felt a dull pain hearing her words of recovery. If only that had been her mom's story.

"So sorry to hear that. Excuse me, but you must be tired. You are still in the same room. Do you want to head up for a rest?"

"I am not sure what I feel is fatigue. It's disappointment. Either way, a rest is welcomed."

Helen squeezed Emmeline's hand. Emmeline saw her gaze drop to the finger missing the ring.

●●●

Emmeline walked the steps, remembering how she felt doing this in 2023. She hoped somehow it was all wrong and Nicholas would be stretched out on the bed reading. She opened the door to their room. A flannel shirt was hanging from a hook on the wall. She walked to it and lifted it to her face, inhaling the familiar woody scent of Nicholas. She lingered with a few more breaths before going to the dresser, opening the drawer, and seeing socks and other clothing. She didn't believe he meant to leave for good, but this was reassurance. She walked to the writing desk and stood with her hands on the back of the chair, exactly as she had in 2023.

Pulling it out and sitting, she ran her hand over the wood that was welcoming her back. It flashed in her mind he would leave a note. She pulled the small drawer from a cubby.

There was a new note. It was sparse like the others since it was expected she'd read it in the future.

Had to leave. Be careful of Mr. Jameson, the coin collector. Asking questions. He's implied my coins are stolen. Need to be careful. Hoping he loses interest.

Her hand flew to her mouth, and she took a sudden breath. This was the first time someone in this world had questioned who they were. Listening to her breath move in and out, she uttered, "Nicholas, where are you? Where would you go?" She moved over to the bed. Slipping out of her pumps, she laid her head on the pillow and her wrist over her forehead. Her eyes closed.

She woke to voices downstairs. Laughter to be exact. She listened to the distant voices, curious who Helen was entertaining. She couldn't hide in the room forever. Running a comb through her hair and dabbing some lip color, she went downstairs.

"Emmeline, great, you're up. I have a guest. This is Mr. Jameson. I believe you met him when you first arrived, at the curio shop."

Attempting to conceal her rising panic, she swallowed hard and pasted a smile. "Nice to see you again, Mr. Jameson. I didn't know you two were acquainted."

Jameson's smile was more a sneer. "Oh yes, we met when I stopped by to ask Nicholas a question about his coins."

Smiling coyly at Emmeline, Helen said, "He has stopped by a couple times since then."

Mr. Jameson stared at Emmeline but then as an afterthought, he flashed a smile at Helen, but Emmeline noted it held more force than warmth.

"I came down to get a glass of water; our pitcher in the room is empty. Excuse me for a moment." Once in the kitchen, Emmeline clung tightly to the enamel edge as she watched water pour into the sink. She inhaled long slow breaths to calm the suspicion. What did Jameson say or do that caused Nicholas to leave? Did she need to feel threatened by his presence? And poor Helen. Was she being used to watch Nicholas? She ran water into a glass and walked back into the sitting room.

Emmeline wanted to avoid staying to talk. "I don't mean to be rude, but I am quite tired from my travels. Please excuse me." She worried Mr. Jameson had noticed the glass shaking in her hand.

As she was turning away, Mr. Jameson said, "I had heard you were out of town, but I was hoping to see your husband while I visited with Helen."

Her breath catching, she turned partially around. "No, it seems we crossed lines somewhere, attempting to surprise each other. I am not sure how long it will take him to get back." At that moment she despised Jameson, confident he was using Helen to get to Nicholas. She squared her body, looking directly at him. "What is it I should tell him you want to talk about?"

"Oh, it is men talk. Nothing you would be interested in."

"I assure you, Mr. Jameson, my husband and I share many interests." Emmeline chose to avoid a standoff when she glimpsed Helen's smitten face. "I will let him know."

Turning away, she climbed the stairs, considering her level of worry. After closing the room's door, she leaned back on it. Was

Jameson an annoyance or a threat? She would ask Helen how Mr. Jameson came to be at the house and get a sense of how she was feeling about him. She sat in the chair by the window re-reading Nicholas's note.

Awaking after dark, still dressed in her street clothes, she sat watching the shadows from the streetlamp. It felt more natural to be looking upon that and not the tall arcing streetlight of the next century. She wondered where Nicholas would go. It wouldn't be far. He knew she was trying to get back to him.

A body was moving just beyond the dim circle cast by the streetlamp. Emmeline slipped over to the side of the curtain. It'd been quick, but she worried it may be Jameson. She closed the curtain without moving into the window view. Anxious to shed the creeped feeling, Emmeline locked the room door, drew a hot bath, leaned her head against the high back, and inhaled cleansing breaths.

●●●

The next morning, Emmeline found breakfast already prepared and people gathered at the table. Helen introduced the new tenant, and Emmeline welcomed the familiar and friendly smile from Clara, who had continued living in Glenwood. Their friendship had been budding when she left.

Emmeline turned to Helen. "I fully intend to resume my duties of helping with the food preparation and I look forward to helping with the children too."

"Emmeline, since you were gone, Nicholas has been able to fully pay for boarding with his work at the butchers. He also brings fresh meat. You are officially relieved of your meal duties. However, I never turn down help with dishes or help with Ruth and Richard."

Emmeline offered a slight nod and smile. "Nicholas's letters did say he was feeling successful at the shop. But I would be happy to spend some time with your kids."

As she gazed at the orange yolks and the crisp bacon, she loved how untainted this food was. Seeing it, savoring it, she renewed her commitment to the second reason for returning. She watched extra yolk dripping from the bakery fresh bread, "Helen, I would love to go to the bakery with you. I miss the heavenly scent of baking bread."

"You'd be most welcome. I go on Tuesdays and Fridays."

The new tenant excused himself and Clara said she needed to get ready for work. She had become a phone operator and Emmeline ticked it off as one of the few work opportunities for women of this time. Wanting a quiet moment in the kitchen with Helen, Emmeline rose to help carry dishes from the table.

"I will send a telegram to my family today, so there isn't alarm on anyone's part when Nicholas shows up at my mother's house. It's the most efficient way to send a message. I don't want the long-distance charge and it's not right to reverse the call."

Glancing over to Emmeline, while scraping the dishes, Helen mentioned, "That is a strange turn of events, his leaving just before your return."

Emmeline wasn't sure if she detected suspicion but chose the innocent route. "I had a completely different welcome home pictured in my head. Alas, the wait continues."

Once dishes were washed and dried, Emmeline made her way upstairs. She bit her lip as she paced the room. The worry for Nicholas was building and she had envisioned a very different greeting. She had made such gains with not needing control over every detail in life, but this was crazy. She seized a pillow and rammed it back to the bed yelling in a whisper, "Dammit. Where are you?"

Chapter 44

When Will the Lie End?

E mmeline couldn't pace the room one more minute. She snatched her coat and shouted goodbye to Helen as she ran out the door. Breathing the crisp air, she devised a plan as she headed to the Western Union office to send her pretend telegram. Once at the door, she placed her hand on the knob, then turned and walked away. It would be the truth if Helen asked whether she went to the telegraph office. She ambled to the library, ready for the distraction of farm journals and old cookbooks. Researching remained her way to relieve stress.

Memories of her and Nicholas's first days together washed over Emmeline as she entered the library. She smiled, recalling their nights at the cabin. She gasped. That's exactly where Nicholas would go. It should have been her first thought.

Marjorie lifted her head from some papers. "Emmeline, you have returned! When did you get back? You and Nicholas must be thrilled to be together. Nicholas was just in a week ago and didn't know when you'd return." Marjorie's expression softened. "He looked so sad when he said it."

Emmeline's heart ached. Her leaving had created that, but she stayed in character. "Ironically, he traveled to surprise me at the same time I was traveling back to surprise him. We completely missed each other. I just sent a telegram to my family to watch out for him and let him know I was back in Glenwood."

"That is tragic indeed! I'm sure he will rush back when he gets it."

"He will probably convince the conductor to go faster. It's been too long," Emmeline said to lighten the mood.

Marjorie nodded and laughed. "True. So, what brings you in today?"

"I was going to do some research, but it's a ridiculous thought. He's all I can focus on."

Now that the cabin possibility had crawled into her head, Emmeline left the library and briskly headed out of town toward the cabin. She stood on the path and stared at the memories flooding in, stared at waking up next to him, stared at their laughing at the table. No footprints marked the mud, but she had to check.

Emmeline lifted a fist and knocked. There were no sounds of movement inside. She hung her head as the glimmer of hope faded. She turned around and sank against the door. The support of the door fell away as an arm thrust around her waist, whisking her inside. The door slammed shut. She caught her balance and whipped around, flailing her arms in defense. She froze, finding herself looking at his face. His eyes glowed with joy, and his grin stretched from ear to ear.

"Nicholas!" she shrieked, throwing her arms around his neck.

He brought his arms firmly around her waist, pulling her so close she thought her ribs moved. Warmth flooded through her body. They clung to each other until they were sure the other was real.

Emmeline pushed back and drank in the sight of him. "I can't believe I'm looking at you. I was doubting it would ever happen."

"When I peeked through the window, I thought you were a mirage! How did you get back? How did you find me?"

"I went to the library to calm my worries. It triggered a memory of this place, and I had to check it out. How did you get in?"

"The key hanging behind the bush, remember?"

"How are you staying warm, eating?"

"I am getting by. The heat is kept on low, and it's only been a few days. The first night was in the woods. I bought a few items from the grocery store before I came. That food in packages has its benefits."

Those words carried a cringe factor, but she ignored them. "I made it back yesterday."

"I know. I was glad you were safe, and it was the hardest thing not to fly up the stairs and wrap you in my arms."

Her nose scrunched. "You knew I was back? How...oh my God, were you the stalker outside my window after dark?"

Nicholas raised his palms. "Stalker? That doesn't sound good. I have been checking the house. I wanted to know you were safe if you came back. I got a glimpse, but then the curtain closed."

"You creeped me out. I thought it was probably Mr. Jameson trolling."

Looking confused again, "I certainly wasn't trying to frighten you. Once I saw you, it was hard to leave. Why did you think it may be Jameson?"

"I'd seen your note. Then when I went downstairs from a rest, I found Helen entertaining him."

"Jameson came back to the boarding house?" Nicholas bellowed.

Emmeline pulled her head back, surprised by the volume. She said, "I'm worried about Helen. She seemed giddy to have a man showing interest. She suspects nothing, even when he said he hoped to speak with you."

His eyes narrowed and his voice was deep. "I warned that pipsqueak he better stay away from you and from the house."

"What is going on, Nicholas? What does he want with you? Why did you leave?"

"Apparently some of those coins are more valuable than he initially quoted and judging by the way he acted, I am quite sure he is not the upstanding citizen he is portraying."

"Did he threaten you?"

"Remember how interested he was in the coins I showed him for exchange? He's asked a few times if he could see them or buy them. Each time, he has seemed more insistent. When I told him it wasn't negotiable, he got angry and said he knew how I got them."

"What did he mean, how you got them?"

"He railed about my not being who I claim to be, and they must be stolen. He snidely said he could report me, but he'd rather just help me out. Then he had the nerve to mention you might convince me."

"Yeah, he didn't seem to be helping anyone but himself that day at the house."

"I warned him to stay away from you if he valued his ..."

Emmeline kissed his cheek and said, "This isn't the gentlemanly side I am used to seeing, but I confess, there's an appeal to it. I never thought I'd be turned on by the idea of a man's protective nature."

Nicholas twisted his fingers into her hair. When their lips met, he parted Emmeline's, slowly gliding his tongue around hers.

Nicholas whispered, "I have been thinking about that kiss across time." He leaned down to lightly kiss her again, then pulled back, "We cannot start this. Not until I can return to the house. We have to resolve the problem with Jameson, or rather I must. I want to leave you out of it."

"Nicholas, hiding makes you appear guilty. How can we find out more about him? You need me involved since I'm not the one in hiding."

Nicholas clenched his fist and groaned in frustration. "There must be other choices."

Emmeline clutched him around the waist pulling him close saying, "I don't want to leave, but I need to. Helen may wonder why I have been gone so long. I pretended I was sending my family a telegram." She switched to a playful tone. "Might I expect a visitor outside my window tonight?"

Nicholas's eyes twinkled. "Absolutely not. If I got that close again, I'd be inside and up the stairs in three leaps. Plus, it might be time for me to pay someone else another visit."

"I can take care of myself, and you don't need to get yourself into trouble. There must be someone we can turn to for help. It is horrid to use Helen, but I could plant a seed for her to find out what brought him to Glenwood."

"That's too time-consuming. We need to know more about this man right now. She can't get too attached. Much too sweet of a person to watch her be bamboozled."

Emmeline smiled. She was back with her nineteenth century man.

"Nicholas, how well do you know Pete, the butcher now?"

"We have become good friends. Why?"

"You should talk to him. He's lived here a long time. Maybe he knows someone who knows someone- or I could approach him."

"Emme. Stay out of this," Nicholas said with surprising sternness. "It's a good idea to talk with Pete, and likely our best shot; I just don't want you involved if it goes awry. I will take care of this."

Emmeline put her hand on her hip. "In case you have forgotten, I have as much to lose as you do. I may be back here by choice, but I'm not who I say I am either."

"That's fair but I refuse to involve you. I would much appreciate it if you stayed in the background." Pausing he smiled. "Is that more to your pleasing, Ma'am?"

"Yes, thank you."

"Approaching Pete is a good idea. The shop is usually empty near closing time. I will go then."

Emmeline rubbed his hand. "Nicholas, be careful. I suspect Jameson is watching out for you."

●●●

Emmeline was in the kitchen doing her best to follow Helen's instructions for dinner. The roast was already in the oven. Helen had put out all the ingredients for macaroni and cheese made from scratch. She'd even measured out the milk and flour. How hard could it be? Still, Emmeline was taking this chef's audition seriously. Helen had gone to watch the kid's school play. The other tenants were still working.

Thanks for the Memories by Bob Hope and Shirley Ross played on the radio, filling Emmeline's mind with thoughts of how Hannah was doing in the next century. A knock at the back door interrupted her shoddy sing-along attempt.

She opened the door expecting a neighbor who might use the back entrance. Jameson slid into view. Whiskey fumes blasted through the screen door. She moved to hook the lock, but Jameson knew his plan better than she did. He ripped it open with a force that banged the screen against the house. He barged in. He shoved her against the wall both hands digging into her shoulders. Jameson pressed against her. A sickly sour stench poured from his breath.

She pushed at his arms. "Get your stinky breath out of my face!" His clutch loosened as she squirmed. She screamed, "Helen!"

Jameson slapped his hand over her mouth. Emmeline's head thudded on the wall. "Shut your trap. I'm not stupid. I know you're alone," he grunted. A fist rammed into her stomach. Emmeline saw his self-satisfied smirk as she doubled forward, breath exploding out.

Jameson hissed, "I want those coins."

She sputtered, "I don't know what you're fucking talking about."

Jameson grabbed her arm and tugged her bent body toward the kitchen, "Don't play the innocent dame with me."

Emmeline swung a kick that only grazed Jameson but sent him off balance. In the moment he teetered, Emmeline centered her feet. She thrust her knee into his groin. He reeled back, collapsing onto the opposite wall. In full clarity, she snatched the broom handle leaning by the counter and tightening her grasp, rammed it into his stomach. "How's that feel, you bastard?" Jameson rolled away, unsure what body part to hold. Emmeline darted from a feeble attempt to grab her leg and stood above Jameson, broom handle held high, aimed at his head. The pitcher of measured milk caught her eye. She flung the broom away and snatched it, "I will break this over your fucking head unless you get the hell out!"

"I know Nicholas isn't here to protect you. I'll be back, bitch," his words snarled as he stumbled out.

Emmeline slammed and locked the door just before her knees buckled, dropping her to floor. She laid a trembling hand across her stomach, realizing the ache. Her eyes stared at the door in disbelief. She had been attacked but also stopped an attack. Did it last two minutes or ten? The drumming in her ears softened as her heartbeat slowed. Relief inched through her body. There might be bruises on her shoulders, but beyond that her body was okay. She noticed the milk bottle beside her. There was no recall of how she'd set it down without a spill. It brought her focus back into the kitchen. That macaroni and cheese needed to get in the oven. She'd work out later what to tell Helen if anything.

●●●

Nicholas had seen Jameson lurking outside the butcher shop the first night he attempted to talk with Pete. A second night of being away from Emmeline approached, he couldn't wait. Nicholas stood, in the drizzle, watching behind the butcher shop. Finally, Pete emerged carrying out the trash from the day. Nicholas scanned the alley in both directions and stepped from the side of the building just before the door closed.

"Hey, Pete." Nicholas tipped his hat.

Recognizing the voice, he whirled around. "Nick! You surprised me! Why are you out here in the back?"

"Can I come in and talk with you?"

"You know you can. Is something wrong?"

"You could say that." After a final scan of the alleyway, Nicholas stepped through the doorway and checked that it locked behind him. When they reached the back office, Pete plopped into the office chair and crossed his feet on the oak desk. He watched Nicholas shifting from one foot to the other.

"Nick, I didn't know you were back. You look troubled. What's on your mind?"

"I apologize, but I wasn't straight with you when I said I was going to surprise Emmeline. Truth is, I have been hiding."

"Hiding? Hiding from what? Who from?"

Nicholas weighed telling him the whole truth but continued with the story as the town knew it. "How well do you know Mr. Jameson, the curio/pawnshop owner?"

"Can't say I know him well at all. He has only been here a year and often keeps to himself. Talk is he is friendly to customers and made some nice donations to the community. Other than that, I know very little. Why?"

"Before we came to town, I cleared out my grandfather's house and found a bag of coins under the mattress. Emmeline and I arrived mighty cash strapped, so I traded some in. Apparently, some hold great value."

"What makes you say that?"

"Mr. Jameson has been trying to persuade me to sell them. He has even implied they must be stolen, otherwise I would let him see them again."

"That's absurd. Wanting to hold on to them has nothing to do with how you came by them."

"I assure you they are not stolen. I am worried he will go to further extremes to obtain them. He has struck up a relationship with the widow Helen, owner of the boarding house in a ruse to get to me. He also said he would have Emmeline persuade me. I think I have stopped that behavior well enough, but I worry Helen is being taken advantage of by his advances."

Tossing back his head, Pete gave a hearty guffaw. "I passed him on the street today. Are you the one who gave him that shiner?"

Nicholas blushed. "I needed him to understand the lines he could not cross. These ladies are two of those lines."

With a cackle, Pete said, "I know you are a hunter, but it's hard for me to picture you punching anything. I am forewarned."

"I question if he is as clean cut as he claims to be. I'd like to find out more about where he was before coming here. I don't know how to go about that. If I am wrong about him, I don't want to raise concerns by involving local police."

"You may be in luck. My cousin is a private detective in Chicago. I could contact him."

A deep sigh was released. "That would be outstanding, Pete."

"Does this mean you will come back to work? Having you these months has already grown the business. It's now a challenge for one man to handle."

"Until we know more, could I work primarily the hours the pawn shop is open? I am hesitant to leave Emmeline alone. I have a bad feeling about this guy."

"Please work it however you can. It will be great to have you back. Tomorrow then?"

Nicholas beamed and vigorously shook Pete's hand. "Tomorrow it is."

Nicholas felt his neck and shoulder muscles relax and now he was free to see Emmeline. Hustling the few blocks, he flung open the front door, catching it before it banged. The children were asleep, and he only wanted to wake one person.

● ● ●

Nicholas's long legs bounded three steps at a time. As the door flung open, Emmeline leapt from the chair with the rifle in hand pointed toward the door.

He reared to a stop. "What the hell, Emme?" Relieved to see Nicholas, she pointed it down and collapsed in the chair.

"As you can imagine, I wasn't expecting you," frustrated by her quivering voice.

He walked cautiously to her and crouched down to eye level. Forcing down his alarm, he quietly asked, "What the hell happened the past two days?"

"I know you won't believe me if I say nothing happened. But I can predict your reaction when I tell you what did."

"It was Jameson, wasn't it?" Nicholas growled between clenched teeth.

Emmeline lifted her head and met his fiery eyes. She nodded, "Bastard."

He casually took the gun and leaned it against the far wall. "Emme, tell me what happened. You don't intimidate that easily."

"Yesterday afternoon Helen was out with the kids at a school play. The other tenants weren't home yet either. I was preparing dinner, so Helen didn't have to."

Emmeline stood and paced, fists clenching and unclenching. Nicholas gently took her hand and led her to the bed. "Sit. I am here. Tell me what happened." He sat beside her.

"There was a knock at the back door off the kitchen. Only neighbors or milk delivery use that door. It was Jameson, a drunk Jameson. I tried to lock the door, but he barged in pushing me up against the wall."

Nicholas hissed. "Did he harm you?

Emmeline scowled remembering the scene. "He tried, but he hadn't met a twenty-first century woman. I kneed him in the groin and rammed the broom handle into his stomach. I was ready to pummel his head when he stumbled out."

Emmeline turned her full gaze to Nicholas and saw his beet-red face. His jaw clenched so tightly she heard grinding. His shallow breathing became a growl from his throat.

She placed her palm on his chest. "Nicholas, breathe."

"I am going to kill that asshole."

"No. No, you are not. This is not the nineteenth century. You are going to do nothing."

"You were going to shoot him."

"No, the gun isn't even loaded. I don't know how to load one."

"That's ludicrous and we'll be fixing that. What century doesn't train their women to shoot a gun?"

Emmeline laughed and Nicholas asked, "What is funny about this?"

"Well for one, women aren't 'trained' to do anything. It reminds me of that first cultural discussion we had. If you remember, that ended in..."

He pulled her hand to his lips and nibbled it, "Oh I remember, I remember. But that is hardly how I want this night to culminate."

She pulled his hand to her thigh and wrapped her fingers around his, "Nor do I."

She shifted farther onto the bed and pulled her legs into a cross-legged position. Nicholas swung a knee onto the bed to touch hers.

"One more thing," Emmeline said. "Jameson had quite the black eye. I didn't do it. Do you know anything about that?"

"Apparently, when I paid another visit after seeing you at the cabin, I didn't make my point as well as I thought."

They sat silently, reveling in being together, tension melting from their bodies. Then with a wry grin, Nicholas slid her from cross-legged and pulled her closer to him. He then put his hands on her shoulders and guided her flat on the bed. Nicholas gracefully laid his body on hers and stroked the hair from her forehead. Getting a glimpse of a bruise on her shoulder he snarled but then leaned down for a feather light kiss. Emmeline slid his face to hers, brushing her lips across his cheek hungry for a languishing kiss.

She ran her hands through his wavy, but now trimmed hair. "We can figure out how we fix all this tomorrow. Who we tell what to. Let's just be happy we are together. I heard you come bounding up the steps. Settling a score is not what you were thinking before you opened the door."

"Hmmm, yes, let's get back to my original thoughts." He slid a hand down her thigh, grasped her leg, and in a swift motion flipped to his back, bringing her on top.

Giggling and kissing his Adams apple, "Ooh, is this nineteenth century or twentieth century Nicholas?"

"Does it matter?"

"Absolutely not. Continue."

He hiked her up and spread her legs more fully across his body. "I fully intend to."

Chapter 45

All is Not as it Seems

They woke as dawn light was being diffused around the room. Their arms and legs were comfortably entangled. Nicholas drew his finger gently along her jaw. "Good morning, Emme. Welcome back to 1939."

Pulling her arms out of the body entanglement, she stretched her arms above her head then flung them around his neck. "I'm happy to see it wasn't a dream. Are you able to live here again? I didn't even ask that last night."

"Yes, I will be returning to the shop, but Pete understands that right now, I don't want to leave you alone when the pawn shop is closed. What I didn't get around to mentioning is Pete has a cousin who is a detective in Chicago, and he will find out more about Jameson. Turns out Jameson has only been in town for about a year. I think he's strategically integrated himself in the town's affairs, but no one knows much about him."

Emmeline smirked. "So, no killing today?"

He slid down past her hips, then murmured, "No, I doubt I need police looking into my past either. With that plan set aside, it appears we have some added time this morning for bringing the past and future into the present."

●●●

A portly woman stepped to the counter. "Hello Mr. Jones. It's nice to see you back here. Did you have a nice vacation?"

"It is good to be back. There's no place like home, is there? What can I get you today?"

"That's the truth. Today I will take a pork shoulder, please. Will you be out hunting soon? I love the fresh birds and wild game."

"It's a favorite part of this job. Paid to hunt." Nicholas handed the customer the wrapped meat and welcomed the next. The shop cleared out after the late morning rush. He stood back at the work counter, arms crossed at his chest, head down, acquainting with the joy he'd rarely felt in past years. He lifted his head when he heard Pete's footsteps approaching.

"Howdy Pete. It's nice to be back. I look forward to getting back into the old routine once I resolve the Jameson issue."

Pete answered. "I sent a telegram to my cousin. I will probably hear if he can be of help within a day or two. I hope you won't be throwing more punches in the meantime."

Nicholas said, "Emme helped me regain my senses regarding that. Jameson has proven himself a threat, and I won't let him bring harm to my wife or hurt Helen. She's lost a husband. She doesn't need a cad of a man in her life. He should know to keep his distance now."

"It's not only good to have your help here at the shop, Nick. It is good to have you around. Something about you reminds me of an old-fashioned man waking up to new things. It's refreshing. Customers stand in line for the meat you bring in. Maybe they long for those old days when people were more self-sufficient, not getting all their food at the new markets."

Nicholas smiled. Would there ever be a day when he could share this secret with his friend?

● ● ●

Emmeline heard the door open and footsteps in the hall. Nicholas's look shot from twinkling anticipation to fury as he stood staring at the back of Jameson and Helen's heads in the sitting room. His gaze met Emmeline's sitting in the chair across from them.

She was swiftly by his side. His attention turned to her as she lightly kissed his cheek. She leaned up to his ear and whispered, "Not today, either. Not today." She looked into his eyes, her back to the room and mouthed, "We are okay."

A muscle bulged in his tense jaw. She lifted her voice and took his hand. "Look, Helen has a visitor. You must remember Mr. Jameson from the curio shop."

Nicholas sat in Emmeline's seat. She stood next to him with a hand on his shoulder; partially to prevent him from flying across the coffee table and strangling Jameson. Instead, Nicholas glared at the man as he squirmed in his seat.

Nicholas seethed when Helen rested her hand near Jameson's.

She looked at Nicholas asking, "Why Nicholas, you look very cross. Whatever happened in your day?"

Only glancing at Helen, he returned his glare to Jameson. "Probably adjusting to the routine after a long trip seeking my wife. We did have one customer that was very rude to a woman in the shop, and I would have loved to grab him by his collar and kick him out. I don't think he was from around these parts. He is probably moving on soon, so I won't have to deal with him again. If he was wise, he would. We don't take to that kind of behavior." Emmeline detected a snarl as Nicholas continued. "Mr. Jameson, whatever happened to your eye?"

Helen confidently jumped in, "Oh, he was bending down getting something under the counter, and forgot a drawer was open. He hit the side of his head. He's lucky he didn't pass out."

Nicholas continued to poke at Jameson. "Yes, Mr. Jameson, it's wise to look all directions since we never know what might be waiting if we are not paying attention."

Jameson cleared his throat and adjusted in his seat but held the testosterone standoff glare before he switched his gaze to Helen. He forced a smile. "This has been a most pleasant visit, Helen. I closed early to catch you before dinner. I should get back to some paperwork at the shop." He stood. "Thank you for the tea. Perhaps we can go to dinner sometime." Helen's face lit up.

Emmeline abruptly stood. "Thanks for stopping by. We don't want to keep you from important work." She gestured a 'stay' sign to Nicholas. She went to the door and held it open for him. Jameson's steely gaze met hers. She quietly and firmly spoke. "I don't think you want to set foot in here again."

He tipped his hat. "This isn't over."

"It's closer than you think, Mr. Jameson." In truth, Emmeline only wished it was close.

When she returned to the living room, Nicholas was hitting his fist on the arm of the chair, his face aflame. Emmeline told him she'd be right back. She went to the kitchen counter where Helen was tenderizing a flank steak with a mallet.

Helen glanced sideways at Emmeline. "It's hard enough for a widow with two young children to be of interest to a man. Yours and Nicholas's behavior was hardly helpful and most mysterious. I wouldn't be surprised if he never returns."

Emmeline flinched at a particularly stern pound of the meat. "But Helen, Nicholas and I don't believe he is who he says he is. I fear he's a wolf in sheep's clothing."

Helen's eyes stayed directed to the steak. "If you know something, you should tell me. I find him quite engaging."

Should she just tell Helen what a worm Jameson was? Emmeline moved possible responses around in her head like pieces on a chess board. Considering the era, how open could a woman be about assault? If she told her, would it lead to suspicions about them? "Please be cautious, Helen. I understand it is flattering and quite hopeful, but I don't want you to get hurt."

Helen turned her head to Emmeline. Her voice was gruff. "You have no idea how much hurt I have experienced. I can take care of myself."

"I apologize if we've overstepped. Of course, it's your life. Now. Can I help you do something here?"

"I am fine preparing on my own. I will see you at dinner."

Wishing that had gone better, Emmeline said, "Alright, I'll check in on Richard and Ruth."

Helen's tone softened as she offered a little smile. "They do enjoy their time with you and with Nicholas."

Emmeline's time with her mother opened a door to nurturing. It didn't have her wishing for a house full of kids, but she saw a joy in their eyes she hadn't before. She heard Nicholas belly laugh as she entered to see him play-straining while arm wrestling with Richard. Ruth was standing next in line, eagerly exclaiming, "I'm next, I'm next. I am stronger than Richard."

Emmeline hadn't been around many children, but they sure had the power to bring someone out of their funk, or at least set it aside for a time. Nicholas glanced over and pointed to Richard. "This guy is powerful! Let's see you take on Ruth."

Glad she had worn her wide-leg pants today, she dropped to the floor, propping her elbow on the table, hand at the ready. "Ruth, you are officially challenged. Keep in mind you don't win just because you are a child. I'm competitive."

In a swoop, Ruth giggled, sat, and took Emmeline's hand. "Ready, set, go!"

Where would this moment remain for Ruth? Would it land in a time where they grew older side by side, or with a leap across time with Emmeline only a vague memory in an old woman's past?

● ● ●

Tenants were savoring the chicken divan when Mr. Markum said, "I saw something I can't say I have seen before walking home from work. I was passing by that curio-pawn shop walk and saw cops taking the owner out the door. He wasn't going quietly, even though he was handcuffed. He shouted he'd have someone's head. I couldn't make out the name."

Everyone at the table stared at Mr. Markum. Emmeline didn't dare look at Nicholas, but she glanced at Helen with pity and worry. Helen shifted from her usual erect posture upright to shoulders slumped and downcast eyes.

Richard took a sudden interest in the dinner table talk. "Oh boy! Real cops and robbers stuff! Can I walk by there after school tomorrow, Mom?"

"Let's not jump to conclusions, Richard. Mr. Jameson may not have done a thing wrong. Innocent until proven guilty."

Nicholas mouthed to Helen. "So sorry."

The tenants were in the sitting room drinking coffee after dinner. Emmeline jumped when there was a knock at the door. Touching her arm gently, Nicholas said, "You stay, I'll go."

She could make out Pete's voice. Nicholas said, "What a great relief. Would you like to come in?"

"That would be nice. It smells wonderful in here."

"That's apple pie Helen made for dessert. Please have a seat. Her pie is out of this world."

As Pete was sitting, Helen came from the kitchen with two plates of pie. Pete popped back up, tipping his hat, "Good evening, ma'am."

Helen smiled her hostess smile and said, "I see we have another. Let me..."

Emmeline cut in, "No, you sit. Let me serve the others." Helen uttered a thank you and took a seat.

Nicholas said, "Everyone, this is Pete. Helen, you may know him from the butcher shop. He stopped by to give me my paycheck." He pointed to the other tenants. "This is Mr. Markum and Clara."

"Mrs. Miles, Nick has said so many things about your generosity and your good cooking. You still resist the canned and boxed foods."

"Please call me Helen. I believe the body was meant to have as fresh of food as is available. Having canned pears in March that came from California just doesn't seem right; I put them up fresh."

"We have that philosophy in common, then," Pete responded.

Conversation continued while eating. After a chorus of compliments, Helen said the pie was made with apples stored in the root cellar since the last harvest season.

Emmeline's head popped up. "How did I forget you still have a root cellar?"

"Still? Why wouldn't I? These new refrigerators are handy, but throughout the year, I prefer to use what I put up in the fall."

"I hadn't considered where all your food comes from. Or maybe I should say I presumed you bought most at the store."

"Of course, I can slip into the convenience when I am in a hurry, but what I can store and use or make from scratch, I do."

Clara interjected, "Many women I work with are loving the ease of finding prepared foods in the grocery stores. They are freer. They can grab and store several days of food."

Looking at the faces and gauging interest, she continued, "Until men begin to do more cooking in the home, or child rearing, women need to embrace anything that eases their time and allows them to possibly make some money of their own, to boot."

Mr. Markum spoke with a misguided attempt at humor. "Ah yes, first the vote, now women want help in the home, too?"

Clara reared forward at the words. "You were obviously alive in the 1920s, Mr. Markum. If you read even a single newspaper, the right to vote was much broader than only having a say in our government. It was about freedom to dream of more and for equality."

"Maybe it faded because most experts concur men are destined to be breadwinners, and women fare best in the home. It's how the family works."

Emmeline was trying to maintain a neutral expression. It helped that Nicholas was distracting her by tightly squeezing her hand in case she needed a reminder of the current year. Emmeline envisioned walking banner to banner with Clara through the streets as suffragettes. She was sitting this debate out, but Clara required no back-up. She had argued this before.

Clara's body remained rigid, and she spoke in a clipped tone. "Maybe it faded because there were no jobs for women during the worst of the Depression, and it isn't much better yet. The jobs were all offered to men. Maybe things stalled because the so-called experts were espousing their opinions of the status quo. It's hogwash."

Mr. Markum shook his head. "This is not a conversation for honoring this delicious pie. I apologize for stirring the pot particularly, with a new guest present."

Pete took it as an opportunity to stand up. "I should be getting home anyway. I always enjoy lively conversation if people are listening to each other."

Emmeline played the devil's advocate. "Yes, I am sure your wife is expecting you."

"No wife, no wife at all." Pete looked at Helen as he put on his hat. "Since we both enjoy food so much, maybe we could have dinner sometime soon." Emmeline saw Helen blush as she gave a quick wink to Nicholas. She knew Pete's suggestion might shield Helen from the blow of Jameson's fate. She hoped that fate would involve being behind bars.

●●●

Sitting at the table by the window of their room, Nicholas looked at Emmeline, his lips pulled to the side in a half smile, "Emme, you know as well as I do, Pete is divorced. What was really at work there, as if I didn't know?"

Emmeline gave a tiny chortle. "I picked up on their common interest and saw a potential for softening the blow that will come when she finds out Jameson's true story." Sitting forward, she asked, "What did happen to Jameson? What was the story behind what Mr. Markum saw, and what were you and Pete whispering about? Can't believe I let matchmaking take over my mind."

Laughing, Nicholas said, "Maybe women are the lesser species. They can't stay focused."

Emmeline kicked his shin just hard enough for impact. "Just tell me. What's the story?"

Nicholas let out a teasing laugh. "I knew it was a risky statement." He switched to a serious face. "Turns out I wasn't the only one hiding. The flaw in Jameson's plan was to hide in the very town where the investigator's cousin lives. Pete's cousin had been looking for Jameson since his disappearance over two years ago. He is wanted for a break-in and attempted murder of a man in his home. Jameson stabbed him twice. Get this, the person he attacked was an avid coin collector."

"You say attempted murder? So, the man lived."

"Yes, he recovered. His daughter heard the commotion and raced downstairs with a pistol and shot over his head." He laughed again. "Evidently, some women are trained in gun use."

Emmeline flew at him hands out, and Nicholas caught her hands and pulled her onto his lap. He was still laughing, "Anyway, it caused Jameson to run. She called the police, but they never found him."

He moved away from the enjoyment of the rhetoric. "More seriously, what did you think of all that talk about women's freedom and place in the home? You managed to remain calm."

"Unfortunately, I could hear that same basic conversation in my time. Some neanderthal thinking still exists. Something I know now that I didn't before is there was a deliberate effort to market these conveniences toward women, offering ease of food preparation."

Emmeline wiggled deeper into Nicholas's lap, resting her head against his shoulder. "Why is it that you accepted my views so easily? You certainly have old-fashioned ideas on other cultural issues, so why does a woman who swears, considers herself equal, and has sex before marriage not shock or anger you?"

"I told you my mother was quite educated. She chose a rural life with my father. Whatever you may think about my era, farming was arduous work. Women were taking care of the home and any livestock while the man was working fourteen hours a day tending the fields. Women knew how to fend for themselves, like how to shoot a gun."

"Stop with the gun talk! Women shoot guns in my day. It's just not something every woman learns automatically. Plus, the whole issue of having guns is a hot political topic in my era. That's a discussion for another day. Tell me about your family. I don't know the details. You didn't have any siblings? That'd be unusual in this era and more so in the 1800s, wasn't it?"

"Mother lost two children after me. I was too young to recall them. When I was older, I found out the doctor told her she couldn't have more children and live."

"Was that difficult for them? Families were so large, weren't they?"

"Not every family, but yes, an only child was unusual. They didn't talk to me about how it felt. That is different from your time. People didn't talk so much about their feelings."

Emmeline concurred. "Yeah, admittedly, there is a big movement to process all our events of life. I will keep in mind it may not feel necessary to you."

Nicholas stood, lifting her with him and onto the bed. Laying her down, he sat at the edge. "There are a couple of things we should talk about." He took her left hand and twirled the garnet ring. "Should this pretend marriage be made official?"

"Is that important to you?" Emmeline asked.

"If we are having sex, what is preventing you from getting pregnant? That isn't fair to a child. Life isn't good for a bastard."

Emmeline flinched hearing the term. "I'm not used to thinking of it like that. Women can choose to have a child without being married. But since I'm trying very hard not to rear at every sensitive term, I'll just say that it's also common for women to keep prevention in mind. Luckily, this time-travel thing allowed for a suitcase. Have you heard of birth control?"

Nicholas responded, "Now who has a misperception of an era? Birth control has always been around, but it also was a more private issue. I don't know what this era has. Do you have a something available?"

"I do. I did have many options, but I brought back a hefty supply of something called the Pill. It's taken daily and prevents pregnancy."

"That is reassuring, but back to the original question. Yes. Marriage feels important to me. Think about it if you need time. People think we are married already."

He leaned closer. "I know I haven't said it again, but I love you, Emme. Your absence and occasional communications confirmed it wasn't just the shock of the time travel that bonded us together."

Emme sat up and kissed his lips with light kisses from the left to the right. "I had told myself this would be a summer fling, a relationship forged by circumstance. I thought when I got into my 2023 daily routine, my caring would diminish. That didn't happen. Initially, the return was thrilling, but soon so much seemed unnecessary and too noisy. I assumed my thoughts of you would fade, but they increased. I re-played that first kiss and our making love so many times.

Smiling, Nicholas said, "I hoped it might be worth remembering."

"My point is, I love you too. I came back fully intending to be with you."

Their eyes remained locked until Nicholas popped over her, landing on her other side. He gathered her into his arms, gave her cheek a peck, and released a contented sigh.

Chapter 46

Moving on

Nicholas offered to break the news to Helen about Jameson's arrest. He helped her scrub the potatoes. Emmeline knew she was being immature eavesdropping from the dining room but did it anyway. She was certain she was in love with a wonderful man when she heard his kind voice breaking the news.

Helen said, "I was a fool to be taken in by him. I haven't had a man interested since Harry died. Why did I think a woman with two kids would appeal to someone?"

"Helen, you are a very charming woman. Even a con artist like Jameson can have good taste. Heck the entire town liked him."

Nicholas handed the colander of potatoes to Helen. He smiled and said, "Besides, I happen to know Pete is planning to call later."

From the other room, Emmeline gleefully bounced up and down on her toes. Helen winked at Nicholas. She said, "Emmeline, it is okay to come in now."

Emmeline laughed aloud and peeked around the door. She sang a few words from the hit song, "*Too Marvelous for Words*".

●●●

Emmeline and Nicholas eagerly accepted watching the kids while Pete and Helen went out. During dinner, Ruth asked if it was time for "*Challenge of the Yukon*" on the radio. The kids got little radio time. It was like Christmas. They had no idea how technology would change in their lifetime.

They all bunched onto the couch. Ruth beside Emmeline and Richard next to Nicholas. Emmeline leaned over and whispered to him. "A calmness floats in when I listen to a story crackling through these wires and tubes." She put her arm around Ruth and pulled her closer. She didn't miss high-speed chases and flashy visuals. At that moment, Emmeline knew she was becoming comfortable in what was now, early 1939.

●●●

Nicholas and Emmeline settled into a daily routine. Nicholas enjoyed his work at the butcher's and had to adjust to new hunting regulations limiting when and what he could hunt.

Emmeline was learning to play the woman's place game even though the antiquated notion some men held about what women could understand made her blood boil. She read newspapers and magazines from front to back. There were so many social or cultural issues she wanted to take on, but Nicholas kept her directed. The farming process was mechanizing more. Their crop yield increased with fewer hours of labor tallied. But she also knew what was coming down the pike. New technology right now meant a grain elevator or a thresher to separate the grain from the plant. That was for those farmers who could afford it.

Months had now passed since Emmeline had returned. The spring of 1939 was poking through but at elevation, winter could return without notice. Within their routine, Nicholas and Emmeline still began each day weaved in the other's arms before the day forced them out of bed. Each night ended the same. Time was not capable of extinguishing memories of their longing while apart.

One night, Emmeline stroked Nicholas's muscled arm and she spoke with a nonchalant tone. "Remember some time ago, you asked if we should officially get married?"

"Did I say that? Was I drunk?"

"You barely drin...." She turned to see his mischievous eyes. "You brat. You do too remember."

"Of course, I do. I hope I'll like whatever is on your mind."

"I have been considering two things. First, I'd love for us to marry. I'm not sure how we do it without tipping everyone off that we aren't already."

Linking her fingers between his, he said, "We have become quite skilled at fabricating a believable lie by keeping it as near to the truth as possible. I'm weary of contriving stories. Once married, maybe we can end that chapter. Uhm, you said two things?"

Emmeline said, "The second is that Helen and Pete are growing closer. I wonder if we should be considering our own place. I wouldn't mind going back to the cabin for a bit while we look. The weather will be warming, plus it's private." Her eyelids lowered as she used her index finger to slowly circle his lips. "We wouldn't have to be so quiet all the time."

Grabbing her, he pressed her hips against his. "Let's think about those issues while our bodies just react."

"Mmmmm, brilliant idea."

"Can I presume those pills are still plentiful?" he asked while sliding up her nightgown.

"We are good for a few more months. I really need to figure out birth control in 1939 life."

Nicholas said, "Or not. That is also a possibility."

"First things first, Mister."

He slid down her belly, using light flicks of his tongue along the way. "First things first. Is this what you mean?"

"Not exactly, but I will go with it for now."

"I thought you might."

● ● ●

Emmeline lay staring up at the ceiling. She said, "Nicholas, the institution of marriage is probably completely different from your era to mine. Not that I have changed my mind, but what does it mean to get married in your mind?"

Nicholas stretched his arms over his head and yawned. "That's quite the question for early morning. What is it you are truly wondering?"

"I know Colorado women had voting rights in the late 1800s. But when they married, was it with a vow to obey? Could they own land?"

He spoke with a chuckle. "No matter what I might have thought before I came to this era, the last thing I would anticipate now is you vowing to obey anyone." His lips curled up. "Not that it couldn't come in handy sometimes."

She poked his ribs with her elbow and rolled her eyes, "I will let you know next time obeying has any appeal."

Nicholas faked pain. Then he said, "More seriously, my parents had a marriage of partnership, both intellectually and day to day work. Decisions were sometimes made unilaterally but not until after much discussion with no resolution. It seemed whoever knew the most about an issue decided. As devastating as it was at the time, it's probably good they died within months of each other. I can't imagine one without the other. Does that help your worry?"

"It does about you, but I still wonder legally. I should make a run to the library to look it up. Seriously, I'm not back peddling. My life in this house with Helen is matriarchal. She owns the house, so there is that. I could look up details at the library without scrutiny. It would feel odd asking Helen or Marjorie."

"I believe women could own land even in my era. I don't know about now. That kind of thing rarely goes backward. Are you at all aware this discussion is dulling the romance?"

"Sorry, but you know it's my nature to question and investigate. I don't do many things starry-eyed without knowing what to expect."

●●●

Emmeline didn't learn much new visiting the library. Things were more limited for women. But illegal wasn't mentioned. Once married, it was standard for women to stay home with the children, but it wasn't illegal for a married woman to work. Working in government only allowed for one spouse or the other to hold the job, favoring the man.

That evening she nudged up to Nicholas as he stood in the bathroom brushing his teeth, "Let's do this marriage thing." He removed his toothbrush, then planted a big, foamy toothpaste kiss on her cheek.

Chortling, she reached for a towel. "I must be insane."

Chapter 47

Take Me to the Chapel

Nicholas asked for one day off. Just enough time to take the train to Denver, get married at the justice of the peace, spend the night, and take the early train back. Even though some months had slipped by, people understood their wanting time away after their separation, followed by the fiasco with Jameson. A night at the Brown Palace was a splurge.

Emmeline's nickel remained behind in a cubby of the desk. They wanted to get married and back to Glenwood Springs with no unintended surprises. Approaching the time travel area, they jokingly held their breath and looked around the train.

Nicholas wore a dark brown sports jacket. Emmeline wore a simple navy suit with a powder blue Basque beret, her curled dark bob showing from one side. Office staff served as witnesses. The ceremony was over in minutes.

Emmeline gave a quick eye roll and Nicholas squeezed her hand when the justice said the word obey. Emmeline mouthed the word with a smirk. Before placing the ring on Nicholas's finger, she spoke the etched words. "I will travel across time for you." Even though they had kissed a million times before, that first kiss as a married couple was like none before. It was raw and carried depth.

●●●

They worked their way to the Brown Palace, ducking into alleyways for stolen kisses. This was Emmeline's first trip to Denver in 1939. The vitality of the busy city surprised her. So many cars. She didn't know there'd been trolley cars. The buildings were fresh, and the colorful awnings over entryways beckoned people inside.

They sipped a cocktail in the hotel's Churchill Bar. Not wanting to draw attention to a woman drinking whiskey straight, Emmeline ordered a highball. Nicholas ordered a Four Roses bourbon on the rocks. They toasted to Mr. and Mrs. Jones.

Nicholas offered only brief objection when she planned to use her maiden name for all the writing she would submit. "Call me old fashioned, but why is that necessary?"

Emmeline was careful to hold her tone in check. This was not a day to start a cultural debate.

"It's still customary for a woman to change her name in the twenty-first century, but nobody bats an eye when a woman keeps her own. I love having my name connected to you, but many authors have used pen names. Even Mark Twain." She admitted to herself she would always be Emmeline Hammond and seeing it in print would establish a thread to the future.

Drinks finished, Nicholas arched an eyebrow and mouthed, "Let's go to our room."

Returning his flirtish behavior, she raised her brow, along with nodding an enthusiastic yes. Tab paid, Nicholas briskly pulled her to standing, "Let us go, Mrs. Jones."

Playful in the moment, she spoke softly into his ear. "I did vow to obey. Here's your one shot at it."

Nicholas yanked her hand and started toward the door, "I intend to savor my opportunity,"

They greeted the elevator doorman and stepped in behind him. Each floor gate passing slowly, they finally reached the fourth floor. Thanking the attendant, they hurried to their room. Nicholas motioned her through the door and closed it. Emmeline leapt up, her arms encircling Nicholas's neck and legs wrapping his waist.

"Let me guess. You are a virgin."

"If that's what you want to play," she giggled.

He tightened his grasp under her thighs. "Not particularly. It's one part of the twenty-first century that sounds quite appealing."

Their lips pressed firmly; their tongues slipped in each other's mouths. Nicholas walked over and dropped her on the soft mattress. He removed his coat. She grasped his shirt and raised herself to kneeling. After unbuttoning it, she unbuckled his belt, then his pants. He gently eased her hands to her side and slid off her suit jacket, followed by unbuttoning and sliding her blouse from her shoulders. Reaching behind her, he unbuttoned the skirt and glided his hand across the silk of her panties. Her audible sigh expressed her delight as she pressed into him, causing a pulsing of connection.

"You are still wearing too much," she said, removing his shirt. Her fingers ran through the blonde hair on his chest and down to his naval. "I love you."

As he slid her skirt down over her hips, he kissed her bare shoulder. "You are the love of my life, but I still worry you might regret returning here."

Her mind pulled from the tickle of her shoulder. "No regrets. You are the love of mine. You make it worth learning to navigate this world. That food dilemma thing isn't going anywhere."

Nicholas paused his kissing. She saw his stop-talking look. "Oh, I'm done. I have zero regrets," she said.

He guided her back to a seated position and stepped out of his trousers. Emmeline scooted farther onto the bed. He pulled her laced panties down, dropping them beside his pants. His full weight on her, Nicholas rolled his hips across hers.

She wrapped her legs around him and rose to meet him. "I think you have forgotten to remove an important garment."

Boxers quickly removed, he returned. "Now where were we?"

"You were about to fuck me."

Nicholas jerked his head back, eyes widened in surprise, hearing the phrase from her. Seeing her sultry look, he smirked and said, "Glad you were paying attention."

●●●

The alarm went off so they could catch the early train. After taking quick baths and gathering their items, they walked in the brisk mountain morning air to the train station.

Once comfortable and snuggling in their seats, Nicholas turned his head to Emmeline. "Well Mrs. Jones, have you figured out that plan for trying to influence food production?"

"Maybe. Marketing to women is in its infancy right now. Promoting convenience is one of the starters. I don't dismiss the value of conveniences but if women can see how they are targeted for marketing, they may recognize when it's more about bumping sales than a true benefit. Writing articles for magazines may reach the most people in cities where the packaged foods are even more pervasive."

"Farmers and the housewife care about the health of their families," Nicholas said.

"Yes, but ease, novelty, and variety are hard things to resist for very long. Especially when you see other people embracing it."

"But your argument isn't against easing housewives' lives, it's the methods for increasing the shelf life of food and some methods used for increasing farmer's yields."

"Both of which are in the primitive stages of their ugliness," Emmeline added.

Nicholas said, "You are a focused woman." He added, "Letter-writing campaigns have long been a successful method for spreading the word. Ladies' magazines will welcome your unusual perspective."

"Not sure *unusual* is what the male editors of the lady magazines are seeking, but there might be success."

The train pulled into the station. Neither were ready for the honeymoon to end, but Nicholas had to return to work. They strolled hand in hand to the shop. Words of love were murmured before they parted ways.

Nicholas went inside. He waved as he passed Pete to go wash his hands and grab an apron. Pete saw the faraway look in Nick's eyes. "Can I presume your night away was quite good?"

"Indeed, it was."

●●●

Emmeline was vibrant as she chatted with Helen over tea. She had no control over her giddy voice and plastered smile.

"Isn't this ring beautiful? Nicholas gave it to me to honor our new phase." Emmeline ran a finger across the tiny diamonds spanning the band.

She slipped it from her finger and read words Nicholas had inscribed. "Our love is timeless." Emmeline's energy was kinetic. She couldn't stop talking. "What's uncanny is, I had a ring inscribed for him with almost the same words."

Helen asked why this felt so fresh. Emmeline said, "I think being apart and then facing the danger with Jameson jarred us. It deepened our connection."

Emmeline knew she'd been blabbering; she switched her attention to Helen. "I hope you don't mind my saying, but you aren't wearing your wedding ring anymore."

Helen nodded and rubbed her bare finger. "It felt like time. I will save the ring for Ruth when she's older. My friendship with Pete is deepening. When we're together, I feel almost as giddy as you are acting. I had forgotten those early emotions." Helen's eyes twinkled.

Emmeline said, "Love is in the air. It allowed me to open in ways I would never allow before I met Nicholas." She stood and yawned. "I'm going upstairs. I didn't get much sleep last night, not that I'm complaining."

With a lively tone, Helen said, "Then, I must say, fatigue suits you."

Chapter 48

Getting Down to Business

E mmeline sat at the desk, writing out notes and thoughts to help arrange her thinking, hoping for an action plan to unfold. She wrote questions. I know how it started, *but who was the driving force?* She wrote words as they came to mind. Technology-refrigeration, long-distance transport, fatigue, hunger during the Depression, hunger during the Dust Bowl, convenience, easing the housewife's workload, marketing, attraction, money. Marketing bubbled up a second time. She remembered reading the public had been trained. Trained in consumerism. Marketers were skilled at shaping our thinking, our perceptions. People were trained not to care where their food came from or the distance it traveled. They didn't need to consider how it was produced, only that it was pretty and spotless, or uncomplicated to prepare. They were told they were too busy attending to other important issues, and this was taken care of for them. Yet she couldn't only blame the marketers. Companies only make what people buy.

She rolled the chair away from the desk. But who in this era could she collaborate with now? Helen? Clara? Emmeline had to tread cautiously with those she knew. There was that woman, someone Colson in Georgia, who was on a personal mission to keep pesticides away from her farm, but that was the late '40s, so still a decade away. She couldn't approach people notable a decade from now. Nutritionist, Adele Davis was writing right now but obscurely and on unrelated topics. Yet Emmeline needed them to notice her.

She made a list of women's magazines. What was happening in Colorado was happening everywhere. If she could help people continue to care who grew their food and where it was grown, then when pesticides became a thing, there might be stronger objection. She drafted her words:

Who is growing my food? Where is it coming from? As a housewife from Colorado, I am always asking myself these questions. My husband works at a local butcher shop and sometimes hunts wild game that is sold in the shop. People line up out the doors on those days. None of the shop's other meats arrive on refrigerated rail cars traveling from east of the Mississippi. All meat comes from local ranchers.

Living at a higher elevation in Colorado where it's difficult to grow enough vegetables to put up and last through the winter, I understand the draw of the grocery store. However, I wish I could determine how many nutrients remain in my food that traveled a thousand miles.

I am a modern woman who appreciates the convenience of the refrigerator and a quick visit to the grocery store. But I equally appreciate the bakery for freshly made bread I don't have to make daily. I am a modern woman who, before marriage, enjoyed my own income with reduced time for food preparation.

I encourage every housewife to discover who is growing your food and its origins. I prefer to give my money to a farmer I've met. Not to big businesses whose ads tell me how easy my life will be or how vital their product is for my well-being.

I have survived a pandemic. I have lived through wars. I have witnessed droughts and struggled for money. I know what is best for my family. The ad agencies do not.

Emmeline had been working and totally ignoring the urge to pee. She popped up and dashed to the bathroom. So immersed in crafting her words, she had forgotten Ruth was in the corner practicing her needlepoint.

● ● ●

Emmeline walked out the bathroom door to see Ruth staring at an object in her hand. It was Emmeline's cell phone.

"Wow," Ruth said. "This looks like it came from Buck Rogers! What is it?"

Emmeline avoided her first instinct to rip it from Ruth's hands and shove it back into the desk. Instead, she said, "Oh, that old toy? Wait a minute, were you in my desk?" Emmeline knew it wasn't right- trying to snare Ruth, making her feel she had done something wrong. She was a kid, of course, she was going to snoop.

Ruth placed the object in Emmeline's outstretched hand as her lip quivered, "I am sorry, Miss Emme. Please don't tell Mom. She hates it when I snoop. I thought I heard something, so I opened your drawer."

"Heard something? Like a mouse?"

"No, oh I don't know. I was just being nosey. I'm sorry."

Without looking at it, she put it back in the drawer. The phone had been turned off; it couldn't have beeped. The battery must have died long ago.

"Ruth, I won't tell your mom. My having this old toy can be our secret. It's a silly thing to have." Emmeline forced a stern look, "I don't want to find you going through my desk again. Okay, Ruth?"

Ruth choked a swallow, "I won't, cross my heart."

Emmeline was relieved when Helen called up the stairs. "Ruth, you have been up there long enough. Come help me and leave Miss Emme to herself." Ruth bolted from the room.

After closing the door behind Ruth, Emmeline went over to the desk and pulled out her cell phone. It was turned on. She wondered now if it had beeped or dinged. But how could that happen? She was sure she'd turned it off. If it was on, the battery would surely be dead. There had been no reason to look at it lately. She would ask Nicholas if he had become curious. Stroking the familiar object, she let herself think of Hannah and her mom before she switched it off and placed it farther back in the desk. She closed the flap over the top of the desk and headed downstairs.

● ● ●

Clara was home from her shift and the third room had turned over. It was occupied by the man now smoking a cigarette in the living room and reading the newspaper. Earl Thompkins was a clothing salesman in from New York looking to get his company's brand into Colorado stores. Emmeline suspected Clara preferred Mr. Tompkins over the previous tenant. She had barely tolerated Mr. Markham. Her nostrils had flared each time he spoke his snooty, but just kidding, words about women.

Emmeline enjoyed getting to know Clara, who had moved from the East, leaving a wealthy family in her quest to forge a different path. She walked away from her anticipated life of marrying a family friend. Clara had listened to a woman who climbed peaks outside Denver. It inspired her travel to Colorado nearly two years later. Marriage was far from her mind. Their conversations were ones of freedom and it felt as if there was not a century between their births.

Emmeline worked her way into the kitchen to help Helen, who kept insisting that as a paying customer, it was unnecessary. As she entered, "A Tisket a Tasket" was playing on the radio. She had thought it was just a nursery rhyme, but today it was a hit song.

"I'd rather be helpful, Helen. I prefer it." Emmeline looked around the kitchen. It was warm, and the golden yellow walls brightened the room as the daylight faded. She carried the carrots and potatoes to the light pumpkin-colored butcher-block table with spindle legs.

"Helen, I've loved living here. Nicholas and I both have. It is so comfortable, but the time to move into our own place is nearing."

"I was expecting it and dreading it as well. I am accustomed to people coming and going, but you have become a dear friend. I will miss you when it happens. Are you eager to start a family?"

"We haven't talked about that since Denver, but who knows when it could happen." Emmeline slid beside Helen. "We'll see each other often. I have never been a socialite, but you're a true friend." She smiled. "Besides, I have much to learn about cooking."

Emmeline moved a little closer and lowered her voice. "I wonder if you know anything about preventing pregnancy?"

Helen's eyebrows flicked up and lowered. As Emmeline returned to peeling, she wondered if birth control was something women talked about in this era.

"I have never used anything but haven't needed it in recent years. I have heard there are natural herbs that prevent pregnancy, and something called a diaphragm. I wonder if a husband must approve it for a woman to get something from the doctor?"

The table was a refuge from the cringe she was inhibiting. She continued her peeling, letting it slough off. "Nicholas and I stayed at the historical cabin when we first arrived and found it rustically charming. We might try that short term while we look for a more permanent place to live."

"Is there even heat in that old place?"

"It has a small wall heater. It was surprisingly comfortable, even though the sleeping arrangement is tight." Emmeline whispered across the kitchen. "But that makes for a greater likelihood of lovemaking, doesn't it?"

Helen giggled. "I suppose it does. Maybe I will experience it if Pete and I continue down the road we are going."

Emmeline said, "Seems I can find anything at the library. I will let you know what I find out about preventing pregnancy—it could come in handy for you."

"Oh Emme. Such talk!" She muffled a giggle.

"Helen, you always seem happy, but lately you have been radiant. Nicholas says Pete mentions you a lot. I believe he is smitten too."

Helen turned her head with a smile spread across her face. She changed the subject, "When are you anticipating a move?"

"We haven't talked about that since Denver either. We will give you notice, though."

● ● ●

Nicholas was relaxing after dinner in the chair by the window. His long legs stretched out, resting on the sill. Emmeline was wrapping up her opinion piece to submit to Charm Magazine. Getting a sudden whiff of smoke, she stared at Nicholas for a moment, processing what he was doing. He was shaking out a match after lighting a cigarette. "What in the world? You don't smoke!"

"Yesterday was my first day. Seems all the modern men and many women smoke cigarettes and sometimes cigars. It is very flavorful."

"What it is, is very addicting. Please put it out."

He inhaled another long drag. "What do you mean, addicting? It's advertised as calming."

"The nicotine in it only makes you want more. It has been proven to lead to lung cancer. Do you sit around a smoking fire and inhale the smoke? No. You move away. That cigarette smoke is even worse."

Nicholas continued with another slow draw.

Marching over, she reached for the cigarette. "How about if I save your life?"

His hand recoiled. "What are you doing?" he said with surprise and annoyance.

"Like I said, saving your life. Are you already addicted?"

"Emme, I can't imagine you stopping anything because I asked. I am not sure what the big deal is here."

"It's not just unhealthy, it's disgusting. You got through life this long without needing it. I don't want you to start."

"So now I am disgusting?"

"I'm not saying you are. The habit is."

"It's not a habit. It's a pleasure."

"Until you start coughing up chunky phlegm. Science has drawn a clear line from smoking cigarettes to lung cancer!" She went to the window and raised it to let the smell out. "In my day, most people don't smoke inside. They step outside when they do. That's where you'll be if it becomes a habit. Does Pete smoke?"

"Sometimes."

"Have you been sneaking cigarettes at work?"

"Emme, I already told you— yesterday was the first day. Besides, why should I need to sneak anything?"

Nicholas's voice carried an edge of irritation. "Emme, I will put it out this time, but I don't like being lectured or ordered around anymore than I see you tolerating it."

"Thank you," she said, returning to the desk.

"Emme, I have heard about your era for months now. I understand you have the luxury of foresight, but you could work a bit to embrace more aspects of this time. There are good things about it, too." Nicholas shifted his legs over to the table and began reading a book.

Emmeline spoke her next words with a tone of desperation. "I probably overreacted to one cigarette. But, Nicholas, I didn't come back here...I cannot watch another person I love die from cancer."

The tension lessened with some silence. Emmeline folded the letter and addressed an envelope. Then she went over and sat opposite Nicholas. She gently edged her feet against his toes and slowly rubbed, wishing for peace. He gazed up, the fire gone and replaced with a softened gaze.

Emmeline said, "I meant to ask you if you turned my cell phone on for any reason."

"I am not sure where that telephone is. So, no I didn't. Why?"

"I keep it in the center of the desk. Anyway, Ruth was up here playing before dinner, and I went into the bathroom. When I came out, she was holding my phone in her hand. She said she'd heard something beep in the drawer."

Nicholas's eyes widened and his voice startled. "She saw your telephone! What did she say, what did you do?"

Emmeline explained how the incident unfolded and about being saved by Helen calling Ruth downstairs. "I think she's too afraid of getting in trouble with her mother to risk mentioning it to anyone."

"Emme, why are you holding on to that telephone? It's no use for nearly a century."

"I re-read notes I'd put in before coming back."

"Emme, you have those committed to memory by now. So why are you really keeping it?"

Emmeline looked down at her hands. "I suppose it helps me feel connected to that era, to my sister."

He took her hand and spoke slowly. "If you aren't still considering returning to your century, I think it should be destroyed."

"Destroyed? Why? I have no plans to return to the twenty-first century. It's more like a memento from the past, but in this case a memento from a time yet to be."

"We can't risk the wrong person finding it. There is no way to explain it. Yes, an eight-year-old may believe it's a toy, but an adult would not.""I'll be more careful. I'm not destroying it."

Nicholas went to the desk. He pulled out the phone. Emmeline lunged for it. Nicholas held it over his head and looked at Emme, raising one eyebrow, "You mean you have no intention of doing what I ask? What if I order it? Would you do it then?"

Emmeline's eyes narrowed. She'd been caught in her own double standard.

He smirked. "What say you?"

"I say I still wonder how the phone got turned on. Someone may have been in our room. Would Jameson have ever been in?"

Nicholas reddened when she said the name. He said, "If not him, we only have a few other possibilities. Either way, locking our door may be needed for now."

"I can't imagine Helen was ever in here, but what do we really know about the renters?"

Holding an edge of irritation still, Nicholas jerked Emmeline close. "It may also be an indicator that it is time for our own place."

She pretended to yawn as she leaned back into his arms. Emmeline gave her most innocent smile. "All this tension has made me very tired."

"I definitely agree bed is in order." Nicholas walked Emme back toward the bed, his arms wrapped around her waist. He broke the grasp and Emmeline dropped back onto the bed. Nicholas climbed on top of her.

He raised up on one elbow and stroked her hair. "Promise me you will think about getting rid of the contraption before we get brought up on spy charges. Neither of us is oblivious to the world events."

Her hand slipped between his legs, rubbing until she had his attention. In a sultry tone, she said, "I have more important things on my mind right now. But I will consider the phone and embracing what I can of this era, if you tell me you will think about never lighting another cigarette."

Chapter 49

Moving Time

They offered Helen a month's notice. During that month, Helen and Pete decided to marry. The ceremony was with the local justice of the peace. Nicholas and Emmeline served as their witnesses. The six of them, including Ruth and Richard, celebrated with a luncheon at the Pullman. In a century, it would be known as a Farm to Table establishment, a novelty for 2023. Nicholas had gifted Helen and Pete a night at the Colorado Hotel. The butcher shop closed for the morning, but Nicholas opened it in the afternoon. Emmeline entertained the children with repeated games of Sorry and the card game, Slap Jack. Pete and Helen never shared whether they enjoyed the hot springs pool that evening or never quite made it.

Pete and the children mutually adored each other and were excited to be a family. Clara was invited to stay on as long as she needed, but the short-term rental room was redecorated for Ruth. Richard stayed down near Helen and Pete. Emmeline asked to pay for their room to remain available as a place for her to write. The cabin was small, with no devoted space. She wanted access to the writing desk cubby, even though there'd been no communication from Hannah after her return.

Helen released a happy sigh. "What do you think of a trade? I may start doing the books for the butcher shop, and the children will miss you terribly. Frankly, I will too. Could I offer a trade of you keeping an eye on the children two days a week after school? I can be at the shop. You are welcomed to come to write any other days of the week."

"I love your kids. It's made me consider kids more seriously. I've said I never had a bunch of friends. I'd love any reason to be here and see you."

●●●

They returned to the cabin on a month-to-month basis so they could save for a house of their own. She and Nicholas settled in quickly as they had accumulated little. Some clothes, a few books, and a typewriter.

Nicholas bought hooks for their clothes. The four-drawer dresser was adequate for folded items. Helen loaned a floor rug she didn't need. Emmeline adjusted to much of the 1930s but having to use an old icebox versus the era's refrigerator thrust her even further back. The no plumbing would wear on her quickly. She still didn't embrace the camping lifestyle.

Emmeline hadn't anticipated the satisfaction from shopping one day for the next day's meal. The food was fresher, and Emmeline understood where it came from, and became acquainted with the merchants.

Emmeline's letter campaign took less of her time each day. Looking for a job might alleviate the building anger from rejection after rejection. She was sure getting her message in front of women could have an impact, but no magazine was managed by women. Male editors projected what they thought women wanted. A grocery store clerk would be a strategic step. The grocery store was owned by a couple and Emmeline had frequently seen the woman working. All they could say was no.

●●●

They sat opposite each other at the table one evening. Nicholas said, "Emme, I want to say something, and I hope it won't annoy you."

Emmeline raised her eyebrows. "I know it sounds defensive, but I think I have gotten better at listening to another perspective."

"That's true, and it relates to what I have noticed."

"Okay. I promise not to bite your head off. Go on."

"Since you have been back in this time, you seem...maybe the word is gentler." He paused with a playful grin. "Don't get me wrong. Some of your language—your cuss words, can still surprise me— but you seem more caring of others."

Emmeline sat for a few seconds; her lips drawn in. "It's interesting you say that. I do feel more tuned into people. I'm not just hearing their words. I understand their feeling more. Taking care of my mom, watching her deteriorate, and wanting to fix for her whatever I could on any given day opened me to something that wasn't part of my life. I adored my dad, but we were kind of a team. We didn't necessarily, or at least I didn't nurture him. Caring for my mom, and becoming friends with Hannah, who is...was unlike me, were defining moments. Does that make sense?"

"I loved the feisty-you early on. The feisty, gentle Emme is even more alluring."

"When I think back, I remember wondering if I was insane to stay with a man I didn't know in a secluded cabin. I had a gut feeling about you though. We had both experienced the same bizarre trauma. You looked crazy-eyed but not like a whacked lunatic. The worry went away when you hung the blanket as a curtain for me."

Nicholas walked around to her side of the table. He scanned her up and down with a flirtatious grin. "I remember noticing your body in those tight night clothes with polar bears and questioning what women were allowed to wear in your era."

She stood and kissed his cheek. "You soon learned we can pretty much do whatever we choose."

He took her hand and walked to their small but big enough bed. "Yes, plus I discovered all the benefits that went with that."

Chapter 50

Not Alone

Nicholas walked into the cabin just as Emmeline crumpled a letter and tossed it toward the fire. "Fuck you, Mr. Bosworth!"

"Whoa! Emme, what's that about?" Eyebrows raised; he remained in the doorway.

"I got yet another rejection from yet another magazine."

"You don't usually get so angry. Typically, you just get busy submitting to another one."

Emmeline walked over to the crumpled paper. She picked it up with two fingers and shook it in front of Nicholas's face. He pulled his head back.

"I have been told in many ways I'm a woman and not to worry my pretty head." Emmeline's anger could have set the crumpled paper on fire. "But this man suggested I enter their contest for a year's supply of Velveeta Cheese!"

"Oooh that cheese is pretty good," Nicholas chortled.

Emmeline threw her hands in the air. "It's not even cheese!"

Braving a little chuckle Nicholas said, "Okay, okay. It was a joke. Not fitting now, but technically, you said it is cheese right now."

"That's not the point!" Emmeline heaved the paper back to the floor. "The point is they think they can turn my head with a silly contest. They believe their tactics can shut me up. They don't know me!"

"No, they do not," Nicholas said. He was still holding a slight smile.

Emmeline stamped her foot, her eyes ablaze. "You think this is funny?"

"I'm sorry, Emme. No, no, it's not funny. It's insulting. I smile because they don't know what I know. They don't know trying to dissuade you only stokes the fire."

Emmeline's chest rose as she inhaled and released a slow sigh, relaxing her shoulders. She walked closer to Nicholas. She put her arms around his waist and squeezed, hard. "Men!"

Nicholas kissed her neck saying, "We are useful for some things."

Emmeline giggled. "Indeed," and pulled away. It was her turn for a devilish grin. "Like cooking dinner."

"In our case, yes, though that wasn't exactly what I meant."

Nicholas was more accustomed to cooking on the wood burner. Emmeline knew how to get it roaring now, but Nicholas cooked the dinner meal. They sat at the table after sharing stories of their day. Emmeline propped her elbows on the table and put her head in her hands. Her anger had simmered to doubt. She spoke slowly. "I'm so discouraged. My gut says this is important, even if it wasn't processed food or pesticides that caused my mom's cancer. Maybe I should just let it go."

Nicholas's hand slapped the table. "Nope, can't do that. I have been thinking too. You are accustomed to starting and finishing everything on your own. Your mom's illness, connecting with Hannah, and Edmund, each put a chink in that armor. They are here now in spirit only. But Emme, I am and will always be here for you."

Emmeline watched his face. His eyes were gentle. He got her. He may know her better than she knew herself.

"I never wanted to save the world. I wanted to be productive and tick off my goal list. Mom getting sick spun me around. I stopped prioritizing my own forward movement." She leaned slowly back on her chair. "I'm open to hearing more ideas. Beating my head against the misogynistic 1930s editors' machine isn't working."

"I have two things. Three but the third is unrelated...I think."

"Okay..."

"When you came back to me, you spoke of some women who around this time were also working to wake people to the potential health hazards. There has always been strength in numbers."

"True but the real work of two of those women is ten years away."

"I doubt those women woke one day and decided there was a problem. They are probably stewing about something right now. Who knows in this nickel loop existence what set the first thought in motion? How do you know it wasn't you?"

"Wow. That's quite a thought." Emmeline pondered gliding her fingers across her lips. She dropped her hand. "There's a saying, 'When one door closes, a window opens.' What's your other idea?"

"I heard the other day the couple who run the grocery store want to sell it. It could be one way to address the issue from the front line."

"I don't know anything about running a grocery store. Or any store."

Nicholas flipped a hand, dismissing her words. "Emme, remember it's no longer just you. I have been at Pete's for some time now. I have watched and learned. Plus, what did you attend college for?"

"Business." Emmeline giggled. She'd been snared. Of course she was capable.

"Mmm hmm." Nicholas's eyes twinkled in return. "We don't have to take action, but we have options."

Nicholas's happiness was as important as her own. They were in this loop together. "Business owners. Sounds appealing, doesn't it?"

Nicholas stood, breaking up her thought. "There's one more thing. We need to go to the outhouse."

"Outhouse?"

Nicholas had already walked to the door and was standing, waiting for her to follow. Emmeline stood, her eyebrows raised, "This oughta be good. Why the outhouse?"

Nicholas was striding away as he looked back saying, "That's where I put it."

Nicholas stepped inside. Emmeline held the door.

"No, I need you to come inside, too," Nicholas motioned a wave to her.

Crossing her arms, she planted her feet. "Nicholas, this is weird."

"Just get in here. It's not like I want sex in the outhouse."

"That's a relief but still a little weird," she drawled under her breath and stepped inside.

Nicholas reached high to a shelf, grabbing a slim, rectangular device. Holding it in his palm, he showed it to Emmeline. They both stared at it. Emmeline gingerly took it holding it with both hands. It had a metallic exterior with a dark screen.

"It resembles my phone."

"That's what I thought."

Emmeline turned it over, seeing what looked like serial numbers on the back. "I wonder what it is?"

"I have no idea. I thought you might recognize it."

"I don't." She felt along the edges for hidden sensors but found nothing.

"Wha...where did you get this?"

"I found it yesterday in the woods. It was lying on the ground by a tree. Are you sure you don't recognize it?"

"I don't see any way to turn it on or wake it up. There were things being developed all the time, but this doesn't look like anything I remember."

Their eyes slowly rose from the device to meet each other's gaze. They didn't need words to know they were both thinking there was yet another person in their loop.

The End

Epilogue
The Next Day

Nicholas and Emmeline waited in the woods. Distant enough to be hidden but close enough to see someone approaching the tree. About to give up, Emmeline nudged Nicholas's foot and pointed. Someone emerged from a thicket and scanned the area. The man knelt and scraped around in a bed of leaves and twigs. He stood, widening his circle, and wildly raked more leaves.

"Oh shit!" Emmeline whispered.

Nicholas leaned in while watching the stranger, "What? Do you recognize him?"

"Yes, yes I do."

Nicholas reached too slowly to stop Emmeline from bursting into the open. "Detective Kelly, are you looking for something?"

The detective leapt to his feet and turned with a jerk. Their gazes collided, eyes wide. Nicholas darted to stand between Emmeline and the man. He looked between them bewildered. Tired of waiting for words, he intervened, "How do you know this man, Emme?"

She continued to stare, her breathing shallow. Slowly shifting her gaze to Nicholas, "This is the detective—the 2023 detective that investigated my disappearance." Her gaze jumped back, "What are you doing here?"

Detective Kelly began to move toward them, but Nicholas put out a hand indicating to stay put. Kelly stopped then said, "The simple answer is I have a message from your sister, Hannah."

Her stomach gave a quick churn, "Hannah! Is she okay?"

Detective Kelly smiled softly and reach into a pocket. He pulled out two items and stretched forward to hand one to Nicholas. Returning to her side, "You'll want to see this."

Tears rimmed her eyes as she peered at a picture of herself and Hannah. Nicholas wrapped his arm around Emmeline and leaned down placing a tender kiss on the top of her head. The photo was a selfie they had taken with an old polaroid camera they found clearing out their parent's attic. The detective spoke in a steady voice, "Hannah is very well and misses you— her words, like crazy."

"So, you and Hannah, you know each other? I mean more than from the investigation."

"We met again a few months back. I don't know if you thought my words cryptic when we met in the bar, but I decided to chat with you again, only to discover you had once again disappeared, left."

"Why did you want to see me again?"

"The investigation of you as a missing person never completely added up. There was never a record of you being admitted anywhere. No matter privacy laws, I should have been able to verify your existence. My curiosity was piqued. Since I am here, obviously you know I also time travel."

"It might have been nice if you helped me out when I was in 2023."

"I only had suspicions at that time. It was a wild guess and I completely understand broaching the topic of time travel isn't something one does lightly."

"Well, how did you get here?"

"You were hiding in the woods watching for something. I wouldn't need to be a detective to surmise you know the answer to that."

Emmeline hung her head, massaging her forehead with her fingers. She thought back to the first days with Nicholas and explaining the term mind-blowing to him. It was her turn to be stunned. As if the detective sensed this, he sighed, saying he would put aside his urgency to have his device back. He held up a piece of paper. "It wouldn't be right to exchange this for my device. It's a letter from your sister. Hands trembling, Emmeline reached for it and slowly unfolded the handwritten letter.

Dear Emme,

How the hell are you? Our desk communications seem to be defunct. Did the detective tell you I miss you like crazy? I do. I have met my own ten. Chris is his name. Tom, Detective Kelly introduced us. No, Chris isn't a time traveler.

I think you'd want to know Ruth passed away very peacefully not long after you left. Before she died, she told Susan she was delighted to meet you twice. Susan passed it on to me but attributed it to the confusion.

Edmund has kept watch here and says hi.

Something else you should know. Your food system efforts—they're rippling. Carry on.

NANCY HOUSER-BLUHM

Emme, we were always sisters but not always friends. Our second chance at friendship fills my heart and spans across time.
Love you,
Hannah
The Real End

Fact or Fiction

While initially researching the history of Glenwood Springs I too was surprised to find out that it served as a hub during the 1930s. People came from surrounding areas to do their shopping. There was a grocery store, a department store, car dealership, movie theater, and an airport. There were restaurants, including Lucy's but under another name. The train depot was built in 1904. It is updated but remains very similar. There were numerous boarding houses in Glenwood Springs, and it was one of few entrepreneurial opportunities for women.

Glenwood Springs, Colorado does not revive an era for the holidays, but wouldn't it be grand if a town did such a thing. If a person stayed at a developed hotel in Glenwood Springs during the 1930s it may have been the Glenwood Hotel or the Kendrick House farther from the station. The Star Hotel did change to the Denver Hotel at some point in 1938.

Amtrak does run west from Denver. The exact path and landmarks are fiction.

Nicholas's cabin is fictional.

There have been small earthquakes documented in the areas mentioned in TNL, but there is no recorded slow-slip in the area, nor other seismic activity in physical Glenwood Springs.

My first of many stays at the Denver Hotel was in a room with a window overlooking the train station. That stay and hearing the train whistle at night, was the inspiration for this and another story. The hotel has an interesting history you can check online or, even better, plan a visit.

If you have other wonderings about the degree of literary license, feel free to email me at n.houserb@gmail.com. Better yet, visit the Glenwood Springs Historical Museum. There's a great display and staff were a wealth of information.

About the Author

Photo © 2022 Betty Agnes of Betty J Agens Photography

Nancy Houser-Bluhm hails from the Mitten State, aka Michigan. She considers herself a hybrid, having lived half of her life in Michigan and nearly half in Colorado (along with some years in the Northwest.) She enjoys all things nature whether it's the mountains, water, or forests. She loves spending time with her husband, extended family, friends, and pets. Colorado was the inspiration for both her novels. Seeing re-run of shows such as Land of the Giants and reading the children's book series, Half Magic fed an early interest in time travel and magical realism. With her return to Michigan, she's excited to soak up new inspiration while exploring trails, local farms, breweries, and wineries.

Nancy has written her entire life. She wrote her first newsy letter in second grade when a friend moved to another town and has been writing ever since. Nancy dabbles in poetry. She is a lifelong journaler even though inadequate time is devoted to it as of late. Nancy has written opinion pieces, vignettes, and blogs about this and that, which is why her blog is named <u>Minderings, a place for the wanderings of your mind.</u> Numerous articles have appeared in local newspapers.

Authentic communication with herself and others continues to be a life quest and she believes our gift of communication is meant to build bridges, spread joy and belief in those around us.

Nancy loves when readers reach out to her. You can do this in multiple ways or follow her on Instagram (@jnbpine) and Facebook (Nancy Houser-Bluhm-author).

n.houserbluhm@gmail.com

nancyhouserbluhm.com

Please leave a review, or even better, a rating plus a review on GoodReads and Amazon.

Thanks to so many...

B ringing the Nickel Loop to a published state has taken a bit of time. There's a whole village of people who cheered me on along the way. While writing TNL, I weaved in and out of numerous groups that made all the difference.

Kat Caldwell, of Pencils&Lipstick, has contributed encouragement, brainstorming, advice, and edits. She is a well-rounded creative writing coach and author. I cannot thank her enough. You will love her Pencils and Lipstick podcast.

Kat's worldwide band of authors lent levity and expertise. I offer a huge thanks to Raine and Madison. Madison Michael has a way with book blurbs.

The Rocky Mountain Fiction Writer's critique group provided welcoming energy. Reading their works in progress and listening to their insights, amplified my writing craft.

Thanks to Joyce and Ami, who have been with me since day one of the "I can write a novel," whim. Our Creative Chicks Check-ins have held me accountable.

My beta readers, Raine, Jen, Kat, and Melissa each offered a lens that made me ponder TNL's story and character arcs. Stacey Juba, of Short Cuts for Writers, edited my manuscript deepening and expanding its quality.

Then there's my newsletter subscribers who not only opened my emails since Whispers for Terra but also responded with excitement.

I must give a shout out to my dear friend Mo, who birthed this title, The Nickel Loop, as well as my first novel, Whispers for Terra. She might have a niche. She's also handed over her beautiful photos whenever I was in need. You can find her photos at moonbeamphotos.com

My dear friend Mary did a very early read while Molly did a much needed proofreading. If you find a spelling error or two don't blame her. I am incapable of <u>not</u> messing with my manuscript. My friend Ed proofed one last time. Can't blame him either. Any mistakes are all mine.

Mary, Molly, and Karen are my super fans, and I am theirs. I must thank the whole Martin family. Not only were they the best pet sitters for years, but the girls provided aged 20-something insights. Kelly's feedback from the detective lens improved this peace-lover's scenes from pedantic to at least a little edgy.

I want to thank my LGBTQ friends who provided great feedback as sensitivity readers.

My siblings are not so engaged with my writing process, but they have always been there for me.

Can't consider ending this until I thank Jon, my husband. He understands my passion for writing no matter where it leads. He's creatively funny, has a way with words and is kind of a great cook. Not that the last one has anything to do with writing, but a girl's got to eat. It's been a lifetime of adventures with that man.

Printed in the USA
CPSIA information can be obtained
at www.ICGtesting.com
LVHW042118220724
786226LV00005B/72

9 781736 212325